PENGARRON RIVALRY

Recent Titles by Gloria Cook

The Pengarron Series

PENGARRON LAND
PENGARRON PRIDE
PENGARRON'S CHLDREN
PENGARRON DYNASTY *
PENGARRON RIVALRY *

The Harvey Family Series

TOUCH THE SILENCE *
MOMENTS OF SILENCE *

KILGARTHEN
ROSCARROCK
ROSEMERRYN
TREVALLION

LISTENING TO THE QUIET *

* available from Severn House

PENGARRON RIVALRY

Gloria Cook

New Lenox
Public Library District
120 Veterans Parkway
New Lenox, Illinois 60451

This first world edition published in Great Britain 2004 by
SEVERN HOUSE PUBLISHERS LTD of
9–15 High Street, Sutton, Surrey SM1 1DF.
This first world edition published in the USA 2004 by
SEVERN HOUSE PUBLISHERS INC of
595 Madison Avenue, New York, N.Y. 10022.

British Library Cataloguing in Publication Data

Cook, Gloria
    Pengarron Rivalry
    1.   Cornwall - (England) - Social life and customs - 18th century - Fiction
    2.   Domestic fiction
    I.   Title
    823.9'14 [F]

    ISBN 0-7278-6075-5

3 1984 00224 2350

Typeset by Palimpsest Book Production Ltd.,
Polmont, Stirlingshire, Scotland.
Printed and bound in Great Britain by
MPG Books Ltd., Bodmin, Cornwall.

To my dear sister Sylvia and brother-in-law Michael
With warmest wishes and heartfelt thanks
For all they have done for me
For being there
And a special mention for my niece, Sarah

One

The ledgers and documents on the ancient oak desk had all been rearranged. Not one was in the careful order she had left them in the day before. The silver lid of the inkwell was open, the pens dropped in a different position, and dusting sand was scattered on the desk and the floor.

Luke!

He had done this. How dare he interfere? Their father may now be journeying up to Bath but he had entrusted her with the management of the estate, under the direction of the steward. It was unconventional to allow a young unmarried daughter to be involved in business matters, but Sir Oliver Pengarron had never lived by the measure of society's expectations. He had occasionally sought her advice on estate affairs, even venturing to agree with her once or twice over the wishes of the steward. Although Luke was the heir to the Pengarron property he had not lived at the manor for some years, and had his own small estate. He had no right to look over her preparations and plans for the coming weeks, to write in his own instructions!

She would have something to say about this. Doubtless, she would find him still abed, too weary to rise after writing like some demented scribe far into the small hours on one of his plays – his passion – while drinking too much brandy.

'Come along, Rex.' As always, her big black retriever was with her. 'I fear we have a battle ahead.'

The dog rumbled a low warning. Kelynen whirled round

1

and found her bleary-eyed brother in the doorway. He was already dressed and well groomed, but only because a reproof from his father that he was turning into a sluggard had made him take on the services of a valet. Unsurprisingly, he was slouched against the door surround.

'Sister. Good morning to you. It was a splendid farewell meal that Mama gave us last night. Am I too late? They've not left already?'

'Of course you're too late! Father distinctly said they were starting out before dawn. You've missed saying goodbye to him and Mama. Samuel and Tamara were disappointed you were not up to see them off.' Samuel was their young brother, and Tamara an infant niece and ward of Sir Oliver.

Luke tilted his mouth to the side, unrepentant. 'I said goodbye to them yesterday. The house is quiet. Have Kane and Livvy gone too?'

'Kane's got a farm to run. Livvy was keen to return to the parsonage and get the children settled.' To convey the more thoughtful behaviour of her other siblings, Kelynen used sarcasm.

If Luke noticed, he did not care. 'So she can torment poor Timothy into allowing her more time to go about her paintings, no doubt. I've never seen such a hands-tied husband. I almost feel sorry for him, but I agree with Father that it's time he took charge of his marriage. A man of the cloth should be perfectly able to get his wife to obey him.'

Tired, weak, his head thumping and stomach queasy from the foolish amount of food and alcohol he had consumed the night before, Luke slunk across the polished, dark oak floor to a leather armchair and sank down in it.

To Kelynen's mind he made an ungainly heap, yet despite his disability – a pain-ridden, stiff right arm and shoulder, the result of a foolhardy act of childhood disobedience – he had a strong sense of presence, of power. Like their

2

father had. It annoyed her to realize how much Luke looked as if he belonged here.

'Are you going to scowl all day?' Luke asked, calling Rex to him and stroking the dog's large friendly head. 'Your mistress is a sour-sides, isn't she, boy? Kelynen, what is the matter? You are beginning to annoy me.' Luke was inclined to be impatient and stubborn and could throw a fit of temper as fierce as any storm.

'You have touched the things on the desk.'

'So I have.' His hand falling away from Rex, Luke settled himself to sleep off his hangover. 'What is that to you?'

'Father left me in charge.'

'In charge of what?'

His disinterest, his light dismissal of her concerns, made Kelynen angrier. 'I'm talking about the estate.'

Luke could not be bothered to open his eyes. 'I know you like to feel useful. I won't get in your way. I hope you're not going to be argumentative all the while Father and Mama are away. I abhor living with rebellious, nagging females.'

Kelynen stared at him. Dismay crept over her. 'Are you saying you intend to live here until Father and Mama return?'

'What? I am head of the family while Father is away.' Luke waved at her to leave the room.

How dare he demand she leave when she had business to attend to! There were rooms enough in the two-centuries old manor house for him to loll about in and waste his time sleeping. The thought of her spoiled, overbearing brother coming home to live for even a short time filled her with frustration.

'You've been away often of late, to Bath or the capital. Should you not be seeing to your own affairs? And you shouldn't sprawl so. You are getting fat around the middle. You're out of condition. I've heard you puffing while climbing the stairs. You look haggard, older than your five-and-twenty years, and jaded and dissolute.'

Luke was instantly up on his feet. The attack on him made him rock steady. To gain support, Kelynen shot a look at the magnificent portrait of her father shining down from above the mantel over the fireplace. Luke might favour Sir Oliver in looks – tall, black-haired, dark-eyed – but he had little of the fine, benevolent ways of the aristocratic gentleman she revered.

'Polgissey is run well enough,' Luke hissed. 'I've an excellent steward there. And whether you like it or not, the Pengarron estate *is* my affair. Kelynen, has it not occurred to you that no matter how much the estate profits from your conscientious labours, you will never inherit it? One day, when it is mine, the wife I shall have taken by then will have precedence over you, and you will be pushed into the background. A sad, dried-up spinster. Is that what you want?'

Kelynen stared at him from eyes flared and appalled. His words had flung her down into a dark pit. A deep, winter-filled abyss called Truth. Working with her father had brought purpose and fulfilment to her life. Yet it had all been a waste, for in the end it would mean nothing. It was of no benefit to her.

'You should marry and bear children.' Luke flung up his right hand and winced as pain sliced through his shoulder. 'It's shameful the way you resolutely stay unwed, refusing every suitor. You have a substantial portion settled on you. What excuse do you have?'

Wetting her dry lips, she hurled back, 'Why shameful? The King and Queen have made it plain that they never intend any of the princesses to marry. And how old do you think I am? I am but nineteen, hardly an old maid!'

The steel went out of Luke. He surveyed her with thoughtful, honest eyes. 'You seem older, older than Livvy, older even than Mama. Of course, beauty and grace will never own you as it does them, but you're becoming plain and unattractive.' He sighed, rubbing frantically at the pain

4

throbbing all the way down his arm. 'Kelynen, dearheart, I never meant to be cruel. Listen to me. As you have pointed out, I've reached my quarter century. It is time I sought a wife, produced an heir of my own. Let us seek matrimony together! It will be fun. We'll make it so.'

Kelynen looked at him as if he were mad. How dare he spring such a suggestion on her after flinging her hopes and aspirations out into the cold? Luke was wholly insensitive. How he differed from their father. Their beautiful, youthful mother, too. She found no pity over his discomfort.

Weariness and a raging headache gained advantage of Luke. His voice was faint and indistinct. 'Invite your friends here so I can look them over. I might find someone tolerable among them. One of the Harrt girls, perhaps. Or a Ransom. Don't care particularly what they look like. As long as they're manageable and able to breed.'

'I would not wish you on any of my friends!' With Luke having so much to offer he would find them easy prey – except for Sophie Carew, a young widow she had recently formed a friendship with.

'You had better sit down, Luke, before you fall down.' All at once she wanted to reach out and push him over. It wouldn't have to be a hard push. He would fold and plummet, like a drooping flower in a gale. But it was not her way to be cruel or childish. She waited until he spilled again into the armchair. 'Am I to seek a husband who is just like you, then? Bind myself to a man who will show me no respect while he keeps a mistress and spends just as many hours at the gaming tables and his own selfish pursuits? Subject myself to that sort of meanness? As a wife I shall be at another man's beck and call. A possession. A chattel. I think not, Luke.'

He laughed, an offensive, mocking sound.

Kelynen had no more to say. Luke would never understand her feelings and she was not about to waste her breath.

5

She made for the desk. 'If you must stay in this room, I'd appreciate it if you did not snore. I have the plantation accounts to see to.'

'Done them. Signed them. I see that a sizeable consignment of timber for the Wheal Lowen is to be delivered there today.' Luke was almost asleep. 'You and Father have brought everything else up to date. Go out.'

It was an order, not a suggestion. 'You are impossible,' she whispered because it was never any use shouting at Luke. Tugging gently on Rex's collar, she made a dignified withdrawal.

Two

The blanket of dark, sulky cloud and the waves lapping over the little shingle beach as if they were in mourning suited Kelynen's mood entirely. She was sitting on her cloak, thrown down on a low shelf of jagged rocks near the shoreline. If she did not move soon she would get a soaking from the approaching tide. She did not care.

She was alone. Rex had deserted her, for she was making nerve-jangling scratching noises with two black-and-white streaked pebbles, rubbing them together, making them rasp, spoiling their smoothness, taking off the shine made by millions of years of being tossed about by the waters. She likened the irritation of the pebbles to the discord between her and Luke. There was little chance of them living in harmony at home, even for a short time, without their fine and noble father in charge, and their kind and patient mother keeping the peace. They would get in each other's way, jar on each other's nerves. It was Kelynen's nature to be peaceable, but Luke could be selfish and egotistical and was often a boor. He had made her feel something of a stranger in her own home. As if the only right she had there was to pass through it.

At that moment she was wildly jealous of Luke. One day he would step into a smooth-running concern, made so partly by her efforts. He would be lord of the manor in the house she loved and felt she could never bear to be parted from. It would be equally unbearable to live there as Luke's spinster sister, pushed into a lower position than the unfortunate woman he would take as a wife.

Luke! Damn you!

But it was not all Luke's fault. It was the way of things that the heir of a property should inherit everything. And she did love him. He might have the natural arrogance of a first-born son but there was lots about him to love. He was loyal to the family. He could be gallant and he was courageous. Three years ago, up in London, he had raced into a burning house and rescued a lady, and then his man-servant, Jack Rosevear, whom he had made his friend and then the steward of Polgissey. She did not suppose she would ever do anything as brave or as exciting.

Luke would make a dreadful husband, though – unless he fell in love, and that did not seem likely, at least not at the moment. He was not looking for love, and in fact had once declared that if love wanted him, it had better come and claim him, if it dared!

She asked herself if *she* wanted to fall in love, to marry and have a home and family of her own. She had given it little thought until now, although lately her parents had started to throw hints in that direction. She could only consider a man who would treat her with absolute respect and love her with passion, as her father loved her mother. Someone she could love deeply, with utter commitment, as her mother loved her father. Yet, even her parents, whose love story was the most ardent and romantic of all that she knew, had been beset by many problems. Was it worth hoping to fall in love? Her brother Kane had a happy marriage. On the other hand, her sister Livvy did not and was dreadfully unhappy, although that was largely her own fault, for she was every bit as selfish as Luke, and inclined to neglect and even be spiteful towards her spouse.

Kelynen tossed the pebbles into the next incoming wave then got up to deny the waters from giving her a malicious soaking. 'I'm not going to clutter my mind with all this unnecessary confusion,' she told a black-backed gull on the wing.

Why should she marry just to please Luke, or even her parents, or to fulfil the role society expected her to? To be required to see to mundane things while her husband might strut about and assume the role of a great hunter, as vital as the sun, as noble as a god. No indeed! There had to be more to gain from life than that. And anyway – she was back to her most significant argument – did such a man live who could match her father? Livvy often teased her that she saw him as a god, an extraordinary human being with unattainable qualities. Sir Oliver Pengarron was the measure she used against all men.

The wind sifted through her fair hair, tormenting her. A shiver raced down her neck. She was surprised, then acknowledged that although it was nearly spring, winter clung on still, invading the air with a spiteful chill. The air was thick with brine and seaweed and growing darker and heavier. Soon a mist would cling all the way along the coast from Land's End to the Lizard, obliterating everything where she was: Trelynne Cove, a tiny horseshoe-shaped inlet in Mount's Bay on the southern Cornish coast.

She called Rex and he came bounding up to her. Friendly and faithful, he made his mistress smile briefly, thankful to have him. She had Rex's unconditional love and the same from every member of her family. She had no need of a husband – at present anyway.

Her steps crunching over the shingle on the way to her pony, she mulled over how much of her family history was to be found in the cove. To regain this place as part of Pengarron property her father had, in effect, bought her mother as part of the bargain, as his bride. Sir Oliver had been angry at being forced to take a working-class bride, and at the time Kerensa Trelynne had been betrothed to someone else, but eventually they had discovered they were soulmates. Sir Oliver ran some of his smuggling operations from here. The seller of the cove, Old Tom Trelynne, Kerensa's grandfather, had been murdered here, retribution for betraying a smuggling run to the Revenue men, which had led to a boy's death. Kane and Luke, much to Sir Oliver's chagrin, had also made smuggling runs here in their youth. And even as innocent maidens, Livvy, and Jessica, Kane's wife, along with a Pengarron cousin, Cordelia Drannock, had attempted the same. Their first and only escapade had gone badly wrong, ending with Jessica being kidnapped and then imprisoned on a ship a little further down the coast, at St Michael's Mount. The three young women spoke of it now with excitement, an adventure before marriage and motherhood.

All of this suddenly made Kelynen feel she had not really lived. She found herself agreeing with what many had light-heartedly accused her of, that she was altogether too serious, too studious and solemn. She had given no sway, as each of her grown-up siblings had, to rebellion, exploration or fantasy. She must seem dull and boring, a thought that had not bothered her before. She saw herself to be a hazy sort of person, uninteresting, blurred at the edges. She had experienced little excitement, never known anyone outside her family that she could call fascinating. And one day her position at the Manor would be superfluous.

She winced to banish the dreariness and apprehension she had generated within herself. She rubbed at her temples to soothe her mind. If she did not alter this perception of herself, she was in danger of becoming a sad little phantom. Decisions came easily to her and she made one now. She would seek something new, make herself a person in her own right, even if it meant she must move out of her beloved home.

With Rex dashing on ahead, she rode Tegen, her lively chestnut pony, bred at the Pengarron stud, up the winding path to the cliff top. She would not return home for hours. Returning to firm ground, where there was scrubby vegetation and a few skeletal wind-bent trees and gorse and heather that had yet to flower, she set Tegen at a gallop, intending to beat the mist before it made her passage to Marazion difficult.

She would visit Sophie Carew for inspiration. Although left in reduced circumstances, Sophie was not touting herself as fresh bride material. Sophie was surviving alone. Kelynen would do the same. Consider a different kind of future. Most of all, she vowed, she would *live*.

Three

Kelynen was in the great hall. The servants were lined up across from her on the vast oak-planked floor. They were waiting for Luke to come downstairs and perform the daily morning prayers.

'Shouldn't be long now, my 'andsome.' Beatrice, the longest-serving member of staff, grinned lopsidedly at her. The former nursemaid was held in great affection by the Pengarrons and was now more a confidante to them than a servant. Peculiarly ugly, fat and piggy-eyed, she was the only one to be seated, in regard of her ninety-three years and frailties. She fell back into her habit of humming and hawing to herself, of sniffing and snorting noisily. She was waiting patiently, amused that Kelynen was not.

Next to Beatrice, neat and straight in contrast, and firm on all the proprieties, was the housekeeper, Polly O'Flynn. She bent in one swift movement to pick up Beatrice's fallen handkerchief. Beatrice snatched it from her, coughing and spluttering without shielding her mouth before pushing the scrap of cloth down into her huge drooping bosom. Beatrice could never be persuaded to wipe away the constant drip from her nose, or to wash herself regularly, and Polly was poised at an angle to escape her overripe smells.

Kelynen allowed another three slow, awkward minutes to pass. Where was Luke? Why must he be so inconsiderate? The staff wanted to get on with their duties and she wanted . . . well, she wasn't sure what she wanted to do today, but it certainly wasn't to be kept waiting by her ill-mannered brother. There was no excuse for his tardiness. Luke had breakfasted in his room after a night spent in Marazion, probably in some house of ill repute. The chief maid, Ruth King, had reported that Elgan, the valet, had passed out an empty tray from the bedchamber and informed her that his master was now getting dressed. That was an hour and a half ago. The valet was a hooked-nosed, distant-eyed, waspish individual, procured from a fine London house. Kelynen and the servants loathed him for his patronizing, sometimes mean ways. He had arrived for the prayers a full minute after everyone else and was standing aloof. So where, Kelynen fumed, was Luke?

'Excuse me.' After a look of apology she mounted the mighty stairs and presented herself in her brother's room.

He was sitting at a leather-topped desk. He had ordered it lugged down from the storage attics to save him a foray into the library or study. The lazy so-and-so! He was scribbling away intently and did not hear her come in. She crept up behind him and stared down over his shoulder.

'Luke! You're working on a play. How dare you! You're intolerable. While the rest of us are waiting like ninnies for you downstairs, you are, as usual, serving your own ends. Stir yourself at once!'

Shocked by her sudden arrival, Luke broke his nib, splashed ink on the paper and jarred his painful shoulder. 'Hell and damnation, Kelynen, you've made me lose the thread of what my character was saying.'

'Never mind your character, and mind your language. The King sisters have complained to me about how often you swear. Prayers, Luke. Now! And don't you dare ring for Elgan. You're perfectly capable of putting on your coat yourself.'

Kelynen expected Luke to bawl at her to get out of the room, but to her consternation he swivelled round, leaned back and laughed. 'Why, baby sister, I believe you're turning into a termagant. I shall make peace with Ruth and Esther.

That's the trouble with Father employing Methodists; too much prudery in the house. I refuse to have dissenters at Polgissey. What shall we do after I've sent the godly Matthias Renfree – yet another Methodist, and a lay preacher to boot – on his way today? Ride to Marazion and take tea with the mayor? I'd like to acquire the latest gossip in the Bay. He has a son. Don't worry, he's a gawky youth as I recall, too shy to bother you. I'll find you a more fitting blade to pay you court. Dear, dear, how you do frown. I'll make sure he will be a merry fellow.'

Kelynen's irritation turned to fury. *He* would send Matthias Renfree, the steward, on his way! No mention of her taking part in today's discussion on estate matters. And no matter what Luke did, people always forgave him, were always eager to dance attendance on him. Later in the day, when it suited him, he would dawdle into the kitchens, where Esther King would be cooking, and poke his nose round the door of the laundry room, where Ruth King would be supervising the younger staff, and after a minute or two of sweet cajoling he would have the plain-faced, middle-aged sisters fawning all over him, promising him his favourite pudding and special attention to his shirts.

She was also furious at his poking fun at her. 'I hate you.'

'No, you don't.' He stretched up carefully and grinned. 'You adore me like everyone else does. I know life's not fair to women, dearheart. You must learn to manipulate it so you're happy, like Mama does. Is she not on equal terms with Father in everything?' It was their mother's Methodist origins that accounted for the faith of a good number of the servants.

'That is because Father loves her so much. That sort of love is uncommon.'

'Well, from the letter we received from them yesterday, they seem quite settled at the house Father is renting in the Royal Crescent. Now, what you need, my dear, is to go out

14

more often, make new friends. You've sulked for a week, returning sadly, after starting a keen exploration of new and fresh ideas, into your little self-made shell again.'

Rising, Luke slipped on a well-cut coat, finished without a cuff but with a band of buttons in the new style, over his short, quilted waistcoat. His shirt frills were small and he pulled them down to protrude fetchingly over his wrists. He made an arresting, rugged sight, despite his overindulgence of food, drink and late nights. He looked at his sister ponderously. 'Now, what else can I suggest for you?'

'Don't trouble yourself, Luke,' Kelynen said as quietly as if speaking in church. Suddenly she had endured enough of him. 'I don't think anyone you could introduce me to would be of the slightest benefit to me. I shall not neglect my responsibilities to the estate, but I think I'll stay at Livvy's for a few days.'

'I'm so glad you're here, Kelynen. You can come with me tomorrow to Chenhalls.'

'Does Timothy approve of you going there so often, Livvy?'

Kelynen was up in her sister's attic painting studio, in the parish parsonage at Perranbarvah, two miles from home. She was gazing down on the little fishing village below. The sun was bright and a sparkle of green-blue and white marked the water's edge. The fleet of rented luggers, all dramatically red-sailed, were safely ashore, and tiny figures in rough clothes were busy with tar brushes or repairing tackle. Small, ragged children with a couple of scraggy mongrels were playing among the rocks, their older siblings working with their fathers or with their mothers in the salting cellars. She knew all the fisherfolk and every child in the district who attended the charity school built under Pengarron benefaction, where sometimes she taught the lessons. A stroll down the steep hill later, a word or two with a fishwife or an old net-maker was an appealing idea.

Luke would not bother to enquire personally how they were faring.

'No, but I don't see why,' Livvy Lanyon snapped, her quick temper rising. She was occupied with packing oils, powders and brushes. 'He's been a particular friend of the Tremaynes for many years, long before he came to this parish. He made no objection at first when Sir Rafe suggested he commission me to paint his portrait. Timothy is being unreasonable, as usual. He'll be back soon from saying the morning prayers in church and he'll get difficult if you don't agree to come with me. His attitude is unfair. He was supportive about my painting for a while, even suggesting that Luke take my work up to London to be viewed by the critics, but now if he had his way I'd only venture out once or twice a week. You must say you've been looking forward to a visit to Chenhalls for some time. After all, Father does business with them, and you are involved in that, so it's time you met the Tremaynes. Also, tell him you're interested in the nephew who resides there. Yes, that will help my cause. Josiah Tremayne is eminently eligible. Timothy will be pleased if he thinks you're paying regard to matrimony. It's all he thinks a woman should ever concern herself with.'

Kelynen was silent for a while, reflecting sadly that the London art critics had considered Livvy's works under-developed – certainly not up to the standard required to grace the most discerning of walls or public galleries.

'You want me to say it's already arranged for me to accompany you to Chenhalls? Livvy, you are such a liar. I'll not allow you to make me one too. Timothy is within his rights to take issue with you. You are the unreasonable one, don't you think? You spend many a day, all of the day, out at your portraits and not enough time with the children or applying yourself to parish duties. Anyway, I thought you would have finished Sir Rafe's portrait by now.'

'Well, I haven't. He wants his favourite cats in it with him. Lady Portia wants me to portray her next.'

'Just paint in some cats and tell the sister she must wait. I can hardly take Rex where there are a lot of cats, and it wouldn't be fair on Mrs Wills to leave him here in her care for a whole day.'

'Oh, really! If you'd seen Sir Rafe's cats you would know they are of particular exotic breeds, each with its own traits and personality. And why should I ask Lady Portia to wait? She is at least two-score years older than Sir Rafe. Time is not with her. She looks more in the next world than this one. I need the commission. I'd hardly have a decent gown to wear if I had to rely on Timothy's stipend alone. There are dogs too at Chenhalls. You can take Rex. Come with me, do, Kelynen. Please! It will give you something to do. It's got to be better than moping about. I thought you were going to treat yourself to new experiences, find a new purpose. Chenhalls might give you both. You've allowed Luke to unsettle you. He should never have said what he did to you. Father will ensure you have a good future whether you marry or not. And you're sure to marry eventually – only look more carefully at what you desire in a husband than I did.'

'Livvy! You are unjust to Timothy. And you've omitted that you have your own money, which he refuses to touch. As for me, I'm more duty-conscious than you are.'

'Oh, tush! Forget duty, it can be horrendously suffocating. Even if Luke had not moved back home, Matthias Renfree could easily run the estate alone. And I am not unjust to Timothy. I'd never have married him if I'd known he would become so predictable and tiresome.'

'Livvy, what a thing to say! Timothy is a fine man, honest and kind and non-judgemental. He's thoroughly likeable.' Livvy's views saddened Kelynen. The Reverend Timothy Lanyon was a sympathetic parson, excellent with the anxious and bereaved. His sermons were long and detailed, but delivered with such fervour that his goodly numbered congregation usually went away each week satisfied or inspired.

17

'You think him fine? You wouldn't consider my comments so awful if you had to endure my life. Timothy used to be outrageously informal and boisterous, remember? He liked to shock people, especially women. Now he's just like any other mature man, content with the mundane. He's dull and dry, like someone all used up.'

Kelynen might have remarked that perhaps the change in her brother-in-law's attitude had something to do with the constant war he was engaged in to stop Livvy disgracing him by living more as a single than a married lady. But that would enrage her sister. It was Livvy who shocked people now, by her neglect of many a wife's duties, by sometimes being rude to those who called at the parsonage on parish concerns. There was speculation outside the parsonage walls that she had deserted the marriage bed. In fact she had, declaring that she had no intention of adding to the two small children already in the nursery.

'Timothy has a son and a daughter; if he wants anything more out of me then he'll be disappointed.' Livvy came to her side, linking her arm entreatingly through hers, inveigling to get her own way. She had inherited the lovely dark-red hair and oval-faced beauty of their mother, but while Lady Pengarron's looks were always gentle, Livvy's were often hard. 'Anyway it's time you met some people who are more entertaining than your usual circle. Sir Rafe is amiable and delightful and fascinating. He's well travelled and has filled Chenhalls with all manner of intriguing effects. He's a most attractive man, his age about forty-seven, I should think. He's sympathetic towards my aims and says he prefers my raw interpretations to anything Hogarth-style or any other of the great masters. You know already that he's outlived his two wives and sadly all his children. Women adore coming under his attention and wit. Come with me, Kelynen. We'll have fun, I promise you. You'll find Chenhalls captivating. The gardens are divine. And . . .' Livvy smiled to beguile. 'Josiah Tremayne has a particularly appealing face, a splendid physique and a pleasant disposition.'

'Think him more interesting than the mayor's son, do you?' Kelynen asked in a sudden drift of dry humour.

'What?' Livvy's puzzled frown metamorphosed into a triumphant smile. 'A thousand times more! Good, so you'll come?'

'I suppose, as you've said, it's something to do,' Kelynen replied doubtfully, adding quickly and sternly, 'But I'll only go if Timothy agrees that you may.'

Livvy squeezed her arm and kissed her cheek. 'I knew I'd talk you round. We'll have to rise early. I need plenty of time to paint in good light. Now the weather is kinder, Sir Rafe is posing in the gardens, where the painting is actually set. I'll slip downstairs and tell Mrs Wills our plans.'

'After that shall we take Hugh and Julia out in the gardens? The air is fresh and sweet. It's a lovely early-spring day.'

'No. It will only disturb their routine.' A second later Livvy was pattering down the attic stairs.

Kelynen wandered about the well-lit room, made up mostly on the south wall of glass. She looked over the assortment of Livvy's work: still life, land and seascapes, but mostly portraits. She liked Livvy's carefree application. Livvy came alive with purpose and creativity when she painted. She sparkled, oozed energy. Such a pity she could not find a similar passion for Timothy.

Kelynen hoped to alight on a stranger in the portraits who might be Sir Rafe Tremayne. But, of course, his portrait would be at Chenhalls awaiting completion, and there it would remain. She was suddenly curious about Chenhalls, an ancient secluded estate, several miles up the coast in Mount's Bay. Chenhalls had always evoked gossip and rumour. Ghosts were said to haunt it. Disappearances and other mysteries were said to abound there. Insanity was supposed to have knocked on many a Tremayne head.

Kneeling down to Rex, she hugged his comforting neck. 'It will pass away some time for us, my old love.'

She slipped away quietly to the nursery to enquire if she might view her two-year-old nephew and niece of fourteen weeks, but before she could speak to the wet nurse, she heard furious shouting from the floor below. Livvy and Timothy were involved in a quarrel, not an unusual occurrence, but it sounded so bitter that Kelynen thought she had better go down to them.

Her sister and brother-in-law halted their fierce words as she entered the spacious, well-furnished parlour. Both were shaking in anger. Kelynen appealed to Timothy's red blustering face. 'If this is about the visit to Chenhalls, then of course I withdraw my desire to go there.'

'It's not that, it's about this!' Livvy stabbed a forefinger towards a bundle of pale pink silk on one of the sofas.

'One of the maids left it there?' Kelynen asked disbelievingly. It seemed a trifling matter to row so violently over.

'Look closer,' Livvy said in a low dangerous tone.

The Reverend Timothy Lanyon threw up his hands in exasperation.

Kelynen shot him a sympathetic glance. She went to the sofa, peered down at the bundle of silk and wrinkled her nose at the strong fetid smell coming off it. 'Good heavens, it's a baby, quite newly born by appearance. Where did it come from?'

'I found it abandoned on the church steps.' Timothy glared at his tight-lipped wife with meaningful intent. 'Poor little mite.'

'Where do you think it comes from?'

'Some unwed trollop,' Livvy replied with distaste. 'And because of her stinking brat, he –' she glared at Timothy – 'has forbidden me to go to Chenhalls.'

'The poor unfortunate child wasn't consigned, as so many others are, to a rubbish heap, the depths of a mine shaft or

20

the bottom of the sea, but has been entrusted into my care. *Our* care, for everything that concerns me should concern you too. Why won't you see that?' Timothy was not far off exploding. Kelynen had never seen him so agitated. 'Of course you can't go gadding off at a time like this.'

Kelynen watched in horror as Livvy strode up to Timothy and smashed a hand across his face. His head spun round at a right angle. A scar in the middle of his chin, caused many years ago during a wrestling match, was noticeably whiter than the rest of his reddened skin. 'How dare you suggest we actually adopt the disgusting creature! How dare you even think of putting it with my children in the nursery!'

Timothy threw out an arm and grasped Livvy by the wrist. 'What I actually said is that we must show the child Christian charity. You panicked, wife, because you saw it as some sentiment, some ruse on my part to tie you to the house. I should not waste my breath! I have long given up hope that you will pay heed to your rightful course. It is not I who needs to get my priorities right. You have that dubious honour. You wilfully neglect your own children. You were out of the house about your art before barely a fortnight was up after being in childbed with Julia. Hugh doesn't even know who you are. Think this makes you a good mother, a credible lady in the neighbourhood? Well, I've had enough of your cold disregard. On no account will I allow you to go to Chenhalls or anywhere else to paint for several months. Do you take note? Disobey me and I shall dismantle your studio and make a bonfire of your things. You may write to your father and urge him home to take me to task, but I shall no more mind if I had Old Nick despatched to my doorstep. In fact I'm sorely tempted to build a bonfire this minute and put you, Olivia –' he used her proper given name in a menacing tone – 'upon it!'

He let Livvy go and for once she was speechless, her red mouth working but empty of words.

Timothy smoothed his straight earth-brown hair, gone wild in the altercation. He took a deep breath to clear his dizzy head and then swept up to the baby. Kelynen jumped back from the sofa. She couldn't help feeling chastened too. She certainly did not wish to stay in this house a second longer.

'Please accept my apologies over what you have just witnessed, Kelynen. The child is wrapped in fine material. It's likely the mother is of high birth.'

'Mama has formed a charity to find orphaned children new homes. I could get in touch with one of the ladies on the board, if you like,' Kelynen offered.

'That is kind of you, but I would like a little time to elapse before I consider what to do with this child.'

'What will you do?' She glanced anxiously at Livvy, who let out a furious huff.

'Don't worry.' Timothy glared at his wife. 'I'll order the trap to be brought round. I'll take the child to your brother, Kane. He understands how it feels to be rejected, adopted himself as he was out of love by your parents. I'm confident he will gladly provide this ill-fated scrap of humanity with the succour it deserves until its future can be best decided. Hopefully its mother will find the means to return and reclaim it. Perhaps you'd be good enough to stay with your sister, Kelynen. She may benefit from your good sense and better character.'

'You went too far, Livvy,' Kelynen said when Timothy had stormed out of the house.

Livvy was staring into space, her face pale and pinched, but her grey-green eyes were glittering with an unquiet passion. She said, one biting word at a time, 'And so did he.'

Four

L ate in the night, Livvy left her bedroom in her floating silk dressing gown and brocaded slippers and crept downstairs.

She had guessed right – that Timothy had not retired and was enshrined in his little dark den. He often stayed up late writing his sermons, and since she had deserted the marriage bed she knew he sometimes did not go to bed at all. Tonight he was drinking claret, had consumed a large amount of it. A near-empty bottle was clutched in one hand and he was leaning against a bookcase, his coat and clerical collars off, his shirt open to the waist.

His mouth twisted to the side as he coldly watched her approach. 'You are intruding, madam.'

She went close to him. 'We've never quarrelled like this before, Timothy.'

'I think you enjoyed it.' He brought the bottle up to his lips, downed the last red drop. 'Leave me in peace.'

She fetched him the full bottle standing by, its cork already pulled. He snatched it from her.

'It's not your way to get intoxicated, Timothy. I really must have unsettled you.'

'Turning to drink to escape the rigours of being wed to you is a tempting prospect, but I shall indulge in such for this night only.' He looked her up and down with a kind of abhorrence that made Livvy shudder. Timothy had only looked at her before with desire, kindness, or a lame pleading or anger. 'However, I might take to beating you. Now that *does* appeal to me.'

'Why not throw me out of the house during the throes of a violent storm without a farthing in my purse?'

'Bitch!'

Livvy had made to mock him further, show him yet again that she was not afraid of him, that she held superiority over him, but his venom pulled her up sharp. 'Kelynen was right. I did go too far today.'

'Is she still here?'

'Yes. Reluctantly so, I think. She probably thought one of us might have need of her.'

'You, Livvy, *Olivia Pengarron*, have no need of anyone. And I no longer have need of you. Get out of my den.'

'I'll leave when I'm ready to.' Livvy was determined to disguise how troubled he was making her. Determined also to talk him round concerning Chenhalls. 'I'm curious about the abandoned child. Is it well? Is it male or female? Has there been any information about its parentage?'

'I will not discuss the child with you. You are not interested in it anyway.'

'I am,' she lied, moving to a single breath's distance from him. 'You may bask, Timothy, in indignation and marital self-righteousness, but nevertheless you are nothing more than a mere man and you do have need of me. Don't you?' Keeping contact with his eyes, so grey and dark and menacing in the low candlelight, she undid the lavish cord of her dressing gown. 'Come to me, Timothy. We'll discuss our differences later.'

Without breaking his sight from her he took a deep draught out of the bottle.

She gave a feline smile. Ran her fingertips along the curve of her chin and down over the central column of her throat, carrying on down until she reached the soft stuff of her nightgown, which she slowly edged off her shoulders. She moved over to Timothy, placing a thigh against his leg. 'I'm sorry about today, beloved. I know I can be difficult, but isn't it part of what you love about me? Come to my room. Or we can stay here. Whatever you choose.'

'What I want, Olivia . . .' He drank some more wine.

'Yes, dearest?' She put her hands on his waist, began a slow journey inside his shirt, up over his skin until she was stroking his neck behind his ears, where he liked to be touched. Timothy had kept his body slim and well toned, while the few other clerics she had deigned to meet all seemed to be portly, with unsightly paunches. She wasn't a willing bed partner nowadays, but suddenly this haughty change in him – this hint of cruelty, even – was sensually appealing. Her woman's regions were on fire and she was hungry for him. She tilted her head, making her long, glossy auburn hair sway provocatively over her shoulders, before reaching up with her lips for his.

'What I want, Olivia –' he brought his face to within a fraction of hers – 'is for you to get the hell out of my den and to never bother me again. Your cheap ploy at offering me sex to get your own way doesn't appeal to me at all.'

It took a moment for Livvy to comprehend the full meaning behind his harsh words. She whipped her hands down from him and backed away.

'In fact, dear wife, I no longer care about you at all. Go tomorrow to Chenhalls, or anywhere else you desire. Henceforth, all I shall require of you is that you attend church every Sunday and make a convincing pretence of acting as a parson's wife on two days of the week. If you do not, I shall order Mrs Bevan to forbid you entrance to the nursery and I shall carry out my threat to destroy your studio.'

With an effort, Livvy found her voice. 'You unspeakable swine! My father gave you the living of this parish and he can just as easily take it away. He will not allow you to treat me in such a manner.'

'Sir Oliver will never learn the circumstances of our marriage, will he? I'm sure you'll not take your disgrace to his or your mama's ears. Because that is what your attitude towards me is, a disgrace. Now be gone. The very sight of you makes me sick and I find you utterly boring.'

'How dare you speak to me like that! I'll make you suffer—'

'What! More than you already have? That, Mrs Lanyon, is impossible. But you know the old saying, he who has the last laugh . . .'

Livvy felt she was shrinking; she felt abused. But Timothy was not finished with her yet. 'Face up to it, woman, your skills with a paintbrush don't measure up. The experts said so. Your work is good and always will be, but nothing more. You have sacrificed me for a stupid dream.'

Five

'Are you sure you'll cope with this, Livvy? Perhaps you'd
be better off at home.' Taking one hand off the reins
of the parsonage trap, Kelynen wrapped Livvy's cape more
closely round her tense shoulders.

The early-morning chilly grey mist still had its grip on
the coast road and little could be seen ahead, but it wasn't
the weather that was making Livvy shiver at alarming intervals.

'You mean to continue with the portrait at Chenhalls?
Of course I'll cope. Sir Rafe's diverting company is just
what I need right now.'

Kelynen knew her sister's good spirits were false. After
the quarrel in the den, of which Kelynen, in the room overhead, had heard the rumblings, Livvy had run up to her
own room and cried all night; a child's crying, lonely and
distraught. Kelynen had waited an agonizing hour before
going in to her, not wanting to get in the way if, as she had
prayed, Timothy did so. 'Livvy, Timothy will come round,
won't he?'

'I care not if he doesn't! At last I'm free, as free as a
man, to come and go as I please.'

'Not entirely,' Kelynen pointed out. 'Timothy has put
restrictions on you.'

'I'm as free as a married woman can be; that makes me
content. If it wasn't for the children I'd leave him.'

Kelynen paid close attention to the dirt road, fearing a
pothole or unseen obstruction might be their undoing. They

27

had travelled through half a dozen hamlets and villages since leaving Perranbarvah and were now passing, from a comfortable distance, the shadowy cottages and shanties of Trewarras. The squat, bleak homes, on scrubby moorland that barely supported a potato patch, of the miners from the Wheal Lowen copper mine. Kelynen knew without a close view that there would be roofs that needed mending, ditches needing to be dug or cleared. Many of the children would be weak and marked by disease. The mongrels could be heard barking, emaciated and ferocious. Although all were skilled in their trade, their wages more than farm workers, these people were the underlings of society. Some were fiercely religious, some were fierce drinkers, all were fiercely proud, a breed apart and somewhat feared.

'I'm sorry things are so bad for you, Livvy.'

'Let's not talk of it again. The sun should burn off this mist very soon and I should complete an excellent day's painting – no matter what my miserable husband thinks of my ability. And you'll be able to walk Rex through the beautiful gardens.' Rex was jogging along, protectively close to the trap.

Kelynen was pleased to see Livvy brightening.

On the road now were miners trudging home after their eight-hour core, lugging excavating tools, usually three or four of them on their sturdy but weary shoulders. They stared at the trap from under their wide-brimmed hard hats, nodding in respect, for their burdens prevented the touching of forelocks. Kelynen fancied one or two scowled at her; jealous, impatient or angry, perhaps, that others should be well bred and better off. They had dirt-streaked faces, worn-out eyes, most were short in stature and all seemed bent over. It was a long walk home after a hard night's graft in hazardous conditions. Long after they had passed the last man, the ominous, hazy outlines of the mine workings itself could be seen near the cliff edge, the mist and distance thankfully muffling the demonic clankings, booms and creakings of the machinery. Sir Rafe Tremayne owned this mine, the largest in the area.

After another mile they were approaching Trewarras Head, a wide finger of land protruding out into the sea. They had half a mile left to go. Chenhalls was sheltered between the headland and the next one, Mearnon Point. Minutes later, Rex scurried on ahead. The mist was thinning, shapes were beginning to show normal and clear, and Kelynen felt the first warmth of a promising sun shining through.

'Tell me more about Sir Rafe.' From what she had already heard, the baronet was firmly in her mind as a man of independent spirit, apt to suddenly dart from Chenhalls to his various homes in Truro or London, or to sail overseas. In his youth, he had captained a privateer ship for the benefit of the Realm. He was a flagrant freetrader – a smuggler of untaxed goods. Livvy had mentioned he was good-looking. So was their father: fourteen years older than Sir Rafe, he was still turning the heads of women of every age. Kelynen smiled to herself. Perhaps she should look over the widower as a likely husband for herself. What would her family think of that?

The next instant she was bringing the trap to a halt. 'Oh, my goodness!'

'What is it? Have you seen something on the road?' Livvy craned her neck to see over the horse's head.

Taking away the hand that had flown to her face, Kelynen broke into a strange little smile. 'There's nothing I can do about it now but I should be at home today. I'd invited Sophie Carew to call on me.'

Polly O'Flynn knocked on the door of the library at the manor and entered on her sure, quiet step. 'Mr Pengarron?'

'Mmm?' Luke glanced up from the rambling table spread with open books and his steadily growing manuscript. When his brain and imagination were in tune he could finish a

29

play in three months. He was researching some obscure African mythology. He favoured to create fantasy plays, with all manner of strange animals that could talk, and with gods, fairies, giants and the like. 'Surely we've not long had breakfast? Throw another log on the fire will you, please, Mrs O'Flynn? The chill from the mist entered my bones and has stayed stubbornly with me.'

'It's because you will sit around, sir. You need to get up and send the blood circulating.' Polly could speak like this to her young master. She had come to the manor long before his birth – had married the Pengarrons' Irish gamekeeper and head forester – and Luke held an affectionate respect for the older servants.

'I'll take a long ride later.'

'I'm afraid there's a bit of a problem,' Polly said, throwing a log on the embers of the fire and raking with the poker to bring about a crackling blaze. It produced a peachy-rosy glow to the dark oak panelling. 'A lady has arrived to take tea with Miss Kelynen.'

'Who?' Luke employed his quill in rapid strokes, having gained a lot of inspirational meat from the account of a fire-breathing, multi-winged, half-human, half-bird immortal. He should get through two thousand words by nightfall.

'It's Mrs Sophie Carew, sir. She's the widow of Mr Wilmot Carew, the . . . um . . .'

'Old fool who married again late and shot himself dead over gambling debts,' Luke finished unsympathetically. 'Send her away.'

'I can hardly do that, sir.' This went against Polly's sense of right and order.

Luke swore under his breath. He hated being disturbed from his writing. He had worked out that he would complete the second act today, and tomorrow he would show his face about the estate while mulling over what he had written. Then, after a night spent with a certain married lady in

Marazion, he would edit and resume writing. 'Why didn't Miss Kelynen come home for this?'

'She sent word, remember, that she's off to Chenhalls with Mrs Lanyon.'

'Oh, I'll see the wretched woman if I must, for a minute. And think of some excuse to save my sister's face.'

'Shall I show her into Lady Pengarron's sitting room? It's where the ladies usually take tea.'

'Yes, yes, damn it! I shan't take long in getting rid of her.'

'Sir . . .' Polly intimated his casual attire.

'What? Oh, arrange for Elgan to bring me something more fitting.'

Polly dropped a perfect curtsey and hurried away. Luke stopped her before she closed the high double doors. 'Polly, what's this woman like?'

'Mrs Carew, sir? The word I'd use to sum her up is surprising.'

Luke was intrigued by this description as he allowed the pompous Elgan to change his frock coat, brush him down, polish him up and re-tie his neckcloth and the bow at the back his long black hair. What could be surprising about Wilmot Carew's widow? She was young, apparently, but she had to be dull. None of Kelynen's friends were particularly appealing.

'If I can't get away quickly, Elgan, I'll ring for you,' Luke said grimly. 'Come at once with an excuse to rid me of the lady's company.'

'Promptly, sir.' Elgan always kept his pale eyes dull and disinterested, but Luke had come to recognize the modicum of gleam in them that anticipated a relish. Elgan was a misogynist. Well, Luke was not. He liked women. He liked to have women of all ages dote on him, witty women to amuse him, beautiful, young, creative women in his bed. Perhaps this one was a sweet, quaint soul he wouldn't mind giving a few minutes of his time to.

31

Luke strode into the great hall, which linked most of the ground floor rooms, then down the long passage to his mother's private room. Polly was waiting outside the door. Luke hurried in. The sooner he got this over with the sooner he could return to the library. Hopefully the widow would not make a fuss and would shortly take herself off.

Anticipating Polly's introductions, Luke passed through the door saying, 'My humble apologies—' He was brought to stand stock still, his mouth curved around a half formed word.

Sophie Carew *was* surprising. More so! She was startling, a sensation. And she was a riot of contradictions. She was the essence of finely bred female fragility, yet he knew she owned a will every bit as strong and as powerful as his own. She was fully a woman, yet although having been married, retained an enticing innocence. Her clothes of gunmetal grey – she was half out of mourning – detracted none of her vibrant energy. No woman had ever had such a shocking effect on him before. She stirred him, excited him, thrilled him – but for all that, she inexplicably chilled him and this fascinated him even more. The look in her eyes spoke of her right to be here and said that she would stay for as long it pleased her to.

'You were saying, Mr Pengarron? I take it you *are* Luke Pengarron? Brother of Miss Kelynen?' Her voice was rich with melody.

Like a lovesick blundering youth Luke stared and stared and saw more of her beauty. Eyes of ice blue, finely honed features, skin that glittered with opalescent whiteness and hair of an unusual fairness, as if shot through with crushed pearls.

'Forgive me, Mrs Carew,' he faltered, struggling to recall the excuse he had thought up on Kelynen's behalf. 'Please let me explain. My sister . . . um . . . she had to rush off, my other sister had sudden need of her. She asked me to extend her apologies to you. I'm afraid I'm a poor substitute for her, but would you care to stay and take tea with me?'

Please stay! Don't go. I won't let you.

'Do you not mean instead, Mr Pengarron, that Miss Kelynen has fled your side? She has told me how she finds you impossible to live with.'

Luke shook his head without realizing he was doing so. He had no idea how to respond to the young woman's calm, almost glacial tone. Then he saw a small smile teasing the corners of her handsome pink lips and he smiled back. 'I fear you may have the measure of me before we can become acquainted, Mrs Carew. Perhaps I may plead my case by pointing out how easily brothers and sisters fall into rivalry?' Pulling up his great height to a more manly bearing, he indicated a plush upholstered armchair. 'Please, may I offer you a seat? Mrs O'Flynn is waiting to ring for tea.'

'I'd be pleased to stay, but I'll take tea with the old woman.'

'Old woman?' Luke swallowed his disappointment and prayed he wasn't making an utter fool of himself. Who could she mean?

'Beatrice,' Sophie Carew explained, and Luke's heart hit his feet, for she was looking at him as if addressing an idiot. 'I understand she goes by no other name. Miss Kelynen sometimes takes me along to her room. I find her entertaining. So there is no need for me to keep you. Thank you for sparing the time to speak to me, Mr Pengarron. Please be good enough to ask your sister to call on me when she returns. I'll show myself to Beatrice's room. Good morning.'

She walked, floated it seemed, out of the room. Luke followed her with his eyes until she had disappeared. He dropped down into the armchair, feeling his legs would not hold him up another second. So there *was* such a thing as love at first sight! A foolish notion to him before, something he had thought only women and poets believed in.

But it was true! The instant his eyes had reached Sophie Carew he had fallen hopelessly and irretrievably in love with her.

Polly was watching him, both amused and worried. She made a discreet withdrawal to order tea and muffins for Beatrice and her guest.

'No! Mrs O'Flynn, come back. Tell me everything you know about her. Every last tiny detail.'

An hour later, trying to look as if he just happened to be there, Luke was waiting beside Sophie Carew's pony when she drifted down the stone steps outside the manor house. He had sent the stable boy away so he could help her to mount.

'Ah, Mrs Carew, I hope you enjoyed your visit. Beatrice is quite a character, is she not? The family set great store by her.'

'I've spent a pleasant time with her, Mr Pengarron. You are a playwright, I understand. Are you currently writing something?'

'I am, actually. It's entitled *The Golden Leaves of Winterland.*' He was elated at her interest. 'How kind of you to enquire. Kelynen has told you much about me, I see.' Polly O'Flynn had told him much about this gorgeous young widow. The remnant of her husband's wealth from tin and copper mining, except for a small house in Marazion and a measly five hundred a year, had gone to the son of his first marriage. Sophie Carew managed without a carriage and only two servants. Her family were of no consequence, there was a vague scandal associated with them. Doubtless, her reason for marrying the tedious old Wilmot Carew had been to gain security. 'Do you enjoy the theatre, Mrs Carew?'

'I do, if the offering is well written and well produced, Mr Pengarron. I really must go. Good day to you.'

Luke helped her up into the side-saddle, careful not to touch her for too long, breathing in her sandalwood perfume.

He watched from the top of the steps until she had ridden through the park gates. His play quite forgotten, he was beaming, more full of purpose than when, in a state of depression three years ago, he had asked his father to release him from estate duties so he could buy his own property and concentrate on his new burning ambition to write for the theatre.

He sent a promise soaring skywards. 'I'm sure we have a lot more in common, Mrs Carew. You won't dismiss me this easily.'

Six

Chenhalls was shielded by high, dense, weathered walls, part of them the original fortress built centuries earlier, when great landowners were forced to protect themselves from rebellions and lawlessness. The gatehouse was granite and Gothic in design, dark and forbidding, as if telling outsiders to keep out, Kelynen thought as she drove the trap in through the solid, studded wooden gates.

A cocker spaniel bounded up from somewhere and growled menacingly at Rex. Kelynen held her breath. Rex enjoyed a scrap and he could practically make a meal of this smaller aggressor.

'Digory, it's me, Livvy. Come here, boy!' Recognizing her voice, the spaniel broke off holding its territory in front of the snarling Rex, leapt up on the trap and settled at her side. The women laughed. 'This is Sir Rafe's only dog. Lady Portia has lapdogs – they hate the cats. She does too. Sometimes there is quite a to-do.'

Trotting along a wide gravelled road they came to the back courtyards of the great house. The front faced the sea. Kelynen experienced a strange feeling, like an awakening, yet more than that. Like an obscure memory, as if she had been here before. The uncanny sensation grew, as if something was pressing on her, *waiting* for her. She told herself not be so fanciful. It was the mystery over the foundling that was making her sense the fantastic. Tomorrow, after apologizing to Sophie, she would go home and attend to the estate before Luke made any unnecessary changes.

Passing under the medieval entrance arch, the sisters entered the cobbled retainer's court where two solemn, blue-and-silver-liveried, bewigged footmen came forward to help them alight. One of them leapt back when Digory shot down off the trap to avoid being bowled over. Digory sniffed Rex, decided the big black retriever was a friend, and then they ran off together.

'Don't worry, they'll come back after they've tired of their adventure,' Livvy said.

Kelynen felt lost and exposed without Rex. Then something inside her soul – the house, she supposed – called to her again and she was eager to see inside it.

While one footman gathered up Livvy's painting equipment, the other led the way through the porter's squint into a second court. It was rectangular, flagged, and surrounded by the three main ranges of the lumbering antediluvian house. A small chapel was incorporated into the north range. Little stone statues of strange leonine creatures were set under the square and arched windows, and larger ones with beautiful faces and wings joined the corners high up on the castellated walls. Gazing up, Kelynen thought their perch precarious and that only a brush from one of the clouds, seemingly just above, would bring them crashing down. They had been added much later to the original building, of course, by someone with a sense of the romantic. Luke should see these statues. They were perfect creatures for his current play.

Had Luke met the guest she had invited to the manor? If so, how had he found Sophie Carew? Likely there would be a letter of slight reprove from Sophie awaiting her at the parsonage this evening. Knowing her brother's fondness for beautiful women, it was unlikely there would be a vexed one from him.

The footman ushered them through the great arched divided door into the vestibule and into the banqueting hall. While Livvy threw off her cloak, Kelynen gazed about, convinced she had stepped back in time. Chenhalls made Pengarron Manor seem very new. There was a feeling of ancient times here, prehistoric times, and she would not have been surprised if a Merlin-like figure materialized and drifted off towards some hidden door to his wizard's den. Doubtless there was a warren of secret rooms and passages in the house. Harking back to the communal living of the Middle Ages there was a table of feasting proportions, and a yawning fireplace on a raised dais, piled high with fragrant logs. The walls were hung with armoury and weaponry. Kelynen's steps were soft on the bare lime ash floor as she tilted her head to the decorated arch-braced ceiling. The Tremayne arms, depicting a rampant lion under a pair of crossed axes, appeared above the fireplace and in the heraldic panels in the windows.

'Take off your hat and cloak,' Livvy prodded her. 'I've told the footman we'll make our own way to the gardens. Sir Rafe is waiting there for me. Lady Portia is with him. She always sits near his side, squawking interference, I'm afraid, but I do find her amusing. You like it here! I knew you would. Why, Kelynen, I've never seen you look so awe-struck or so pretty. The family lives mainly in here. They don't use many of the rooms. We'll be treated to a feast on that table later, on that you can rely.'

Kelynen allowed herself to be pulled through a door in a corner of the room, then along a cold, dark, stone passage. She did not want to go outside but to wander through the rooms and study the old solid furnishings and things that centuries of Tremaynes – and, of course, Sir Rafe – had brought here: Flemish tapestries, Eastern and European pottery, carved chests, folding chairs, the several and diverse paintings and engravings. She was to learn that Josiah Tremayne had sent home many an interesting piece while on the grand tour. She wanted to explore, to stumble on some fascinating secret, solve a long-held mystery. Chenhalls had that effect, on her anyway, making her fiercely curious, wanting to pry.

Of a sudden she was back outside, gasping in fresh air, blinking, for the sunlight was now strong, while Livvy was banging shut a heavy, creaking, planked door. They were at the side of the house, where the coast beyond Mearnon Point stretched all the way to the Lizard. The fishing village of Porthleven was tucked away out of sight beyond the point. Livvy prodded her to look inland. Kelynen gasped, lost in wonder. Down over a gentle slope, amid grounds of natural undulations and copses, and sheltered from behind by an arc of trees, lay a sunken garden, landscaped in the medieval style of the knot, a geometric pattern within a square made up of clipped box hedging and herbs. A simple fountain was in the centre.

Peeping above the trees were the parapets of a square tower. 'What's that? I must see it!'

'Not now, you can't. It's a folly. Sir Rafe's father had it built. Look, down there in that quiet arbour. It's Sir Rafe waving to us.'

Forsaking the steps and formal path, Livvy suddenly took off at a run down the grassy slope, taking Kelynen with her. They raced, gaining speed and squealing as they had as little girls, and were laughing and pink-faced by the time they presented themselves in front of Sir Rafe Tremayne. An elderly lady was sitting close to him on a stout chair. Her maid-cum-companion, a staunch, ruddy-faced woman named Jayna Hayes, was beside her on a high stool.

'My, having a wonderful time already,' Sir Rafe said, flashing brilliant eyes on each sister. 'That's what I like to see. Livvy, beloved, how good to see you. How divine you are, as always.'

Embarrassed after her abandoned moments, Kelynen watched, amazed, when the baronet gathered her sister into his arms and kissed her firmly on the mouth.

'And who is this?' Sir Rafe's laughing eyes danced all over Kelynen the instant he let Livvy go. 'Your sister? You are not greatly alike but there is some resemblance.' He lifted Kelynen's hand and kissed it, once, twice, three times. Feeling a fool, all she could do was stare up at him. He was a tower, broad of shoulder, a wearer of gaily coloured clothes, although at present his coat was flung across the companion's lap. His hair was thick and dark and he looked much younger than his forty-seven years. His face was full of strength and hilarity. 'Miss Kelynen Pengarron, you are beautiful! And blessed with a pretty Cornish name; it means holly, does it not?' He kissed her then on both cheeks, warmly, resoundingly.

Shaken, bewildered, unused to affectionate contact with men (unless with her father, brothers or brother-in-law), Kelynen thought she should be offended by this noble taker of liberties. But that wasn't the effect Sir Rafe Tremayne had on women. Kelynen blinked, feeling she could all too easily succumb to the spell he unconsciously cast. He would have been a formidable beau in his youth – still was. She found her voice.

'It's an honour to meet you, Sir Rafe. I like your house and gardens very much.'

Sir Rafe threw up a large hand. 'Do wander about at will, m'dear. Your sister and I will be occupied for some time. She's a tyrant with the brush and forbids me to move for hours, but I'm sure you know that. But first, come and meet the old dear, my sister. And the cats.'

It was then that Kelynen saw the cats. There were eight of them, every one exquisite. None were of the usual breeds. These had oriental features, with eyes of sapphire blue, deep copper or vivid green. Some had long tails, some sharp, pointed ears. Some had sleek coats and others had coats that were long, of lavender, silver-blue or chocolate. All were perfectly groomed. Her father would never stand it here. He was allergic to cats and banned them from the manor and home farm.

'I won't bore you with all their names.' Sir Rafe swept up an armful of the gorgeous creatures. 'This is Lady Portia Custentin, my very much older sister.'

'Dah! Insolent boy!'

'What do you think of this lovely little bud, Kelynen, old dear?'

Lady Portia rose with difficulty, clasping against her flat bosom two small white dogs of an indistinct terrier breed. She was tall and thin and shaky on her feet. Gold-rimmed spectacles sat astride her long nose. She was wearing a pale-green gown, fussily decked with ruffles, lace and ribbons. Kelynen likened her to a reedy bendy branch overgrown with anaemic leaves. Her wig was discreet and dressed with green silk flowers, and her jewels were emeralds. She had a high domed forehead and strong cheekbones, clues to her aristocratic birth. Her voice was loud and boisterous. Every few words her eyes half closed as if clogged with sleep, but Kelynen fancied she missed nothing. 'I bid you welcome to Chenhalls, Miss Pengarron. I've heard about you. You're your father's favourite and no wonder. You look a loyal, sensible sort. Our grandfather was in love with your grandmother, Lady Caroline, did you know, but Sir Daniel Pengarron got to her first.'

'I didn't know that, Lady Portia. What dear little dogs you have. Mine is about somewhere. I'm afraid he ran off.' Kelynen was praying Rex wouldn't show up here. He would run amok among the cats and create mayhem. Sir Rafe might lose his humour, although it seemed he had a constant supply of it. She had the impression it bubbled up inside him like a hot spring, along with a strong amorous drive. Apparently he had never been without a mistress, or two. She was worried Livvy was in danger of being dazzled by him, but her sister appeared set only on organizing her painting things and telling the footman where to place the easel and unfinished portrait. Sir Rafe, after the inappropriate

41

kiss, was speaking to her now in a kindly, professional
manner.

'Bring your dog to show me as soon as you're able.'
Lady Portia wobbled and Jayna Hayes helped her to sit
down. 'My little Cosmo and Hartley like canine company,
don't you, my precious boys? Take my advice, Missy, and
stick to dogs for companionship. I'm happy to say my
husband has been one of the blessed above for the past
forty years and I don't regret a day of it! Rafe, it's time
you and Mrs Lanyon got started. And keep those infernal
cats at a distance from me!'

Kelynen was eager to track Rex down. To explore these
wondrous grounds was an exciting prospect. After receiving
a handsome smile from Sir Rafe, no one paid her any attention, so she walked off towards the trees where Rex was
likely to be. It was her intended destination anyway; she
was curious about the tower folly.

Almost at once she was brought to a halt by the sound
of music, a skilled performance on a violin. It was an unfamiliar tune, sweet and pure and strangely disturbing, evocative of the sort of hazy dreams one had about paradisiacal
places. The music was soughing out through the trees, most
likely from the tower. Had she heard music on her arrival
without realizing it? Was that what had called to her?

'That's my nephew who is playing,' Sir Rafe called after
her. 'He doesn't like to be disturbed when he's composing,
m'dear, so I'd advise you to keep a wide berth.'

'I will,' Kelynen replied. So Josiah Tremayne wrote and
played beautiful music. She was curious to meet him. Livvy
had said many complimentary things about him. Was he
wickedly entertaining like his uncle? she wondered.

Once within the oaks, beeches and elms she saw Rex and
Digory crashing on ahead. 'Rex!' she shouted, hoping the
dogs would not interrupt Josiah Tremayne. She dashed after
them. Digory probably knew to keep away from the tower
but Rex was altogether too inquisitive and playful.

Now she was out of the trees, the tower came fully into sight. It consisted of five small rooms, one on top of the other. The lower four were sheltered and private; the highest room and the parapets must afford a fine view over the sea. It was an ugly but fascinating folly and Kelynen's imagination took flight to its purpose. Almost hidden away from the great house, it did not aspire towards ornamentation. If a memorial, the deceased must have meant little to the builder. The music was indeed coming from inside. It was the perfect secluded place to compose and practise music. Josiah Tremayne had switched to the harp, making ripples of sound so beguiling that Kelynen would have stopped and listened if the dogs would only obey her calls. They were heading for the tower and she set herself in pursuit.

A low portal in the side of the tower was ajar and first Digory and then Rex plunged through it. Hoping Josiah Tremayne would not be too angry over Rex's encroachment, Kelynen squeezed inside the gap, trying not to make a sound. She took half a dozen steps, her feet making hollow sounds on the paved floor. Rex and Digory had disappeared. There was nowhere for them to go except up the narrow stone stair incorporated into the far wall.

The music had stopped but instead of leaving a feeling of tranquillity, there seemed a heavy brooding resonance in this first airless, unfurnished room where there was only a small fireplace. The low rectangular windows were of dull stained glass and therefore let in little light. It was quiet now, an unearthly hush, as silent as a graveyard. Kelynen had a sudden horrible feeling of being cut off from all life and purpose. The dark seemed to wrap itself around her. And it was cold. A bleak cold that chilled her flesh and invaded her bones. She hugged her arms to her body and wondered what she had let herself in for by agreeing to come to Chenhalls.

Seven

Feeling it invasive to call out Rex's name, holding her breath, Kelynen crept towards the stairs and mounted them on her toes so her heels would not tap out her trespass. Even so, her steps echoed like unwelcome strangers. She arrived on the next floor. The stair carried on, climbing the next wall. Here there was a narrow landing and an open door leading to the first-floor room.

She peeped inside. It was as dark and gloomy as the room below. She heard a snuffling and gulping. Unnerved, Kelynen swung her head to each of the four walls. Everything was steeped in shadows but as her eyes grew used to the dimness she made out a small fireplace with a grate and ashes. She saw the source of the strange noises. Digory was up on a chair at a small square table, wolfing down the remains of a meal on a wooden tray. Josiah Tremayne's breakfast? Digory had knocked over a goblet. There was an empty wine bottle and a single candlestick on the table, but no cloth. Then she located Rex. Sniffing, burrowing with his paws, he was attempting to get his snout under a heavy iron chest. Sensing his mistress near, he abandoned his exploration and padded over to her.

'Get down!' Kelynen hissed across at Digory. He had cleared the plate. He scrambled down and scampered out of the room and down the stairs.

She knew she should leave. But her eyes stole up the next flight of steps. 'Do you think he's up there, Rex? Josiah Tremayne?'

Rex whimpered. Kelynen put a hand on his collar, felt the hairs rise on his hackles.

She should run away from this cloying, shadowy atmosphere. There seemed so little air it was hard to breathe. Or was that the result of her excitement and sense of fear? The tower smelled like a vault. It was cold, so very cold. Perhaps this was where some of Chenhalls' ghosts roamed and lamented their fate. None were rumoured to be friendly. She swallowed down an irrational surge of panic. She had come this far, she might as well take a quick look about the room. 'Come on, Rex.'

She tiptoed towards the iron chest, interested to see if there was an inscription on it, a clue as to its owner. Rex growled low, warning. 'Shush!' She grabbed his collar. He obeyed, but every muscle of his body was poised to leap forward, to protect her if need be. Her heart thundering, she waited to find out the cause of Rex's alarm. If all was well she would leave and Josiah Tremayne need never know she had been trespassing.

He was coming down the stairs with slow, heavy steps. She prayed he would carry on downwards and leave the tower. If not, she would have to summon up the courage to brazen it out. Then she told herself not to be so silly. Why should she be afraid? After all, the nephew of the jovial and hospitable Sir Rafe Tremayne was unlikely to be hostile.

The steps came towards the door. Kelynen sucked in her breath. A rumble started in Rex's throat. He was stiffly alert, raring to lurch forward. 'Shh.'

There was a groan. Kelynen wished she had run out while she'd had the chance.

A shadowy figure shuffled in. Kelynen stared, hardly daring to breathe. It was a very old man. He was panting, muttering and reaching out with one feeble hand for anything that would aid his laborious passage. He was thin to the point of emaciation, bent over and wearing a thick, fringed shawl over which spilled his extraordinarily long colour-less hair. His breathing came raggedly. He was weak and stumbling. Who was he? A servant? Or some ancient insane Tremayne the family wanted to keep secret? Certainly not Josiah Tremayne, who had been playing such wonderful music minutes ago. This person looked too frail to pick up a violin bow, as if he would disintegrate in a puff of wind.

Rex suddenly slipped away from her and hurtled towards the old man. 'Rex, no!' The old man seemed not to hear her shout.

Rex nudged him on the leg and to Kelynen's horror the old man fell, dropped like a stone, too shocked to cry out until he hit a chair and ended up sprawled in front of the fireplace.

'Rex, get back!' Mobilized by instinct to help and make recompense, Kelynen rushed to the old man, falling to her knees. Rex retreated unwillingly. 'I'm so sorry. Are you hurt? Don't try to move. I'll get help.'

'No,' the victim rasped. His fingers curled round her forearm with a strength that surprised her. For one gut-wrenching second she thought she had walked into a trap. 'I don't want any fuss. Please, just help me up.'

'But you might have broken bones.'

'Please, no fuss I say.' He could only raise his voice in a whisper and she had to bring her ear in close to him. 'I assure you the worst I've suffered is bruises.'

He lifted his head and Kelynen recoiled. The face looking directly at her appeared to have had the life hauled out of it, the eyes burned out. He was not an old man but his face was in ruins. She entreated herself to be calm. This phantom of a man frightened her a little. Feebly, he reached for the chair.

'I'll help you,' she said. Getting behind him, she hooked her arms in under his armpits, around his chest and eased him up high enough to drag him on to the chair. It took little effort. He was no more than an outline of a person.

She had felt the bones of his ribs pressing against her arms. He smelled dusty. His hair had fallen across her face, giving her the horrible sensation of being covered in cobwebs. She wiped at her cheeks and brow. Altogether it had been a macabre experience.

His head flopped down and he was wheezing. She moved to get a better view of him. She was almost afraid to look into his face again, but she could not help herself from wanting to.

'*Look up and let me see exactly what you are like.*'

Slowly, while she stared in gruesome fascination, he lifted his head. She saw that her first impression had been conjured up out of her fear-fuelled imaginings, perhaps even a longing to witness the supernatural. Here was a man of about Luke's age who was deathly pale, ill and exhausted.

His fathomless blue eyes, glassy and hollow, flickered and stared at her. 'I thank you for your help. You are not one of the maids.'

'I'm here at Chenhalls with my sister, Mrs Lanyon.'

'Mrs Lanyon? I'm sorry, I have no idea who she is. May I know your name?'

'I'm Kelynen Pengarron. My sister is presently painting Sir Rafe's portrait.'

His head fell to his chest. Kelynen looked about for water to revive him but there was no glass, no jug. He roused himself. 'Pengarron? I heard that name long ago, when I lived here for a short time. My uncle has commissioned a woman? How odd.'

She ignored his question, moved as close to him as she dared. '*You* are Josiah Tremayne?' He was nothing like Livvy's description, unless she had lied or been joking.

'No. I'm Gabriel. Josiah is my younger half-brother.'

Kelynen's mind worked up an intrigue. Two brothers! Half-brothers. And one of them was starving to death in this old tower. Sir Rafe had warned her to keep away from

47

the music-maker. Was Gabriel Tremayne being kept prisoner? 'Do you live here?' she asked.

'I come here to compose and play, although in fact it's many a day since I've ventured up to the house.'

Kelynen was chiding herself for being melodramatic. He was hardly a prisoner if the door was left unlocked and open. But it was more likely he had not ventured up to the house for many weeks. Surely the generous and caring Sir Rafe would not allow his nephew to languish in this condition. Perhaps Gabriel Tremayne had some wasting disease. Perhaps he was in some way mentally ill.

'Don't you think you should go up there now? Forgive me for being forward, but you are very weak. In need of a nourishing meal.'

'I eat well.' Gabriel Tremayne sounded perplexed. 'My plate is cleared every day.'

Kelynen thought she saw the situation. Whatever the man's condition he had lost all appetite. 'Are you in this room when your meals are brought to you?'

'Never. I am always too occupied with my music.'

'Then, I fear, it is Sir Rafe's dog that has been eating them. Do you drink any water?'

'Not often.'

'Then you are probably dehydrated. Forgive me again, but I think you are near to becoming dangerously ill. Please allow me to fetch someone to help you up to the house. You urgently need food, water and the attention of a physician.'

His gaunt eyes rested on her for a long time before he spoke. 'Miss Pengarron, I fear you are right and I thank you for your concern, and for not mentioning my other pressing need: a bath. Could I press you to go up to the house and ask a footman to attend me? Don't disturb my uncle. My aunt will most likely be with him and she is much given to drama, displayed shrilly. I could not stand that.'

Rex had waited, watching warily. Eager to get outside, he whined suddenly.

'What was that?' Gabriel Tremayne wasted some of his limited strength by looking about in alarm.

'It was my dog. It was he who knocked you over. I apologize.'

'Oh, I have fallen a lot lately. I did not realize I was knocked over, although the ghost is capable of such.'

'The tower is haunted?' Kelynen looked nervously behind her. One could imagine anything in this dark, oppressive, unhealthy environment.

'Yes. With much hostility and bitterness, it is said. I shouldn't have flaunted my presence here for so long. Miss Pengarron, please go up to the house and get help. I am anxious to leave here.'

Eight

Kelynen suffered a night of fitful sleep in which she dreamed of being imprisoned forever in a dark dungeon at Chenhalls, and then being hurled off the top of the tower folly by an unseen hand.

After this, and the bleak atmosphere at the parsonage, it was reassuringly light, airy and calm the next day inside Sophie Carew's humble, pleasant home, looking over the port and castle atop St Michael's Mount, half a mile directly across the waters from the ancient market town of Marazion. The parlour walls were charmingly decorated in block-printed, olive-green wallpaper. Miniature enamels of Wilmot Carew were framed with black ribbon. Kelynen admired the exquisite needlepoint that Sophie was working on, of a bird of paradise on white lace.

'I thought I'd put it on the stomacher of a day dress,' Sophie said. 'It will make a pleasing change from the usual bows or ruching.'

The friends had exchanged a formal embrace on Kelynen's arrival, and, as always, Kelynen had felt a slight stiffness in Sophie, who was not given to displays of affection.

'Why not an evening robe? It would make many a lady envious of you.'

'I've no particular wish to resume a social life yet.' Sophie rang for refreshments. 'Now, no more apologies over your journey to Chenhalls. Of course you had to put yourself at your sister's disposal. Tell me, how did you find my late husband's business associate? Sir Rafe speculates in many tin and copper mines on the cost-book system, where many take up shares, but Mr Carew was the only other shareholder in the Wheal Lowen.' There was a tart edge to her voice.

'I found Sir Rafe the most charismatic of men. If he were twenty years younger I think I could easily be drawn to him. But do allow me to say it's kind of you not to mind that I went there. Did you favour Beatrice with a few minutes of your time?'

'I passed an agreeable hour taking tea with her. I met your brother Luke. Beatrice favours him well. She pressed his good character upon me.'

'Oh, I was afraid he would be there. No doubt he was amiable towards you. He can turn on the charm to the ladies.'

'I only saw him for a moment,' Sophie replied dismissively. 'Now, about the Tremaynes, they cheated Wilmot, you know.'

'They did? Are you sure?' Kelynen was disappointed to hear this. 'I didn't meet Josiah Tremayne but I did meet his half-brother. Did you know of Gabriel Tremayne's existence? My sister, Olivia, had no idea he was living there too.'

'I know that Sir Rafe's brother, Reynold, died young, shortly after the death of his second wife. Sir Rafe also married twice to produce an heir, tragically not to be. I do recollect mention of another nephew. Sir Rafe is said to have doted on both his nephews and was saddened when one was taken away as a boy from the estate.'

'And now they are both under his roof,' Kelynen said, absorbing the information. She wanted to learn all she could about the Tremaynes. 'Sadly, Gabriel is very ill. It appears that Josiah may inherit Chenhalls. Sophie, do you have any evidence that the Tremaynes cheated Mr Carew?'

'I can see the family have you somewhat spellbound, Kelynen. I grant you Sir Rafe is thoroughly charming, but he could never insinuate himself into my good books. He was among those who encouraged Wilmot to gamble when he could ill afford to lose. He is something of a restless fellow. He allows Josiah Tremayne almost total sway in his mining affairs. I am convinced Josiah was cheating Wilmot. There were so many things left unexplained after Wilmot's death. After Wilmot's debts were paid, my greedy stepson sold off the few remaining assets to the Tremaynes, but he got only a quarter of what Wilmot had me believe his interests were worth. The jewellery that was supposed to have come to me had disappeared. My stepson showed me documentation to the effect that Wilmot had taken it out of the bank in the weeks prior to his death, doubtless in a desperate effort to redeem himself, but I fear he gambled it all away too. Sometimes I think I should like to go to Chenhalls myself to take issue with the Tremaynes.'

Kelynen listened closely. She had known Sophie, a native of Helston, for nine months, from the time of her marriage, and she had never before spoken of her husband's business matters or the reasons behind his suicide. 'Did your stepson challenge any of this?'

'No. It was a matter of urgency for him to slip away; he was afraid other creditors of his father's might materialize. I, of course, have no right to question anyone about these matters. I care not about the jewellery. I'm content to abide here quietly. Thankfully Wilmot gave me this house as a prenuptial gift and no one can oust me from it.'

Sophie was sitting with her graceful white hands folded in her lap. Kelynen was struck by the dignity she retained in her reduced circumstances. One reason for her contentment, which she had confided to Kelynen, one of the few people she had declared she could trust, was that her position before her marriage had been even more tenuous. The besotted, cumbersome oaf, the kindly bumbling soul that was Wilmot Carew had saved her from homelessness, of having to become a seamstress or a governess. It was inevitable that people had judged her an opportunist, and now certain gentlemen, impressed by her beauty and good breeding, had ventured since her widowhood to make unseemly propositions to her. Two untrustworthy sorts had offered her marriage. She had rebuffed them all, forcefully, unapologetically.

A maid, young and awkward in appearance, entered the parlour carrying a silver calling-card tray. She dropped a clumsy curtsey. 'Brought this for 'ee, ma'am.'

'Has someone sent me a message?' Suddenly Sophie was animated and alert and already reaching out towards the tray.

'No, 'tis a visitor, ma'am.'

Following her friend's eagerness, Kelynen was now curious about her disappointment. Sophie seemed to deflate before her eyes. She read the card with her face set hard. 'Straighten your cap and apron, Mary, then show Mr Pengarron in.'

'Luke! He's here?' Kelynen spun her head towards the door.

Mary scuttled away, shortly to reappear, tidier but flustered, in front of the unexpected caller. She was given no time to make an announcement. Luke strode into the room, looking, to Kelynen's annoyance – and she noticed, also to Sophie's – as if he was lord and master here. He was dressed in manly, crisp blues, with his body erect and head up, smiling broadly and confidently.

He bowed low. 'Your most humble and obedient servant, Mrs Carew, please do forgive the intrusion. I thought my sister would be here to offer you her apologies. I thought to enquire about our sister, Mrs Lanyon, if that is not too much of an impertinence on my part.'

He looked eager to impress. His eyes danced all the way up to Sophie, and Kelynen saw his self-assurance was in fact a little shaky, but buoyed up by a purpose, an emotion she had not thought to see in her brother for some years, perhaps never. Love. Heavens above! It was as obvious as daylight. In the short time he had spoken to Sophie yesterday, he had fallen utterly in love with her. Kelynen had never seen him looking so boyish and enthusiastic. It was an effort for him to keep his impatience, his hopes, in check.

'Livvy is quite well, Luke.'

'Excellent. I thought not to call at the parsonage in case she was indisposed,' he said. Then he fell into an uncertain hush. What happened next was up to Sophie.

'Do sit down, Mr Pengarron.' Expressionless, Sophie used polite hostess tones. 'Mary, ask Mrs Jago to prepare a tray of coffee, please.'

'Yes, ma'am.' Mary bobbed and hurried away.

Normally, if Luke had noticed the little maid at all he would have glared after her or sighed with irritation. 'She is new to your household, Mrs Carew? Learning the craft?'

'You are correct, Mr Pengarron. I was just asking Miss Kelynen about her excursion to Chenhalls.'

'Chenhalls, Kelynen?' Luke feigned surprise. 'You went there?'

'You know I did. I sent you a note.' Taken back twenty-four hours, Kelynen dropped her scoffing tone. 'Chenhalls is fascinating. The front aspect is peaceful and sheltered while the back of the property looks upon the cliffs and sea. The gardens are glorious. Sir Rafe and Lady Portia are open and friendly, and although she is fast succumbing to senility, the banter between them is amusing. The food Livvy and I were offered was sumptuous, Sir Rafe employs a man as head of his kitchens and this fellow produced all manner of delicious things from the many and diverse countries Sir Rafe has visited.' She babbled on about *côtelettes d'agneau*, a hot spicy sauce from the Caribbean, a new recipe for beef broth brought back from Scotland. She was unwilling to speak of the dark tower and Gabriel Tremayne. For some reason she felt protective towards him and did not want the others to think him peculiar.

As Gabriel Tremayne had requested, she had fetched a footman, ordering him to take great care in helping Mr Tremayne up to the house. A physician-surgeon had been sent for. Despite Gabriel Tremayne's protests, it had been necessary for him to forsake his dignity and allow himself to be carried. The sunlight had been too bright for his eyes and at his exclamation of pain Kelynen had pulled his shawl, which she supposed he wore to keep the cold out of his scrawny body, over his face. She had followed on, all the way up Chenhalls' granite stairs, which were worn down and darkened in parts through centuries of use, and divided off at the top in three directions. Then they moved along the long dim corridors to Gabriel Tremayne's bedchamber, which faced the sea. By this time he had slipped into a deep sleep.

'Does Mr Tremayne have a manservant?' she'd asked the footman. He was one of the fellows who had been there on her arrival and the solemnity he had displayed then had vanished. Older by about five years than the man he had carefully lowered down on the stout bed, he had shaken his head wryly and grinned.

''Fraid not, Miss Pengarron.' Kelynen tolerated his impudence in exchange for the information he offered. 'Never known a gentleman like Mr Gabriel before. Sees to himself in all things, he does. He hardly had a shirt for his back when he come here, and what he did have was worn to death. Sir Rafe ordered a complete new wardrobe for him.'

In between watching the patient to ensure he was actually breathing, for he seemed so still, Kelynen glanced about the room. It was tidy and blank, like an unused guest room. Gabriel Tremayne seemed not to own a single personal possession. 'How long has he lived here?'

'A few months. Sir Rafe got a letter from Vienna. It said for him to come at once, that Mr Gabriel was in a bad way.

Sir Rafe was about to go up to London and he sent Mr Josiah to fetch him. He was badly undernourished when he arrived, his hair like it'd never seen a barber's scissors. He's a strange gentleman. Spent all his time in the music room at first, making up new tunes. Sometimes he wrote 'em down like a man demented. Got a touch of the Tremayne mad—'

'Go on,' Kelynen ordered sharply.

The footman shifted on his heavy feet but didn't seem embarrassed. 'Begging your pardon, miss, I was going to say the Tremayne madness. Well, we had the devil of a job to get him to eat and we used to find him asleep in the oddest places. And he do like a drop of sweet nectar.' The footman made a drinking motion. 'The women servants believe he's grieving over a broken heart. Don't know about that, but Sir Rafe tried speaking to him. Mr Gabriel didn't like that – he's secretive, you see, shy too, if you ask me. Then he took every instrument he could carry down to the tower and forbid no one near him. Well, none of us servants would argue with that; the tower's bad luck. His food trays were left in haste, I can tell 'ee. Sir Rafe said to leave him be, see if he'd come round to some semblance of proper behaviour on his own. 'Tis a wonder Mr Gabriel let you help him, miss. Thank the Lord he did.'

Kelynen had thought it a decisive nudge of fate that had brought her to Chenhalls and the tower folly. Even a day later might have meant different consequences for Gabriel Tremayne. 'And where is Mr Josiah Tremayne to be found at present?'

'Gone abroad, miss. To some business meeting, I shouldn't wonder. Won't be back till nightfall, if he's back at all. Got his own little house, he have.' The footman grinned to himself as if he had some secret.

'And what is your name?'

'Jacob Glynn, miss.'

'Well Glynn, go down to the kitchens and order hot water

to be brought up. I take it I can safely leave you to attend Mr Tremayne? See to it that he's in a fit state for the physician's consultation. I'll inform Sir Rafe of what's happened.'

'You can trust me, Miss Pengarron.'

When Jacob Glynn had gone Kelynen took a closer look at Gabriel Tremayne. Breathing in low gasps, he lay rigid on his back, his hands gripping the shawl. His hair, so fair it was the colour of parchment and as long as his waist, was splayed out over the shawl. Cautiously, gently, she touched his wrist and felt his skin was papery and cold. Was madness the cause of his self-abused state? She thought not. He had spoken lucidly to her. It was more likely his condition was brought about by a broken heart. What depth of love had he lost to reduce him to near death? Had he realized what he was doing?

She touched the shawl. It was of woven patterned silk, a woman's shawl – his lost love's? He stirred fitfully. When she looked back at his face she stifled a gasp. Gabriel Tremayne's depthless eyes were open and fixed on her.

'You will be looked after now,' she said in the soothing way employed for the ill or the young.

'You have been very kind, Miss Kelynen Pengarron,' he croaked through dry lips. 'Please accept my humble gratitude.'

'It will take a long time for you to become fully well again. Please persevere with the physician's directions.'

'Your tenderness commends you. I entreat you to perform one more favour for me. Tell my uncle to send the physician away.'

'I could not do that. Mr Tremayne, you must allow sense and let the doctor attend you.'

'No! I forbid it. If I am bled it will drain the last of my constitution and I shall surely die.' His eyelids fluttered down to his sunken cheeks. 'I have not the strength to stay conscious. Miss Pengarron, my life is in your hands.'

Sir Rafe had looked alarmed when she went outside and

told him about his nephew's adversity and his wishes concerning the physician-surgeon. He thanked her and said he would consider his nephew's request, but decided, in view of his nephew's deep slumber, to allow Livvy to continue with the portrait. Kelynen had stepped aside, introducing Rex to Lady Portia, but all the while stealing glances at the baronet. He made a commanding figure, posed slightly sideways on his feet to form a diagonal composition, with a cat in his arms, another on his shoulder, the rest, induced with nibbles, about his feet. Kelynen did something Livvy hated and peeked at the unfinished portrait. She was impressed, believing it to be Livvy's finest so far, with a good sense of staging and a pleasing lack of drama.

The physician-surgeon summoned to Chenhalls had still been with the patient when she had left. Had Gabriel Tremayne been bled? Was he still alive?

Kelynen came to from her reverie to feel Sophie and Luke's eyes intently upon her.

'Well, Chenhalls has certainly made an enormous impression on you, Kelynen,' Luke said, as if awed by her account. 'I can safely assume you'll be going there again?'

She was embarrassed. It was not often she displayed her feelings, and then usually only to her parents or Beatrice. 'I might return with Livvy to keep her company.' She wondered if she should inform Luke of Livvy and Timothy's estrangement, but decided he did not own the sensitivity to be of any use to them.

The coffee arrived and Sophie poured it out while Mary handed the tiny brittle-looking china cups to the guests. Luke thanked Mary graciously. All the while he gazed at Sophie. She ignored him most of the time. The atmosphere became strained. Luke fidgeted. Kelynen began to feel sorry for him. His feelings for Sophie seemed to be growing deeper by the second, while the adoration he was aiming towards her was making her cross.

Kelynen had complained about his egotism to Sophie

and Sophie would know his reputation as a carousing womanizer. Sophie was capable of destroying a rake's intentions. She was within her rights to shield herself, to maintain her independence and remain a widow for the rest of her life if she desired, but sometimes she came across as a little cold. If she were told Luke was in love with her and was not set on a dishonourable campaign, she would still, in all likelihood, continue to stamp on his heart. Sophie was a lost cause to him, just as it appeared that the country wouldn't win the war in the American colonies. And Luke was no more likely to take advice about it than King George was from his ministers to give into the colonies' demands.

Kelynen alighted on something unrelated to Chenhalls, something that would hopefully ease the tension. 'A baby was abandoned outside Perranbarvah's church two days ago. The Reverend Lanyon came across it on the steps. Rather than resign the child immediately to an institution, he took the child to Vellanoweth. Kane and Jessica have agreed to take the child under their care, to give the mother time to hopefully reclaim it.'

Sophie put her coffee cup down and leaned forward. 'How very sad. Was there anything significant about this foundling, Kelynen? What is its age?'

'It's a newborn and it was wrapped in the finest quality silk.'

'Not the misfortune of some poor village girl then,' Luke remarked.

'I think I should like to view the child,' Sophie said. 'Would your brother mind?'

'You think you have some notion of who the child and its mother is, Mrs Carew?' Luke anticipated the question on Kelynen's lips.

'It's hardly a probability,' Sophie said briskly, her eyes lowered. 'Those of us in more fortunate circumstances have a duty not to ignore the needy or abandoned, don't you think? Could we not ride there now, Kelynen? I'm restless suddenly and would welcome the exercise.'

'Could we not make it on the morrow instead, Sophie? I thought to engage myself with estate business at Ker-an-Mor Farm today, to discuss the tenants, and how next to raise monies for the deserving poor with the steward.' To fend off dissent from Luke she fed him a brusque glance.

'Pardon me, Kelynen, I will donate a hundred guineas to the Parish Poor Fund,' Luke said, hoping it would impress Sophie. 'And there is really nothing so urgent that Matthias Renfree cannot attend to alone. In fact I think he would prefer it.'

'You mean *you* would prefer it,' Kelynen snapped, stung by his latest disregard to her present rightful position on the estate. 'I consider it ill of you to keep pushing me out.'

'Kelynen, dearheart, that was not what I meant,' Luke protested civilly, throwing an anxious glance at Sophie. 'I just thought the child's need was more pressing than any other.'

Kelynen grew red with embarrassment and anger. In two carefully chosen sentences Luke had made her seem selfish and stupid. She hoped he declared himself to Sophie and that Sophie crushed his hopes as if he were an insect under her feet. It was a childish reaction, Kelynen knew, but she was unrepentant. There was little about Luke to commend him; she was foolish to have felt sorry for him. He did not really care about the foundling. He only wanted to go to Vellanoweth to remain close to Sophie and to be seen as caring and compassionate. It seemed that all too often men were liars and cheats, or weak or selfish. Wilmot Carew had wasted most of his wealth and the end of his life. Sir Rafe and Josiah Tremayne, apparently, were lacking in honour. And as for Gabriel Tremayne . . . she could not make up her mind about his tremendous imprudence.

'We'll go now to Vellanoweth, Sophie,' she said. 'Just as you please.'

Hiding the depths of her hurt, she glared at Luke. 'I cannot prevent you from accompanying us – Kane is your brother too. But I give you notice that hereafter I shall distance myself from you and relinquish my connections with the estate until Father's return, for I cannot bear your interference. I shall remain in residence with Livvy, where I demand that you do not seek to trouble me.'

Nine

L uke rode at a respectful distance behind Kelynen and Sophie to Vellanoweth Farm, his dark eyes either on the ground or on Sophie's back.

His first instinct after the haranguing from Kelynen – when Sophie had left the room to change into riding clothes – was to berate his sister for humiliating him. But he had realized Kelynen's hurt and had sought to explain himself. To reassure her that he had no reason to try to eject her from her responsibilities to the estate. Their father was in excellent health and should live another twenty-five years at least. Except for a tragedy it would be a long time before he came into his inheritance, in which case Kelynen would almost certainly marry.

Refusing to look him in the eye, Kelynen had stood at the parlour window and from the high vantage point of Sophie's house had watched the busy scene across at the Mount, of sailors and tradesmen loading fresh provisions or unloading cargo from the many ships in port. More two- or three-masted vessels were out at sea, and with the tide in, rowing boats were ferrying goods and people to and from the Mount and town.

'You're only saying this to gain in Sophie's estimation. Well, you're wasting your time. She loathes you.'

Luke had felt his chest tighten. 'She's said as much?'

'She despises your type. She sees you as an irritation, a pest. She's offended by your addresses towards her.'

He had been aware his presence was unwelcome here,

but was crushed by the fear that Kelynen's assertions may be true. 'I'll pursue my chances.'

'You have none. If you were a gentleman at heart you would step back and leave Sophie alone.'

He had nearly declined to go to Vellanoweth, to retreat and rethink his campaign. But he could not turn up here uninvited again and Sophie was unlikely to yield to an invitation of any kind from him. So he went with them to his brother's farm, praying Sophie would notice his new humility and that an opportunity would arise in which he might make an impact on her.

In the sprawling farmyard at Gulval, further round Mount's Bay, Luke allowed a labourer to help the ladies dismount in the front courtyard. Once inside the farmhouse parlour, which was furnished comfortably and in a slight carefree disorder, Luke remained passive while Kelynen explained to Jessica Pengarron the reason for their visit.

'I'll fetch the baby down from the nursery,' Jessica said. 'It'd be wonderful if the mother could be found, but even though the little mite's only been here forty-eight hours, we're already getting mighty fond of Betty, as we call her.'

Jessica was the daughter of a former tenant farmer on the Pengarron estate. She was lovely in a raw sense, forceful in spirit and inclined to be outspoken. She pinned a golden curl behind an ear and stared at Luke, puzzled by his quietness and his interest in the foundling. She was aware of the fraught mood between him and Kelynen and assumed it was Luke's fault, for she herself had clashed with him many times. She thought it typically selfish of Luke to stay at the manor and interfere with Kelynen's endeavours.

'So it's a girl child,' Kelynen said. 'Is she extra work for you?'

'No. Not in the least. The foreman's wife was safely delivered of a son last week and she's kindly agreed to come regularly to the house to feed Betty, and Betty tends to sleep soundly. She's about a week old, I'd say. Harry and Charlie, my sons,' she explained for Sophie's benefit, 'are fascinated with her.'

Jessica went upstairs and returned shortly with the baby wrapped in a lacy knitted shawl. Kelynen took her, cradling the sleeping foundling with ease, used as she was to babies in all branches of the Pengarron dynasty. She pushed back the baby's soft cotton cap. 'She has pretty, fair hair, of a pearly tint. I took little notice of her before.'

'That's one small clue to her parentage,' Luke said, coming close. He had no particular dislike of children and wanted Sophie to be aware of this. 'She's of a good weight, isn't she? So her mother went to the full term of her pregnancy. Does she have any distinguishing features, Jessica?'

'No moles or birthmarks, if that's what you mean.'

'May we see the silk she was wrapped in?' Sophie asked, also on her feet, staring down at the baby's peaceful face. It seemed lost on everyone but herself that the baby had the same colour of hair as her own. 'It might be a significant clue.'

'It's drying on the washing line. I'll send a maid to fetch it,' Jessica said. She had not met this friend of Kelynen's before and did not take to her, finding Sophie Carew distant and feeling her innocent persona to be deceptive. 'Have you any particular interest in the baby, Mrs Carew?'

'I am merely concerned about its misfortune, Mrs Pengarron.' Sophie's tone was clipped and, Jessica thought, defensive. Jessica noticed the longing, covert gazes Luke was giving her. She glanced at Kelynen and they passed a look of understanding over the sorry condition of Luke's heart. Jessica was astonished. She had not thought Luke capable of heroine worship.

'Darling! Harry! Charlie!' a strong male voice soared on joyful notes through the house.

Jessica's round face broke into a sunny smile. 'Kane, my love, we have visitors. We're in here.'

At their father's call, young Harry and Charles Pengarron

dashed inside from the garden where they had been playing under the supervision of a nursemaid.

After being introduced to Kane Pengarron, a retired army captain, Sophie retreated to a corner. She watched, straight-faced, throughout the affectionate embracing that went on among the Pengarron brood. Kane gathered up his sons in his powerful arms. Sophie decided she approved of Captain Pengarron, an adopted member of the family, a kind-eyed, reddish-haired, commanding man, dressed in good-quality clothes but suitable for fieldwork. He was clearly selfless, even-handed, generous and loving. The silk had been forgotten, but Sophie had no desire to view it in the presence of so many people.

'How good to see you all. You must stay for luncheon.' Kane grinned, putting his sons down so they could peep at the baby. 'Mrs Carew, you are curious about the little one?'

Suddenly all eyes were on her and Sophie could not prevent herself blushing. 'I . . . well . . . I thought, it's improbable I know, but I thought that somehow I might recognize her.'

Her discomfiture made Luke love her more. Kelynen was pleased to see a softer side of her emerge. Kane was sorry he had embarrassed her. Jessica became more suspicious of her.

Someone else came into the room. 'Is there space for another?' He was tall and broad-shouldered, wearing dark, sober clothes, and the hair around his gentle face was fine and blond. He was not unlike the Pengarron children, who in turn were like their mother.

'David Trenchard!' Luke cried. 'I've not seen you for many a year. How well you look. Oh, I am sorry. I quite forgot the reason for your leaving the Yorkshire circuit.'

'It's an honour after all this time, Luke. How fine you look, if I may say so.' David Trenchard was the epitome of courtesy and good grace, bowing to the newcomers as greetings were exchanged.

After the meal, Kelynen and Sophie made to leave the farm on their own, Luke having elected to remain behind – to discuss business with Kane, he said. Kelynen assumed Luke was reviewing his crusade. Sophie had either ignored or politely rebuffed him at the dining table.

'Mr Trenchard shares his sister Jessica's looks but he is quite different to her in personality,' Sophie remarked while putting on her discreet riding hat in front of the hall mirror. 'Why did he leave Yorkshire?'

'David was a lay preacher of the Methodist Connection. He had a twin brother. Philip was murdered three years ago. The perpetrator was a cousin of mine, actually. His father feels David should now take his brother's place on their farm at St Cleer.'

'How terrible for you all!'

'The Trenchard history is closely entwined with my family's. David's father, Clem, was once betrothed to my mother. Clem's first wife, David's mother, was a friend of my mother's. My brothers, Livvy and I grew up to be friendly with the Trenchards. Indeed one result was Kane and Jessica's happy marriage.'

'How fascinating. And Mr Trenchard is visiting his sister just for today?'

'Jessica mentioned he's not returning home immediately.'

'How long is he to stay?'

Kelynen fastened the last button on her brown kid gloves and fronted her friend with a gleam in her eyes. 'Sophie! Are you interested in David Trenchard? I did not think you'd countenance a single thought about someone of his faith.'

Sophie's face was on fire and she pushed Kelynen away from her. 'Don't be ridiculous!'

Kelynen rubbed the sore spot on her arm. 'I apologize for offending you, but there was no need to use such force.'

Sophie stared at her grimly then dropped her eyes. 'Forgive me, Kelynen. I get so tired of people trying to link me with a man. We cannot discuss this here but please let me explain on the ride back.'

'I did not mean to upset you, Sophie.'

'I know. We have not seen the silk cloth yet. Before we leave, can we go to the washing line?'

Moments later, in the back garden, Sophie's heart quickened and a trickle of perspiration wet her brow, but she was careful not to show her agitation in front of her friend. The piece of pink silk billowing in the fresh breeze on the washing line was shot through with darker pink thread in an exacting design and had come from a particular dress. It looked as if it had been torn off. Sophie had a reason to hope she would recognize the silk, but now she was afraid for its owner.

Ten

The following day Kelynen paid her second visit with Livvy to Chenhalls. The fine weather was threatening to break and there would be rain later in the day, but Livvy reckoned she could make useful progress on Sir Rafe's portrait.

Out in the quiet arbour, where trailing roses would soon bloom over the high trellises, and while holding and stroking one of the cats – a proud blue-cream Persian – Kelynen enquired about the welfare of Gabriel Tremayne.

'He's alive, thanks to you, m'dear, but a fearfully rebellious patient. It's a dangerous, yet simple case of malnutrition,' Sir Rafe replied. He was as stately and as handsome as before and Kelynen kept her eyes on him. 'Only time will say if there are to be any lasting ill effects. If you had not come today I would have written to you expressing my profound gratitude at saving the boy's life, and imploring you to attend his bedside. It's not known for him to respond to anyone as favourably as he did you. Perhaps you could encourage him to cooperate with the doctor's instructions, persuade him that he must, if he wants to return to good health.'

'I'd be pleased to, Sir Rafe, although I'm not sure if I'm capable of exerting any influence over him. Mr Tremayne is hardly a boy.'

'I cannot help but think of him as so. I'd not seen him in over twenty years until recently. Now Kelynen,' Sir Rafe laid his hand near hers and joined in with the coddling of

68

the Persian, 'we are friends. I am confident we shall become close friends. You must call me Rafe.'

She answered his handsome long-lasting smile in kind.

'Girl, come here to me. Don't let my brother monopolize you,' Lady Portia cut in, pouting and snorting from her usual position. She was wearing red and orange, with a mass of sequins and yellow bows and a ginger wig. She looked like a riot of wallflowers.

'Ignore my sister. She's bossy,' Rafe whispered close to Kelynen's ear but loud enough for Lady Portia to hear. 'She's been particularly contentious since breakfast. Anyone would think it was my fault she has arthritis.'

'He's the one you should ignore!' Lady Portia shrieked, her crusty eyes blinking rapidly. 'There's not a decent manner to be found in him. I wish I'd died before my husband, then I'd never have returned here to live.'

Kelynen suppressed a giggle, knowing the old lady cared deeply for her brother. Why else spend so much time with him?

'She adores me really,' Sir Rafe declared.

'My brother Luke believed everyone adored him. Now he knows differently.'

'That sounds intriguing. You must tell me about it sometime.'

'Rafe, if you please,' Livvy said, impatient to begin.

Still smiling, Kelynen handed over the cat and joined Lady Portia. Jayna Hayes got up off her stool and Kelynen took it over, petting Cosmo and Hartley, feeling the softer difference in their coats to Rex's smooth curly mane. Rex had long ago chased off with Digory.

'Do you know what he calls that loathsome creature you've just passed to him?' Lady Portia scoffed. 'Octavia. Another goes by the name of Julius, another Caesar. Stupid, eh? Brought 'em all back from his various jaunts. I'll be glad when he takes himself off again. I've asked him to go to China and bring me back a Pekinese dog. I heard about 'em from a sea captain. Apparently, they're so tiny the Mandarins carry 'em about in the wide ends of their sleeves.' Next, she demanded from Livvy, 'When're you going to start on my portrait?'

'As soon as I possibly can, milady,' Livvy replied tonelessly, without looking up from her work.

'Are you well?' Lady Portia studied Livvy with her spectacles on, then off and finally on again. 'Not starting another child, are you?'

'My dear, you are being personal,' Rafe chided.

'If I appear flushed it's because it was something of a rush in getting away.' Livvy had suffered another sleepless night. She had finally dozed off, then found it hard to stir herself when the maid had come to help her dress.

'Would you like me to send for some cordial, Livvy?' Rafe spoke with tender concern and Kelynen wondered how measured his affection was for Livvy. He had given her a thumping great kiss again, had held her far longer than he should have. But then his lips had found their way on to hers also and she had received a prolonged hug. It had felt good – very good indeed.

'I'd welcome some elderberry, Rafe. Thank you.'

The companion went to fetch the refreshment. Kelynen asked if she could hold the little terriers.

Soon Kelynen became more interested in the young man fast approaching Rafe. Tall and clean-limbed, dark, elegant and stylish, poised yet casually at ease, he was exceedingly handsome. This could be none other than Mr Josiah Tremayne. Kelynen straightened her posture and wished she were wearing a prettier dress, and that she had allowed Livvy's maid to style her hair instead of grappling it herself into the muslin cap she was wearing underneath her milkmaid hat. Her heart gave a queer flip. Now she understood how Luke had felt when he first saw Sophie.

Livvy sighed in annoyance but allowed the interruption.

Josiah Tremayne bent over Livvy's hand and kissed it

lightly. 'An enormous pleasure once more, Mrs Lanyon.' His voice was deep and pleasantly cultured.

Giving Kelynen a gallant greeting, his eyes lingered on hers a moment. 'I'm delighted to meet you, Miss Pengarron. My uncle and my brother have spoken glowingly of you. Sir Oliver must be deservingly proud of creating two such beautiful daughters.'

'You know my father well, Mr Tremayne?' She wanted to hold his attention, delighted that he possessed Rafe's charm.

'Indeed, we met in Marazion to discuss business not many days before he left for the spa town. He said he would miss you particularly. May I ask if you have had the opportunity of taking a turn around the gardens?'

He was close enough for her to smell the appealing mix of light cologne, scented tobacco and the masculine freshness of him. To walk anywhere with him would be a pleasure. 'No. Not yet. I am much looking forward to that delight.' She was pleased with herself. She had sounded polite and intelligent without being coquettish and projecting too much enthusiasm for his company.

'I would very much like to have that honour now, but I am vexed to need a few urgent words with my uncle, and Gabriel is asking for you. He is quite insistent.'

Just for a moment Kelynen wished Gabriel Tremayne locked in the tower in the woods. She would have gladly waited any length of time for Josiah Tremayne to finish his business with Sir Rafe.

She lost her bearings on the way to the sick room. With no other soul about, she peeped into chambers and behind long, heavy drapes that blocked off draughts or concealed alcoves and passages. Denied the pleasure of strolling with Josiah Tremayne, she wanted to explore but moved on quickly until she located his half-brother's bedchamber.

She went straight in. The curtains were drawn only enough

to allow in a crack of light; candles provided a dim illumination. The fire was lit and the room was stuffy and smelled of wood smoke and the mild staleness of an ailing human. The patient was propped up against the pillows, his eyes closed. Her curiosity and compassion for Gabriel Tremayne came flooding back.

Jacob Glynn was occupied at the washstand and crept across to her. He whispered, 'Morning, Miss Pengarron. I've just finished washing and shaving Mr Tremayne. He's had his medicines. He should be comfortable for some time.'

Kelynen examined the array of medicines on a corner cabinet. Long botanical Latin names were written on the small brown pots and bottles. It appeared the physician-surgeon was also an accomplished herbalist. 'Is he eating now?'

'He'll take a few spoons of broth but with much protest. Got in a terrible state just now because Mr Josiah wouldn't permit his musical instruments brought up. He keeps asking for them. And for you, miss.'

'I'll sit with him awhile. If he wakes I'll coax him to take some water. Ask the chef to make up some egg and cinnamon custards and syllabubs. Perhaps something sweet will tempt him.'

Kelynen waited until Jacob Glynn had quietly closed the door. She had a different idea on some aspects of what was good for the patient. She drew the curtains back halfway and opened all the windows. Daylight and fresh salt-laden air streamed in, dispelling some of the bleakness. The wash of the sea, hundreds of yards away and eighty feet below the cliff edge, could be heard more clearly, along with the bright chirping of birds in the gardens and the raucous screaming of gulls. There was a magnificent view of the two sheltering headlands, and miles and miles of blue-grey sky and the English Channel. The dark clouds that would bring rain before evening were beginning to gather on the horizon. She and Livvy would have to leave earlier today.

'Please, I cannot bear the light.'

She turned to see Gabriel Tremayne shielding his eyes with a shaking hand. She closed the curtains but not quite as far as before, then poured out a glass of water. 'You must drink as much as you can.'

Close to the bed she saw he was not as grotesque as before. His hair had been cut to shoulder length. 'I'll hold the glass for you.'

'No. I shall feel sick.' His voice was weak and hoarse.

'That is of no matter, Mr Tremayne. You'll certainly feel no improvement until you're eating and drinking something a little more substantial.'

'Are you to be a bully to me then, Miss Pengarron?' He fashioned a smile but that too sapped his energy.

'I shall be if you do not make an effort. My only intention is to see you restored to vigour.'

'I shall endeavour then to repay your kindness as you would have it.'

He sipped, his long fingers clasped over hers. She did not allow him to push the glass away until half the water was gone. He was panting, needing sleep again. She dabbed at his mouth with a napkin, then sat at his bedside. His breathing came oddly, but then she realized it was in one particular rhythm, and then another, as if he was composing some piece of unquiet music in his subconscious.

'Hush now, Gabriel.' She leaned over and smoothed back his hair and felt his brow. He was unwholesomely hot. There was a long scratch down his cheek. How had that come about? Then she noticed his fingernails were long and sharp, harmful to him and those attending him. She went to the washstand and then the dressing table, where she found what she wanted. She carried a small pair of scissors back to the bed.

Gabriel opened his eyes and they widened in panic. 'What are you going to do?'

'Don't worry,' she soothed, pointing to his hands.

'You'll be more comfortable if your nails are shorter.'

He lifted his fingers and studied the tiny daggers on the tips. 'I have neglected myself for so long, Kelynen. Forgive me, I must seem a monster to you.'

'You do not. Not at all.' She smiled down on him. There was something so appealing, so anxious in his expression.

'You are kind enough to lie.' He managed a stronger smile and for an instant Kelynen glimpsed what he really looked like, and although it was gone before she got a clear picture, it pointed to him being good-natured, shy and private. 'Kelynen, might I ask you to fetch my instruments up from the music room?'

'No, you may not. You have no strength to play.'

'I'll settle for my violin.'

'Perhaps in a day or two, but only if you make progress.'

'Does this mean you are staying?' He gripped her arm with a startling strength as he had in the tower. He had reserves of passion too. 'I would like that so much.'

'I am here for the day with my sister, as before. Be still, Gabriel. I wish to employ the scissors.'

'Stay,' he said as she snipped the first nail. 'My uncle would be as pleased as I to have you here. Think about it.'

Staying at Chenhalls was a pleasing thought. She had been asked to do something worthwhile. She could look over the house and, hopefully, stroll with Josiah through the gardens. Thoughts of him took her mind to those outside involved with the portrait, and then on to Rex. Wherever he was she hoped he was not making a pest of himself. To stay here in the company of the generous Sir Rafe and the dear old Lady Portia was more than appealing. And she felt a responsibility for Gabriel. She cared that he recovered and was curious to see how he would be then.

'Stay,' he repeated. 'Please. I give you my word I will make an agreeable patient.'

'My parents are out of the county. I would have to seek my brother's permission.'

'Is he likely to raise an objection?'

'None that I can think of.' It would be too bad if Luke did.

'Then come back tomorrow. Promise me that you will.'

She gently squeezed his hand. 'I promise, Gabriel.'

Eleven

'I forbid this stay at Chenhalls, Kelynen,' Luke said firmly. 'Why?' she challenged.

'Because I don't think Father would approve of it in his absence.'

'You mean *you* don't approve, and that's only out of spite. Sir Rafe is an old friend of Timothy's. Timothy has no reservations about the family. I only asked you out of politeness. I shall go anyway. Ruth is packing my things and she's coming with me as my maid, so I shall be properly chaperoned.' Kelynen would never have considered disobeying the head of the family before – even if Luke was only substitute head – but she turned on her toes and strode out of the drawing room, where, to her mind, Luke was languishing in selfish pity and she was unmoved by it.

He sprang up and went after her. 'Kelynen, wait! I'll give you my blessing if you do something for me.'

'And what might that be?' She narrowed her eyes, comparing Luke's self-centred qualities to the natural courtesy of three Tremayne men.

'Tell me how I might win Sophie. You know her very well. What can I do?' He threw out helpless hands.

Kelynen surveyed him for some moments. Luke seemed to be diminishing in size. It was as if all the strength, the very gist of him, was draining away. He had been vanquished. No longer was he the heartless lover, insensitive to the hopes he bred in hapless females. There was a torment in him which she could not ignore.

76

'Your heart is truly set on her, isn't it?'

'Yes, yes. Please help me.'

Kelynen chewed her lower lip. 'It's a week before I'm to see her again, but I may be required to stay longer than that at Chenhalls and I'm about to write to her to that effect. I could ask her to consider you among her acquaintances, but I fear that is the best you could ever be to her.'

'Why? I know I was brash at the start, but if she saw a different side of my character would she not look more kindly on me?'

'No, Luke, I am afraid she would not.'

'Am I such a terrible fellow then?'

'It is not you in particular. Sophie never befriends men. She's told me she has a particular reason not to consider remarriage for several years, if at all.'

'Did she tell you the reason?'

'She did not confide that much to me.'

Sophie had said the mysterious reason would soon become apparent. From her friend's worried face, Kelynen had sensed it was something demeaning that would need courage to face.

'Is there anything I can do for you?' Kelynen had offered.

Sophie's indomitable spirit had instantly returned, her expression closed, final. 'Thank you, no. I've a little thinking to do. You will be one of the first to know when I have something to tell. It will be necessary for me to live an even quieter life,' she had said.

'Forget about her, Luke. You can never find happiness with Sophie.'

He sagged and put both hands to his face. 'I've written of lost love in my plays. Love stories as tragic as I could make them. I never thought to have my heart broken, to feel this wretched. I am quite undone, Kelynen. I cannot eat or sleep. I cannot put a word to my latest script. I cannot even think properly.'

'I am sorry, Luke.' Kelynen went to him, and he threw

his arms around her and clung to her tight. She held on to him. Then disappointment settled inside her like a rock. 'I'll write to Chenhalls and say I cannot go. My first duty is to be with you.'

'No.' He pulled away, wiping moisture from his eyes. 'You must go, sweeting. There's nothing to be gained by you being miserable also. I can see how excited you are about this event.'

'Will you be all right? I don't like leaving you like this.'

He nodded. 'I'd prefer to be on my own. I shall get through. I suppose it serves me right. I've been a vain pleasure seeker for most of my life and now I've been brought down. Go to Chenhalls, Kelynen. Write, keep me informed how it goes with you. However, let me bid you this one caution. You have spoken enthusiastically of Josiah Tremayne. Beware. Take care of your own heart. Matthias Renfree has written to him again requesting that he settles the Tremayne accounts with us. And Timothy says he regularly changes his mistresses and doesn't appear to be seeking marriage.'

Kelynen thought about this. Many businesses were not prompt at paying their accounts, and Luke had been of the same mind as Josiah concerning women until he had fallen in love; so love and devotion in such a character *was* possible. 'Do not worry about me, Luke. My main concern is to aid the recovery of Gabriel Tremayne. And Livvy will be there for some of the time.'

'Enjoy yourself then.' He kissed her and turned away. The image of his dejection stayed with Kelynen for hours.

In the parsonage, Livvy bathed and changed into a new dinner gown – bought with money of her own – and then went to the nursery to ask for a report on the children.

'The children are well, Mrs Lanyon. And safely asleep for the night.' The nurse used formal tones. Phylida Bevan was highly experienced in her post. Livvy had been impressed by her references and confident attitude during the interview, but now found her frosty and strict.

Livvy stayed fifteen minutes, sitting between Hugh's cot and Julia's muslin-draped cradle. She reached out and caressed each child. She softly sang a lullaby and said a short prayer over them. At regular intervals the nurse pulled in a long disapproving breath.

'Is there something amiss with your sinuses, Mrs Bevan?' Livvy hissed when she was ready to leave.

'No, ma'am.' Phylida Bevan's long severe face was tight and uncompromising while she unnecessarily refolded a pile of linen.

'Then pray do not breathe in that offensive manner. I shall return at ten of the clock in the morning. Please have the children ready for an airing in the garden.'

Bitch! Livvy fumed on the landing. *How dare you show such impudence towards me?*

Before going downstairs she went to Timothy's room, the master bedchamber. He was not there.

She found the dinner table set for one. 'Where's the Reverend Lanyon?' she asked Mrs Wills, the housekeeper.

'He's eaten already, ma'am.' Nancy Wills had been housekeeper to Timothy long before he had taken over the parish. A small woman, normally agreeable, she took little pains these days to hide her condemnation of her mistress.

'Where is he now?'

'I've no idea, ma'am.'

'He never goes out without leaving a message about his destination.' Losing patience, Livvy snapped, 'Where is he?'

Mrs Wills picked up the soup tureen and approached the table. 'He might have ridden over to the manor.'

'Well! Did he?'

Leek and potato soup was ladled expertly into the bowl in front of Livvy. 'I'm not sure, ma'am.'

Livvy banged her hand on the table, making cutlery leap

and glasses ching. 'You are refusing to tell me where my husband has gone. I shall not let this rest. I don't want anything to eat. Clear the table. From now on go about your work in an entirely respectful manner or I shall put you out of the house!'

Livvy went to the parlour. Her insides were trembling, her hands too. She was thoroughly miserable. Gaining the measure of freedom she had desired for so long – or rather, having it thrust upon her – was an empty victory. She had spent a wasted day at Chenhalls, unable to apply her brushes with pleasing results, unable to get the colour compositions right. And she had suddenly missed the children and had been glad to leave early to outpace the impending bad weather.

While the rain beat hostile flurries against the window-panes she huddled over the fire, deflated, discouraged. She had got what she wanted but it had come at a high price. There was no loyalty for her among the servants, and she had no right to expect there to be. She had treated Timothy appallingly, trampled on his feelings and demeaned him in every way. And now she was lonely, horribly lonely. She missed her parents. They had always lent a willing ear. If only she had not dismissed their advice and concerns over her marriage. Tonight Kelynen was not here, but her younger sister had too much on her mind to have given her the companionship she needed. Luke was closer geographically than usual, but he would be of little use.

The front door banged and she sat up straight. She heard Timothy's voice as he handed over his wet outdoor things. He stopped outside the parlour door and she wished him, willed him, to come in but he strode off. Damn Nancy Wills! She had informed him the parlour was occupied.

After several long lonely minutes Livvy ventured to the den.

'Hello, Timothy.' She put on a pleasant smile.

He rose from his desk and gave a formal bow. 'Mrs Lanyon.'

'Don't call me that, please!' She was tapping her finger-tips together, on edge. 'Timothy, I . . . Have you just come back from the manor?'

'I have, for my weekly duty call. Your brother was uncommonly melancholy.'

'Oh?' Livvy was hopeful this snatch of communication meant Timothy was thawing towards her. 'Why was that?'

'That is between Luke and me.'

'He confided in you on a spiritual matter?'

'He did. Now, have you finished? I have much to do.' He sat down and resumed his activity with quill and eccle-siastical register.

'Does he have need of me, do you think? Timothy, please! Give me heed. I have the right to be concerned about Luke.'

Timothy trawled a long, lingering look over her. 'I suppose it is just possible you might be of use to him now Kelynen is to abide at Chenhalls.'

Livvy wanted to smack his face for his insolence. She detested him for insulting her – her station was higher than his and he was seeing fit to forget it. Yet she had treated him wrongly. And she hated no longer being the centre of his life. She hated being the subject of his loathing.

'I'll make my way to see him tomorrow and offer my comfort. Kelynen has hopes of Josiah Tremayne. What do you think? He is not the heir to Chenhalls, of course, but it is thought he has money of his own. As younger chil-dren of two great families they are on the same level in every way.'

'Josiah Tremayne would be unsuitable for Kelynen for many reasons.'

'What reasons? I find that worrying.'

'It need not. I trust Kelynen's good sense to see her right. I'm confident she will not make a mistake in cleaving to a man who is wrong for her.'

His insinuation slashed through Livvy but she was too proud to let it show. 'Before I leave can I get you anything?'

His answer was postponed by Nancy Wills' arrival with a tray of steaming hot food. 'Here you are, Reverend. A hearty bowl of beef and vegetable broth, just the way you like it. And hot herb bread and spiced tea. Now, don't you be letting any of it get cold. The rain's being carried on a south-west wind and you'll need something to set you up if you're working again long into the night.'

'Mrs Wills, you do me proud. How is the sexton's sore leg? It took quite a knock with the spade this afternoon. It was kind of you to dress it for him. The widow of the late Mr Cantor need not worry over his burial tomorrow. The grave is dug strong and true, as always.'

Ignored, belittled, bruised to her soul, Livvy quietly withdrew. She raged to herself for some time, then wept throughout the remaining hours of the night.

Twelve

'At last!' Gabriel stretched out his hands for his violin. 'You were cruel to keep it from me for so long, Kelynen.'

He was dressed and reclining on a chaise longue, his laundered shawl – which he refused to part with – around his shoulders, for he complained always of feeling cold. Kelynen wondered about the shawl. With no explanation over his near starvation, she had decided a broken heart must be the cause of his troubles and the shawl had belonged to his lost love. And troubled he often was, slipping away into a trance-like state when he would hum and sing and his fingers would appear to be writing down the peculiar haunted sounds. Sir Rafe had brought his things up from the tower but locked the score sheets away, declaring his fervent composing unhealthy.

'It was only for a week, Gabriel. You may play for ten minutes, as agreed, and then, as you've also agreed, you will allow Jacob Glynn to help you downstairs. I've arranged a couch for you beside a window in the drawing room.'

'You are rushing my recuperation.' Gabriel caressed the violin strings, making a sweet, mournful sound. He kissed the polished woodwork. 'I have missed you, old friend.'

Kelynen watched and smiled. Gabriel had not been complaining, he was grateful for her every consideration, but he was a determined recluse and it had taken a lot of persuasion to get him to agree to the physician's orders that he must not languish in his room. His appetite was still absent and he had to be constantly reminded to eat. He would avow he was full after only two or three mouthfuls and needed to be cajoled to finish off each meal. The first day of her stay, Kelynen had fed him with a spoon. When he had the strength to employ the cutlery himself she had watched over every plate. For two days now he had been strong enough to leave the bed. Always, persistently, he had pleaded for his musical instruments.

The physician's opinion was that Gabriel was in the grip of an addiction, which would hopefully ease as he recovered. Kelynen liked Dr Menheniott. He was young and jolly and open to suggestions. She had brought herbal medicines with her from home, having consulted Beatrice, who was an authority on natural remedies, on Gabriel's condition. Dr Menheniott was interested in the ingredients of the ointment Beatrice had given her to apply to Gabriel's dry skin, and she had told him it was buttercup and lavender. When she had attempted to rub the ointment on Gabriel's hands he had protested it was too much to expect of her, and Jacob Glynn, who was now attending as his personal manservant, had taken over.

'Must I go downstairs today? I'd prefer to stay here and look out at the sea.' Gabriel put the violin under his chin and used his fingers to feather out a few chords of an overture by Haydn. 'Why not tomorrow?'

'You need a change of environment and the sooner the better. My sister Livvy will be here today to put the finishing touches to Sir Rafe's portrait. You'll have a good view of them down over the gardens.'

'And I suppose all the windows and doors will be flung open.' He put the bow to the violin.

Kelynen knew she was facing a minor battle of wills to pry the violin out of his hands. 'You will benefit from the air. Tomorrow I'll have you sitting outside.'

'I will not be looked upon as if I'm some specimen in a surgeon's jar.'

'Who do you suppose would do that?'

'My uncle. He sits for hours beside my bed when he thinks I'm asleep.'

'You should be grateful that he cares for you so deeply, while you in turn give him much concern.'

'I am grateful to him, and I take into consideration that he hardly knows me.' Gabriel frowned, plucking strings. 'But I prefer to be alone.'

'I know you do, Gabriel, but it's your desire for solitude that has led to your current condition.' Her tone was steeped in understanding but it was also firm and authoritative.

'Not total solitude, Kelynen. I like a little company from time to time. I like yours. I'm looking forward to returning to my friends in Vienna when I'm well enough to travel.'

'I rather think your uncle is hoping you will remain here, or at least not quickly flee his side.'

Gabriel was thoughtful. 'Why do you say that?'

Kelynen did not have to think about it; she absorbed everything Sir Rafe did or said. 'It's what I've observed about him.'

'He knew where I lived as a boy. He did not call on me there. I cannot see any point in us forming a closer relationship now.'

She sat still while Gabriel played, filling the room with tranquil soothing notes, then sad ones; evocative of lost love, she mused. It made her heart want to weep.

She was gradually piecing together Gabriel's history. Josiah Tremayne had been one source. To her pleasure, it had been he who had shown her and Ruth King to their rooms.

'As you've been so charitable to give heed to my brother's pleas, Miss Pengarron, I feel you should know something about him. After his mother's death he was taken by his grandmother for a few months' stay in her quiet country house, on the outskirts of London. She never got round to returning him home, despite numerous requests from our father. When our father married my mother, Gabriel's return was somewhat overlooked. Then my mother died giving birth to me and shortly afterward our father had a fatal hunting accident. Sir Rafe returned from the Caribbean and wanted to rear us both, but Gabriel's grandmother pleaded that he was content and settled residing with her. A few months passed, and, unknown to my uncle, the old lady suffered a stroke and was bed-bound for the remaining years of her life. Gabriel was taught all his lessons at home. You must have concluded yourself that he'd had an inspiring music master. The servants left him much to his own devices. Apart from the many public performances he'd give – including, I'm proud to say, at Court – he lived in virtual seclusion and, I'm afraid to say, he has little concept of family life.

'He lived in Vienna for three years. I found him languishing in his apartment; fine quarters, but he had reduced them to barely habitable. It was the first time I had met him. Our blood gave us a bond and he agreed to come with me. I've learned to respect his desire for solitude. I'd hoped to learn much about him, but he slept during most of the journey here and then locked himself away. I would not say he is difficult but sometimes he is hard to understand.' Josiah had smiled and made a resigned gesture. 'I think you know the rest of the tale, Miss Pengarron.'

She knew what she had witnessed but this new information made Gabriel seem more mysterious.

They had arrived at the room next to Gabriel's. 'My uncle thought it best to put you in here, for your convenience in attending the patient. There's a comfortable bed for your maid in the dressing room.'

Kelynen had swept her eyes appreciatively round the spacious room, its many tall windows looking out over the sea and Mearnon Point. The dominant feature was an elaborate Chippendale bed with an overhead Chinese-style canopy with flowing rich silk, gold-coloured fringed falls.

Oriental cloisonné censers, vases and ornaments and jade and ivory figures were set everywhere. The dressing table was crowded with cosmetics and perfumes in bottles shaped in the like she had never seen before: tall twisting flowers; animal tusks; the female form.

'It's so beautiful in here!' she had said.

'I'm pleased you like it.' Josiah had fluttered his pale, well-kept hands in a circle. 'Sir Rafe saw personally to the little additions. He was anxious to create a pleasing ambience for you.'

'It certainly has that.'

Ruth had declared the whole effect as decadent, yet Kelynen knew she was fascinated by it too. Kelynen loved the overriding feel of femininity and sensuality. She felt honoured and cherished, and it gave her confidence to look forward to the promised walk round the gardens with Josiah. She had ordered Ruth to bring her loveliest dresses, and she daily endured the rigours of having her hair dressed up with horizontal side curls. She would apply a little rouge and Ruth would make a face, but Kelynen caught her maid smiling knowingly, and although she had not spoken of her hopes for Josiah, Kelynen knew the staid, religious Ruth shared them for her.

Kelynen had been kept busy with the patient the first day, and Josiah had not been at home for dinner that evening. During a later talk about Gabriel with Josiah, before he had left Chenhalls for business at Penzance, she had asked, 'Do you have any idea what brought him so low? Jacob Glynn mentioned the possibility of a broken heart.'

Josiah had smiled so strikingly that Kelynen's hopes of a romance with him had climbed. 'I rather think that was the cause. Is it not said that love will do strange and tormenting things to one's heart?'

But to her dismay it seemed love was not prodding Josiah Tremayne in her direction. He had so far stayed formally polite. She now only saw him when he enquired about

Gabriel's health from Jacob Glynn, in confidential whispers in a corner of the room. It had left her feeling slighted and a little foolish at his lack of interest. Was she so plain and undesirable? Apparently not according to Sir Rafe, who plied her with endearments and compliments.

Josiah had mentioned that Sir Rafe had always been most kind to him, and that after the tragic loss of his last little daughter they had grown close. This made Kelynen wonder if, although Josiah appeared to bear an affection for his half-brother, he secretly resented the fact that Gabriel – who showed no interest at all in Chenhalls, or the mines that brought the estate its wealth – would one day inherit everything. Of course, Sir Rafe could change his will if he so desired. Perhaps he already had.

'Sometimes you look so serious.'

'Oh!' Gabriel was suddenly on his feet and leaning awkwardly towards her, his ashen, woefully thin face with its peculiar yawning eyes alarmingly close. 'I did not realize you had stopped,' she said.

'Then you were unaware that I stole another five minutes above the stipulated time.'

'I was thinking of Josiah.' She had no idea why she blurted it out. It might have been instinct, because she did not like Gabriel creeping up on her.

Gabriel put his hand out to a chest of drawers to aid his balance and he straightened up slowly. He stayed silent a moment, looking at her gravely. 'He has a new mistress. He spends as much time as he can with her. But he'll soon tire of her, he always does.'

'It's of no concern to me.' She sprang up, hiding her hurt, feeling silly and exposed. She was sure Gabriel had spoken out of jealousy at not receiving her undivided attention, but she believed his words nonetheless. She had been warned about Josiah's inclinations. Her dutiful ways showed how she was not mistress material. 'Gabriel, take my seat. You're not strong enough to stand this long.'

Jacob Glynn entered and with him was Sir Rafe. Kelynen felt an instant cheer at the baronet's presence.

'Good to see you making small endeavours, dear boy,' Rafe said, coming to Gabriel's rescue for his legs were wobbling.

Together with Jacob Glynn he soon had Gabriel tucked up in a blanket on the couch in the drawing room.

'I'd rather sit at the spinet in the music room, Uncle,' he said, slightly breathless from the journey down the corridors and stairs. 'Could I not have my cello for five minutes? Or a sheet of score paper so I can write down what's inside my head?'

'You've not the strength yet for such an undertaking,' Rafe said firmly. He was feeding titbits of steamed chicken to Octavia, his favourite cat. 'Be a good fellow and give no cause for dear Miss Kelynen to plead with you to be sensible.'

Gabriel seemed about to plead for some other concession, but then he looked at Kelynen. Just looked at her, studied her, as if he had never seen her before. He had not seen her before in such good light, nor had she him. Kelynen was pleased to be at her best, for Rafe's quick eyes were on her too. She was wearing a pale peach and ivory polonaise gown, a narrow silk ruff round her neck, with the perfect complement of dropped pearl earrings and pearl bracelets on both wrists.

When Gabriel spoke next he sounded a little emotional. 'Uncle, please write to Kelynen's brother and ask that she may stay indefinitely. Between us, we must forbid her to leave until I am fully recovered.'

'Write to Mr Luke Pengarron, I shall, and immediately, before I prepare for my last sitting with Mrs Lanyon. Indeed, Kelynen,' Rafe lifted her hand and kissed it while smiling into her eyes, 'I absolutely forbid you to leave. Ever.'

Thirteen

That same morning, David Trenchard was preparing to preach the gospel in the marketplace of Marazion. He chose a spot where a great many people were likely to pass by, where there was room for an audience, and where he would not have to compete too much against the cries of the hawkers, chapmen, stall holders and sideshow entrepreneurs and the noises of live animals and poultry.

He offered up a quick prayer to be given courage and authority over the jeers and heckling he would inevitably receive from the likes of drunken sailors and prostitutes, and the occasional outrage over his beliefs from a hard-line Anglican. He took a deep swallow and with his Bible in one hand – opened at Genesis, for he would start with the Creation – he mounted the wooden box he had brought with him.

'Friends!' His strong voice of conviction carried well across the town's one long straggling street. 'Friends, I bid you one and all, come and listen to the most important story you will ever hear. Come and hear about God, your Father, who was and is the Father of the whole world. Come and hear how he sacrificed His only son to save the world, so that we may all, if we answer His call, live with Him in the world to come.'

His initial nervousness soon vanished, and, with sweat dampening the silky fair hair on his hardy brow, David gained in confidence and fervour as an audience of interested faces grew, overwhelming the scoffers, some of whom stopped poking fun or mouthing obscenities and stayed and listened too. Methodism was thriving in Cornwall, mainly among the ordinary working folk, and David was heartened at the appreciation he was receiving, and the support from local Methodists who shouted 'Hallelujah!' or 'Amen to that!' at his every pause. When he heard his prowess likened to that of the greatest public evangelist, the institutional founder of the faith, the Reverend John Wesley, he felt almost already in Paradise.

Sophie Carew was wandering through Marazion. To avoid the general crush she kept tight to the shops, ignoring the goods inside them, but if she had caught her reflection in the rough windows she would have seen by how much her anxiety was on display.

'What shall I do? What to do,' she was muttering under her breath. Her mind was filled with thoughts about the baby residing at the home of Captain Kane Pengarron. She knew who the child's mother was. She wanted to ride to Vellanoweth and announce, 'I'm certain young Betty is my niece, daughter of my sister Adelaide. Thank you for caring for her, but I'll take her with me now and raise her.' Even though, as a young widow, taking in an abandoned child would cause unwelcome speculation and effectively ruin her chances of a second husband. She had accepted months ago that Adelaide's baby meant little hope of love for herself and children of her own. There was no point in encouraging any honourable gentleman, and she could never become someone's mistress.

But she could not claim Betty yet. Betty was well and safe and that was all that mattered for now. What was paramount was to discover where Adelaide was.

This was only the latest of many struggles in Sophie's life. Last year, after her penniless father died, she had been forced to look for lodgings for herself and her flighty sister. Deliverance from shame and poverty had come in the form of Wilmot Carew, the only faithful family friend. He had offered her marriage, security and status. They had expected Adelaide to live with them, but she had mockingly declared that her lover, whom she refused to name, was setting her up in a secret address. The next time she had encountered Adelaide she had complained bitterly of becoming pregnant and declared she would give the baby up.

'Give it up to what?' Sophie had demanded in despair over her sister's hard attitude. Adelaide had always been cold-hearted.

'It can go to an orphanage for all I care,' Adelaide had stated, cantankerous and intolerant at Sophie's horror. 'Hopefully I'll miscarry the wretched creature.'

But Adelaide's hopes had not been realized and she had presented herself at Sophie's house late one night with a swollen belly. After a fierce quarrel in which recriminations and scorn had flown, an arrangement had been made. Sophie would take the baby, declaring it a foundling she had taken pity on. Hence her interest in the foundling Kelynen had mentioned, its birth falling about the same time Adelaide had been due to deliver. But Adelaide had not planned to actually leave her baby abandoned. Her intention was to have had it brought to Sophie, along with a letter of assurance that all had gone well during the confinement. Why this change in the arrangement? Had she survived the birth? Sophie had to discover what had happened to her sister in case she suddenly showed up and caused trouble. She wanted to know if Adelaide was in good health before she made little Betty her own.

If only Wilmot had not been so careless with money, wanting her to have everything and gambling heavily, despite her protests that she was content as things were, then he would not have been faced with disgrace and would still be alive. He would have found a way to track Adelaide down. If only Kelynen was not at Chenhalls with the wretched Tremaynes then she could have leaned on her wisdom. She should have confided the whole truth to her friend. Kelynen might be unsympathetic now over her lack of faith, and the Pengarrons at Vellanoweth and the Reverend Lanyon were bound to be angry with her for keeping her secret.

A loud voice infiltrated her harrowed thoughts. David Trenchard! He was just the sort of quiet young man she would have liked for a husband. Of course, his faith and class were unbreachable barriers between them. He seemed totally trustworthy and was likely to be sympathetic and discreet. Could she prevail upon him to make enquiries in places where she, as a lady of good birth, dare not? He was smart enough to enter gentlemen's coffee houses, where patrons apparently boasted as much about their mistresses as they did their lucrative business deals.

After a minute of indecision she joined the throng listening to the preacher.

Timothy Lanyon was on his way to Vellanoweth to enquire about the foundling's welfare. He reflected grimly how his wife had travelled away from home in the opposite direction to Chenhalls.

'I'm thinking of making some changes to the nursery,' Livvy had told him over breakfast, the first meal he had shared with her since the quarrel over the foundling.

'You will not, if these changes are to be detrimental to the children,' was his sharp reply.

A comment of this kind would once have provoked indignation and fury in her but she had simply looked hurt. 'Of course I don't intend anything of the kind. How could you think that?'

'I thought perhaps it was something that would make it even easier for you to give them less attention.'

'Timothy,' she had said in haughty but quiet tones, 'if you had consulted Phylida Bevan lately, she would have confirmed that I now spend more time with the children than many other ladies do with theirs. Excuse me.'

She had left the table without eating another mouthful, leaving most of the cooked breakfast on her plate. He had been tempted to go after her, show an interest in her plans for the nursery. He had been unfair. He *had* known she was spending more time with the children – indeed, Phylida Bevan had said she seemed to enjoy being with them. Livvy was quieter altogether. She seemed anxious to be in his company. This pleased him to the reaches of his soul. Was she tamed at last? Willing to become a proper wife? He hoped so, oh, he hoped so, because – leaving aside his anger on the day he had found young Betty – he loved Livvy entirely and with a sort of desperation.

She had changed her attitude towards him at last but only, when out of hurt and frustration, he had railed against her. He had seared through all her layers of selfishness, had shown her what she was in danger of losing. And, as he had witnessed that same night in his den, it had excited her and for the very first time she had offered him her body. It had always been necessary to keep himself under careful restraint during intimacy, even at the beginning of their marriage, when passions for those fortunate to marry for love often ran free, for Livvy had very nearly been raped and murdered by an evil debauched sea captain, a supposed friend of Sir Oliver's. Perhaps he had been wrong in continuing to be passive and Livvy had long found his performance dull and unexciting. He should talk to her. They might be able to finally bond in love and be truly happy now she was willing to compromise, even perhaps to bend to his will.

Or it could be that she was being clever, trying to deceive him with this softer attitude. Perhaps the moment he succumbed and they returned to normal married life – normal for them – she would resume her thoughtless, selfish ways.

No. He could not risk that. He could not stand the pain

in his heart, knowing she did not, and probably never had really loved him. Nor could he bear the humiliation of having his son grow up seeing him as a hands-tied husband, not a patch on the virile, commanding Sir Oliver. The present situation was soul-destroying, but he could endure it better than the other option.

His thoughts moved on to the baby, young Betty Nobody. 'I pray that you will have experience of a happy life, little child,' he whispered to the memory of the pathetic bundle he had picked up off the church steps. 'But I know your future pain at finding out you were rejected by the one person who should love you most.'

Luke was in a gentleman's coffee shop, where he had arranged to meet Matthias Renfree. He smoked his clay pipe without pleasure, leaving his coffee to grow cold. Distracted, morose, he was uninterested in the figures the steward was enthusiastically relating over the price he had just realized from a grain merchant.

'Sir Oliver should be impressed, don't you think? If the harvest's a blessed one, it'll be a penny more a bushel than last year.' Matthias Renfree, stocky and compassionate, at fifty years old had worked all his life for the Pengarrons. Intelligent and learned, he was married to David Trenchard's aunt. He was also vigorous in his Methodist beliefs, and was always eager to offer Christly comfort; he was known locally as Preacher Renfree. He was disturbed by the dark shadows under his young master's eyes and his apparent depression. Disturbed also to have learned he was drinking late into the night and had abandoned his play-writing. The servants at the manor were talking about a broken heart over some beautiful young widow. 'Lady Pengarron's letter this morning sees them well, you said, sir. How long do you think they'll stay up in Bath?'

'What? Oh,' Luke tapped out his pipe. 'My mama sounds excited still. She wrote that she is much taken with the magnificent architecture. They may stay away for many weeks yet.' Luke was not in the mood to discuss estate business or the family. 'I heard the voice of your nephew preaching while I was on the way here. Feel free to leave and listen to him any time you wish, Renfree.'

'I'd like to do that, sir. Thank you.' Before Matthias left, he paused. 'Forgive the question, Mr Luke, but are you ailing? Is there . . . is there anything I can do for you?'

Luke sighed wearily. Never had he felt so low in energy. He was hungry but could not face food. He had lost the extra pounds about his waist. 'Offer a willing ear, you mean? I thank you for the kindness but you cannot help me. And before you mention God, let me tell you that a week's fasting and prayer undertaken in sackcloth and ashes would not prevail.'

'I'm very sorry to hear that, sir. If you ever want to . . . to talk . . .'

Luke replied with a grim smile. 'You are indeed a willing substitute for my father, Matthias Renfree, and I know you would be a good one. But do not worry over me. I shall pull my wits together. I'll have you know that when I leave here I intend to go straightway to Polgissey for a few days. I bid you not to disturb me there unless it's of the utmost importance. After that, I do not know . . .'

Although aware of the fervour and emotion David Trenchard was spreading through the crowd gathered round him, Sophie was too anxious to listen to his message. With her perfumed handkerchief up to her nose to offset the ripe smells of animal manure and unwashed bodies, she kept at a distance, not wanting anyone from the besotted throng to think she was interested in the lay preacher's message. Anglican tradition was enough to feed her spirit, and rightfully so! An hour passed. It seemed a week. She shuffled her feet, sighed, and then huffed in annoyance when suddenly jostled by newcomers. Should not these people, mainly of the lower orders, be about their work? They were stealing time from their employers. Outrageous! Was David Trenchard ever going to finish?

At one point an elderly woman in typical Methodist puritan grey tapped her arm and spoke loudly in her ear. 'Don't you be too proud to step forward and receive the Lord, sister.'

Sophie shrugged her away. 'Don't you dare call me your sister, and how dare you touch me!'

The woman, short and small, peered up in under Sophie's small straw hat. 'Begging your pardon, ma'am. I meant no offence. Why're you here, then?'

Almost in tears of frustration, horrified at having compromised herself, Sophie strode away. She had made a spectacle of herself. If any of the gentry had seen her lingering in such an unseemly manner, in such an unsuitable place, she would be the subject of scornful gossip. She hurried towards home, towards sanctuary. It had been a stupid idea anyway. David Trenchard might be a pleasant, respectable young man, but his only interest in talking to her would be about salvation. And he was a stranger to her. How could she have considered that he might be willing to help her? Likely, he would suggest she tell the Reverend Lanyon the truth of Betty's parentage, and what would the Reverend Lanyon think of her consulting a dissenter? Both men might consider Adelaide not worthy of being found. Part of Sophie thought this too, but Adelaide was her sister and she had to know her fate. With her head down she hastened her steps, afraid she would actually weep in the streets. She ploughed into someone.

'Oh, my goodness! I'm so sorry, ma'am. I wasn't looking where I was going.' Luke had also been bowling along, eager to reach his horse, stabled in a holstelry, and be on his way to Polgissey.

Sophie looked up, first in horror and alarm, and then with some relief. She had feared she had collided with some drunken rogue or one of the vile gentlemen who persistently propositioned her. 'Mr Pengarron, it is I who should apologize. I was gazing down.'

Luke saw her anxious expression and wanted to comfort her. This touch of vulnerability made his heart ache for her, and ache to have her like him, even a little bit. But he must be circumspect. If there was ever to be a glimmer of a chance in gaining her respect, he must show a humble side. He took off his tricorn hat and bowed lightly. 'I trust I've caused you no injury, Mrs Carew.'

'No. No, you have not, Mr Pengarron.'

'Then I bid you well and bid you good afternoon. Your servant, ma'am.' He bowed again and walked on, one of the hardest things he had done in his life. He felt his heart breaking into tiny chinks; each had a name. Love. Hope. Future.

Sophie felt too breathless, her emotions too shocked and bruised to walk on. She had expected overtures from Luke Pengarron but instead had been shunned. Rejection from a man was a new experience. Well, the arrogant, immoral Luke Pengarron could rot in hell!

She glanced over her shoulder, expecting him to be striding away in his most autocratic manner, and received another shock. He was plodding on, head down, dejected. So perhaps there really was another side to her friend's brother. In her letter mentioning her intended stay at Chenhalls, Kelynen had tried to convince her that there was. Flashing over his words just now, she realized they had been delivered with the utmost respect, even a little shyly.

Well, whatever the truth of his disposition, it was of no interest to her. Gathering her dignity, she went on her way. But ... But what? What was her inner self trying to tell her?

Luke Pengarron, she knew, had kept many a mistress. He was not as likely to make high-handed judgements over Adelaide's disgrace as David Trenchard was. And he would have connections, and ways and means. Would he be willing to help her? It was a risk to ask him. He could become a pest again. But she could not let Adelaide down. Now was the time to be brave, to humble herself, to strike out boldly.

She turned on her heel, and, while fighting to keep her decorum, hastened after him. Two steps behind, she called out softly, 'Mr Pengarron. Mr Pengarron, pray stop a moment.'

Luke whirled round the instant he heard her voice. He could not help smiling down on her. If he was in some wonderful fabulous dream, he prayed he would never wake up. Hope was renewed and burned in him like silver being purified; painful, yet utterly desirable. 'Mrs Carew, this is . . .' He stopped himself from saying 'a pleasure'. *Don't ruin it now!* He bowed in perfect civility. 'Your humble servant, ma'am.'

'Pray, forgive me for delaying you, Mr Pengarron. Could you . . . I mean, could I possibly ask you, as the brother of my dearest friend, for your help?'

Ask me anything at all! Heaven be blessed for evermore!

He willed his voice to be neutral and calm. 'It will be an honour, Mrs Carew.'

Gabriel longed to be taken back to his room, but knowing Kelynen would leave him to rest and join her sister in the garden, and wanting to stay where she was, he pretended to be asleep.

She reminded him, just a little, of Caterina. Caterina had inherited her looks from her English mother, and Kelynen had the same delicate feminine build, the same pretty fair hair and deep, dark eyes. But the resemblance ended there. Caterina's whole being had blazed with extraordinary energy, and her gaze had been fierily decadent, her walk superior and seductive. Kelynen exuded a comforting peace, and moved with an unconscious innocence and at times had a beguiling awkwardness. Caterina had shouted or cried shrilly rather than simply talked. Kelynen spoke in soft or firm or considerate tones and was always open to reason. She had a sense of fun and was not easily offended. Caterina had taken even the smallest remark, when not issued in adulation of her or her dancing, as criticism, accusing the speaker of spite or jealousy.

Kelynen had not questioned his self-neglect, showing the same care and understanding as if he suffered from a natural illness or the result of an accident. Caterina had tossed her head and screamed at him not to infect her if he'd suffered as much as a sniffle. 'How can I dance for the Emperor if all my limbs are aching?' she would have accused him, and would likely have slapped his face and stormed out of the apartment they had shared for twenty-one glorious, destructive months, and not return for days.

Caterina, an ardent social butterfly, had never understood his need to be alone and had accused him of being mad or peculiar, as if she were threatened by it. Kelynen willingly granted him the space he desired. Caterina had stamped on other people's feelings. Kelynen spoke glowingly of her friends and lovingly of her family. She expressed sorrow over tragedy. He had been touched when her eyes had filled with tears when Jacob Glynn, after her genuine queries, had explained how his uncle's first wife had died of a ruptured stomach during an early pregnancy, how the second wife had drowned while swimming in a nearby cove, and how his daughters had all died of childhood illnesses. Kelynen was interested in everyone and everything, including the running of Chenhalls and the mines – unusual for a woman to be interested in business. He liked it when she asked about his music, and she'd said she was looking forward to the day she could accompany him on the spinet, while modestly adding he must overlook her lack of skill. He was very much looking forward to the duet.

He had loved Caterina with a blind, dogged devotion, and had felt torn asunder at her sudden death. A quirk of fate, a heavy piece of staging at the Imperial Kärntnerthortheater, had snuffed out her scorching spirit and robbed the ballet world of one of its finest dancers. Robbed him of the only woman he would ever love. No one could ever raise in him the passions that Caterina had – and how grateful he was for that! He could never again bring himself to embark on such a tortuous love affair. If Caterina had not died when she did, she might well have driven him to throw himself off St Stephen's Cathedral, so frenzied, so dazzling – and in the end so spirit-leeching – their relationship had been. His appetite for food had left him long before her death, and his gradual decline had seemed to please her. She had fought always to maintain control of him, and he, loving her so powerfully, had forsaken almost all his own desires to please her. His life with her, her terrible death and his grief had almost cost him his sanity. If Josiah had not come for him he would be dead by now. And now he owed his life to Kelynen.

He tugged in Caterina's shawl tighter, his one precious reminder of her, for her family had claimed her other things. Thoughts of her made his emotions splinter but as he strove to regroup them and clutch at peace they formed a riot inside his head. He was shivering. Cold. He was so cold without her. Then, as in a hundred times a day, his mind clouded over. He was back in Vienna, composing music for a solo ballet for Caterina. She had given him the theme of wild, devastating love ending in tragedy, which she was hoping to perform exclusively for Emperor Joseph and the Imperial Court. He must finish it soon. Caterina demanded it. She demanded it every day, not caring that he was in the middle of composing an opera under the Emperor's personal command. And she complained about every note he wrote for her, wanting more drama, more excitement, something heart-rending, and hellish, it seemed to him. But he was so tired, so weak.

Her beautiful face and flashing eyes were before him

now. 'Work Gabriel, darling, work, work! Then I shall come and make love to you. No music, no love.' He continued to strive for her, struggling towards possessing her, needing her love – needing her, for even in the madness, it was all he lived for.

Then his mind was recaptured by the present and he was working on the ballet in its new form. Caterina's own story, her epitaph, loud and stirring and fierce, and yes, partly hellish. His muscles jerked, his face twitched, his eyes flickered under their closed lids as he mumbled an unearthly tune. His long, desperate fingers reached out for the pianoforte and score sheets.

Nearby, with Rex snoozing at her feet, Kelynen was writing a letter to her mother, describing the beauties and charm of Chenhalls. The unnatural sounds of Gabriel's tortured dreams troubled her. She reached for his hands and stilled them. 'Hush, Gabriel. There's nothing to worry about. You're quite safe now. You are home.'

She felt his hands grasping round hers. She held them for as long as it took to soothe away the spasms, until he fell into a silent, restorative sleep.

The portrait of Rafe was finally finished. Tomorrow it would be hung in the gallery over the main stairway. Livvy had left Chenhalls satisfied with the result, but she was leaving behind a wake of people concerned about her.

'I've never seen her looking so downcast,' Ruth said, pushing up the encrusted silver lace that Kelynen had lowered to reveal a little of her small, shapely bosom. 'Whatever would her ladyship make of it? P'raps you should write to her? Tell her Miss Livvy's wasting away?'

'I'm worried about Livvy too.' Kelynen peered round Ruth to gain her reflection in the long mirrors in the dressing room. 'But it's hardly serious enough to spoil Mama's stay in Bath.'

However, Kelynen was more worried about her sister

than she'd revealed. Livvy had disappointed Lady Portia, putting the elderly lady in high dudgeon by postponing the starting date of her portrait. Livvy had explained she had urgent things to attend to at home. Kelynen hoped her sister's priority was to repair her marriage. Rafe, who was delighted with his portrait, had invited Livvy and Timothy to Chenhalls for an overnight stay at the end of the week, charging her to pass on a letter to Luke, inviting him to the same. Kelynen hoped they would all accept. She was looking forward to playing hostess here – Lady Portia was past that sort of thing and retired promptly at eight thirty.

Kelynen worked the modesty lace down. Ruth pushed it up. 'I'll sew it in place, young lady!'

'It's not fashionable to have coverings up to one's throat,' Kelynen protested.

'Her ladyship'll expect me to protect your honour, Miss Kelynen.' Ruth pursed her narrow mouth.

Kelynen burst out laughing. 'My honour is perfectly safe in this house, you goose. Mr Josiah is never here. Mr Gabriel is incapacitated. And Sir Rafe is, well, he's old enough to be my father.'

'As if that'd make any difference,' Ruth snorted, intimating to Kelynen to sit at the dressing table for the application of her jewellery. 'Sir Rafe's good-looking and in fine fettle. He's also a wicked pursuer of ladies and servant girls, from what I've heard. Don't you think for a minute, young miss, that I've missed the way he looks at you.'

This last remark made Kelynen's heart leap strangely and her hand shot to that region. The sensation had been far more intense than when her thoughts had been with Josiah Tremayne, and her tummy felt queerly agitated. She tried to keep her voice to a juvenile mocking tone. 'Oh? In what manner does he look at me?'

'In a way that he shouldn't! Impiously. You don't need me to impress it on you any stronger, do you? You're in danger from that gentleman, or my soul doesn't belong to the Almighty. Time he got himself decently married again, 'tis long overdue.'

Kelynen held out her wrist for a diamond bracelet while chewing over Ruth's words and liking every one of them. She felt a little afraid and that excited her. Rafe was handsome and captivating and enticing. He stirred her every feminine sense. She recognized that now and gloried in it. She liked the touch of his hand when he lifted hers to kiss it, and the way he tucked her arm through his to take her on a stroll round the gardens and grounds. She liked – and now her feelings grew alarmingly and deliciously keen – the feel of his lips on her cheeks and the persistence of his liberty of placing them briefly on her lips. A lady would be fortunate indeed to have him pay her court, to make him his wife. Being mistress of Chenhalls was a prospect to aspire to – one she found, with growing fright and delight, utterly agreeable.

'Have you finished with me, Ruth?' She was suddenly brisk. 'I don't want to be late going down.'

When Ruth went downstairs, Kelynen once more fashioned a more interesting décolletage. Then she unlocked the connecting door to Gabriel's room and slipped into him, to ensure he was settled for the night. He was deep in sleep – an exhausted, uneasy sleep, she thought. She sat at the bed, holding his hand. When he started up a mournful air she counteracted it by singing softly. 'Sleep peacefully, Gabriel.'

Rafe came in and closed the door gently. Kelynen smiled up at him, glad the room was darkened and he could not easily detect the flush now tingling her cheeks. Was she to feel awkward in his company from now on? She prayed she would not. She whispered, 'He seems a little more settled each day.'

Rafe moved up behind her and placed his hands on her shoulders, and she closed her eyes to enjoy the warm, firm pressure of them. 'It's all thanks to you, m'dear. I'm so grateful for all that you've done for Gabriel.'

'You have a deep affection for him.'

'Indeed I do.' Rafe smoothed his fingers over Gabriel's brow. 'I failed him in his boyhood and in his youth. I want to make it up to him. He and Josiah and my sister are all I have.'

Kelynen's gaze, as always when in this room, crept to the dressing table. The only additions since her first look were grooming items. 'Has Gabriel no belongings at all?'

'There's a trunk somewhere. Glynn took a quick look inside it when Gabriel first arrived but he said it was not worth unpacking.'

'I've been thinking about his grandmother's house. Does he still own it?'

'No. He sold it to fund him abroad.'

'Then he has no one but you and Josiah and Lady Portia. I'm sure when he's fully recovered he will come to realize how much he owes you.'

'I want nothing from either of my nephews except for them to be content.'

Kelynen studied the man in the bed and longed for the day when flesh would fill out his cheeks and eye sockets, when his skin would appear less brittle. 'You've not seen Gabriel since he was a boy. What do you suppose he really looks like?'

'I think he will be a handsome enough fellow.'

Kelynen turned her head, but not before Rafe saw her frown of doubt.

Rafe smiled down on her. 'Are we Tremayne men not an arresting breed? And we always take lovely brides. Gabriel's mother was a beauty. Now, let us go down to dinner before we wake him.' Rafe leaned over the bed and affectionately touched Gabriel's cheek.

After dinner, Kelynen found herself alone with Rafe in the banqueting hall. This was no different to many other evenings when Josiah was absent, but after Ruth's remarks about Rafe, Kelynen felt strangely elated and tense and shy.

While stroking the cats crowded on and around him, Rafe's shameless eyes were on her often, but tonight she lacked the boldness to hold his gaze and resorted instead to bringing up her fan to hide her blushes.

Relinquishing his pets, he got up from his chair to approach her and her heart thundered ever more wildly with his every closing step. He reached out his hand. 'Walk with me through the house, Kelynen. You've not seen much of it yet and I know you are curious.'

She felt special and important to be viewing his domain, and it was such a pleasure to be close to him. Not once while passing through doors and along passages did he surrender his hold on her arm. He peeped into the library, situated at the end of the south range. 'This is where I see to matters of business, which I get through as quickly as possible. There are books on many subjects and languages. Read as many as you like.' He made to lead her away.

'Oh, please may I look around?'

'Anything you wish, m'dear.' Rafe carried in a three-light candelabrum.

There were steps to climb down, an overriding smell of leather and old paper, and a feeling of hush. It was as if the long broad room had other presences, of disapproving, dark-clothed librarians, jealously guarding the literary collections and artefacts, and ghostly, long-bearded professors welcoming them as pupils to whom they could pass on their years and years of knowledge and wisdom. Kelynen gazed into every dark corner to be sure there really were no spectres, and was startled to see two moving, glowing orange orbs before realizing Octavia had slunk secretively in with them. She took little notice of the rows and rows of packed shelves cramming every wall and gallery. She would browse or climb the many ladders to the top shelves another day, make a search for anything that might interest Luke. Uncommon subjects as research for his plays might help heal his broken heart.

There were many tables – some so long they appeared to be ludicrously stretched – with books, microscopes, maps and fossils laid out upon them. She went straight to the desk at the foot of the steps and ran her fingers over the polished mahogany. 'My father allows me many duties on the estate at home. We often work long hours in his study.'

'I hold rather more traditional views to Sir Oliver as to where a woman's duties lie,' Rafe said. 'You're devoted to your father, aren't you? You've spoken of him many times.'

'I do tend to believe there is nothing he cannot achieve or rectify. He was in France when I was born. My parents were temporarily estranged and he had no idea that I was expected. He's always felt he must make it up to me and we are very close.'

'It must be wonderful to be very close to you, Kelynen.' In the light of the candles he saw the vibrancy that shot through her over his compliment. It added to his desire to take her into his arms and kiss her sweet, tender mouth. Rarely had he found someone so engaging. A man could easily grow very fond of this serious, caring, innocent bud, and he admired intelligence in a woman. It would be utterly delicious to exploit her virtue – always a powerful draw to him.

He looked away. Her father would break his neck for merely thinking this way about her. There was a sizeable age gap between Sir Oliver and Lady Kerensa Pengarron, but the years dividing him and Kelynen were more marked. But perhaps Sir Oliver would not be against him making Kelynen his third wife. She would become mistress of Chenhalls, mother of his heir. Doubtless she would produce healthy babies; her generation of Pengarrons had proved themselves good breeders. Of course, young Lanyon's wife would have made a better prospect. There was more vitality in Livvy, more spark and fire. Timothy had not the first notion how to tame or enhance her. Either option for him would have been a pleasure of thrilling proportions.

Kelynen studied the desk. It was bare of paperwork and she was hungry to see inside the drawers. Were documents and ledgers securely stowed away in them? It seemed Rafe was as indifferent to his industry as Sophie had hinted. Sophie. It seemed an age since she had seen her. An age since she had been at home in the manor. Chenhalls and the nursing of Gabriel made everything else seem far away. Or was it Rafe's overwhelming presence making her feel like this?

'Let me show you something, Kelynen,' he said. 'It will require us having to steal past your harridan of a maid on the way up to the attics.'

On the first floor, Rafe picked up a single china candlestick and led her towards a long concealing drape, beyond which was a narrow passageway. She lost count of how many twists and turns and flights of stairs they climbed. All the while her exhilaration at being alone with him, coupled with apprehension, rose and spread. Where was he taking her, and why? Did he have a secret room up in the attics?

She knew a thrill of alarm when he finally ushered her into what seemed just such a place. Did he use this room for assignations? Then she saw it was rigged out as a reading room with shelves of books, furnished only with two armchairs. Long windows were incorporated in the wall, which looked out over the sea.

Rafe put the candlestick down in a dark corner and approached her with a telescope in his hand. 'It's a cloudless night and the moon is strong. You'll get a good view all along the bay.'

She stood at a window and peered through the telescope, first in the direction of Trewarras Head. She could make out much of Mount's Bay and the furthest dark shadow of land of Penlee Point. Not far in the distance were the dark, looming silhouettes of the chimneys and engine house of the Wheal Lowen. In the opposite direction, up-coast, were

Mearnon Point and the final looming shadow of the Lizard. She saw the lonely twinkling lights of a ship out at sea, the tide creaming over faraway sandy inlets and crashing over rocks at the foot of cliffs and headlands. She leaned back to gaze up at the stars in the indigo sky, and with Rafe standing so close behind her it brought her into contact with his body. She was aware of the tantalizing warmth and strength of him.

'Everything seems shrouded with a touch of the mystic in this nocturnal light. It's beautiful. It's awesome.' She brought the telescope down and put it on the window ledge. Every inch of her skin and all her inner regions leapt with delight when he wrapped his arms around her and joined his hands over her midriff.

'That description fits you perfectly, Kelynen.'

She did not reply. She closed her eyes and drifted into him, resting her head against his shoulder. The sense of his warmth and power was like nothing she had experienced before.

Rafe moved to bring the side of her face against his neck. He held her tighter and kissed her cheek, making it a soft and tender salute, a feathery touch, for he did not want to make the mistake of rushing her. He knew women. Kelynen was looking for romance and adulation. Her lips were only a fraction away. He could so easily get carried away with her. With the backs of his fingers he gentled a slow path down over the place he had kissed.

Enjoying the contact, revelling in it, Kelynen turned her face and placed a shy kiss on his hand.

Rafe turned her round slowly. 'You're so lovely, Kelynen, so perfect. I can hardly believe you have come into my life.' He gathered her in and placed his lips with tender restraint over hers.

To be drawn in close to Rafe's solid body, to feel his firm and knowing embrace taking charge of her, to have his mouth on hers, moving over hers, moving with hers, giving more and demanding more, made her aware for the first time of all the realms of life. She burst completely into being. And fell fully and marvellously in love.

Fourteen

Rafe was paying his monthly visit to the Wheal Lowen. The stone engine house, with its arched upper windows, towering brick-topped chimneys and numerous ancillary buildings, were skilfully structured, but to him they were brutal, seeming to encircle and imprison him. The noise on the mine face was deafening, overwhelming the roar of the sea, and the air was choked with dust and grit. The constant rattles and clanks of the great draught bob labouring to pump up water from the lowest depths, the pounding of the stamp, the creaking of the giant-sized waterwheel, the hammering of the ore by the bal maidens, the comings and goings of the necessary tradesmen – from ropemakers to gunpowder manufacturers – all collided and made his head thump.

Here was a foretaste of hell. Heaven alone knew how the unfortunate wretches coped underground, sweating through their eight-hour core, struggling to work in the little ventilation that the cliff-face adits allowed, often bent over in inadequate spaces, risking life, limb and sanity, and certainly their health. There was no such thing as an old miner, rarely even a middle-aged one. Rafe did what he could for them and their families without offending their fierce sense of pride. He distributed blue drill cloth for work coats and trousers, scraps of leather from the tanner's for boots, the occasional beast from his fields, blankets at Christmas, and kegs of ale on his birthday and the parish feast day. Many of his servants originated from here – at least some had a healthier occupation.

Mining was entering a slump. He knew he should sell the mine. Smuggling was more profitable. He would go away soon, to London, but in this year of 1780 there was anti-papist unrest on the capital's streets; bloodshed was sure to follow. The whole country was steeped in discontent. Taxes were high, the realm was drained and exhausted by its many successive wars, and he, a realist, saw there was no hope for victory in the American colonies. England was about to lose one of its empires. He wished he could hand over his. Chenhalls was a burden and a bore. He must leave these shores and go overseas, before the restlessness inside him drove him mad. Only one thing still fed him entertainment and hope. Kelynen. He tried to conjure up the impression of her sweet young body clasped in his arms.

He finished business quickly inside the gloomy claustrophobic shack that served as an office. Josiah was with him, taking a minor role while he consulted the mine captains. All were elevated from the ranks of the working miners, having been chosen as trustworthy, intelligent and loyal.

'Losses?' Rafe demanded, expecting to hear about loss of life before that of yields or equipment or machinery. He sighed at hearing that a boy had 'fallen away' from a ladder on his way up to grass and that a tributer – one of the more skilled miners – had been blinded in one eye from flying debris while driving down to the new level of eighty fathoms. 'Is that all?' Mining was a dangerous occupation, accidents frequent.

'Aye, Sir Rafe,' he was told by Captain Mordecai Lambourne, a hard-faced, sometimes belligerent giant, who was the lander of Rafe's highly efficient smuggling team, responsible for arranging the men and beasts of burden, and the hiding places that were not on Chenhalls land. 'The boy's body can never be recovered but minister came and said a few words for him. Sol Rumford reckons he can

112

manage just as well with only one eye. Put on a patch the next day, he did, and went back to work.'

Rafe put some silver on the rough wood table. 'For the boy's family and Sol Rumford as compensation.'

'Very generous of you, sir.' All the captains agreed.

Neither Rafe nor Josiah had any idea who Sol Rumford was. He did not figure among those who smuggled, and it was hard to keep account of all the hundreds of men and boys who worked below grass, or the women and girls who worked on the surface, cobbing the ore to be taken by mule train to Hayle, to be smelted by the Cornish Copper Company.

After studying the cost sheets and profit ledgers, Rafe dismissed the mine captains. 'Why are some of the accounts still outstanding, Josiah?' He stared at his nephew, who was drinking gin and looking bored.

Josiah shrugged, but a bright flush spread up from his neck to his hairline. 'I pay everything late to build up interest in the bank.'

'That does not concern me. The honour of the Tremayne name does. See to it that the older debts are settled at once, particularly for the Pengarron timber and the horses from their stud. I have a care for Kelynen Pengarron and I do not wish contempt for Sir Oliver.'

Josiah now stared, deducing. 'You desire more than seduction?'

'It's been a pleasant surprise to me and I'm confident she'll succumb all the way to the marriage bed. I need the very thing that Kelynen has a bounty of – freshness and a quick mind. I cannot be doing with another airheaded female. Neither of your late aunts had a thought beyond their next new dress. Now, Josiah, I have a matter of some seriousness to discuss with you. Gabriel has made it clear he does not want Chenhalls. He's requested that I sign it over to you. I shall do that if I don't produce an heir.'

'No! Don't do that, Uncle.' Josiah's blush deepened.

'Chenhalls is unlucky. I've no wish to follow the fate of some of our forebears. Wait a few years to see what happens. I have my own plans to travel.'

'Really, Josiah, what a strange fellow you are with your superstitious beliefs. You are not a common labourer or a gipsy. I shall leave things as they are then. Be assured of the money I have settled on you.'

'Your generosity, as always, moves me deeply, Uncle.' Josiah bowed in respect. When he straightened up his eyes were shifty. 'Uncle, I have something to tell you. I need your help.'

'What is it, Josiah? I've noticed you're not as nonchalant as you'd have me believe. Be quick; I have something I greatly desire to do before preparing for my overnight guests. Do not forget I want you at my table tonight.'

'It will be a pleasure to feast my eyes again on the delectable Mrs Lanyon. Now there's a lady who needs to be brought to a full flowering, and then there would be no end to the pleasures – for a while.'

'Josiah, you tire of women as quickly as a dandy does a suit of clothes. I take it this is why you need my help?'

'I'm sorry, Uncle Rafe. I'm having problems with one of my former amours. She won't accept the fact that our time together is over and she's causing trouble.'

'I take it you've offered to pay her off?'

'I have, of course. Nothing sways her. She's getting violent and I've had to resort to keeping her restrained.'

'Josiah, when will you learn to restrict yourself to married mistresses? They rarely become bothersome when it's time to disentangle oneself. Where is she?'

'I've kept her at an isolated farmhouse for some weeks, but she is now not far from here. Will you come and talk to her? You are more effective at persuasion than I.'

Rafe was expecting to take a short ride, but Josiah led him to a disused shed on the outskirts of the workings. It had been stripped of its planked floor and previous storage and smelled of musty oil and damp, and there was only what looked like a bundle of blankets in a corner. 'Lordsakes, Josiah, you mean you've actually brought this woman here, and so close to home? Why, in heaven's name?'

'I didn't know what else to do. She seems to be going mad and is refusing to eat. Her guardians could no longer keep control of her. They've been paid to keep silent. Mordecai Lambourne helped me. He's willing to do the same again, in reverse, but where to?'

In the dimness, Rafe could just make out an inert form within the blankets, lying on its side. He shot Josiah a furious look. 'Why didn't you tell me before things became so serious?'

'You've been preoccupied with Gabriel, Uncle, and I thought she would see sense eventually.'

Rafe strode up to the blankets, prodded them with the toe of his riding boot. 'Woman, sit up. I want to speak to you.'

The person under the blankets did not move.

'Her name, Josiah?'

'Adelaide. Adelaide Trevingey. She's sister to the unapproachable Mrs Wilmot Carew. I've implored her to go to her sister, but she refuses. I'm afraid it's been necessary to tie and gag her,' Josiah whined like a child complaining that his playmates were cheating at some game.

'Adelaide Trevingey.' Rafe reached down and wrenched her round to lie flat, pulling back the blankets. He winced. She looked as pale and as ill as Gabriel had been when Kelynen had discovered his plight. She had not washed or put a comb to her hair in weeks. Her dress was filthy but might once have been pink. 'You cannot stay here. Accept that your association with my nephew is finished and let us see you on your way. You may go anywhere you wish.' He pulled out the handkerchief, one of Josiah's, gagging her mouth.

'He promised me everything,' she hissed, her voice cracked and weak. 'I had his baby, which he took from me. He ended it with me before I even gave birth.'

'Adelaide, you lie,' Josiah snarled, aggrieved. 'You never wanted the child. I could not stand your ill tempers and possessiveness and that is why I ended it with you. I ensured that you were well cared for during your confinement. I've offered you money. I owe you nothing. I want to be free of you.'

'Don't think I'll make anything easy for you,' she spat, struggling to sit up.

Rafe calmly put his hand over her throat. He used firm pressure. 'There's nothing you can do to cause trouble for Josiah. I won't tolerate it. No one knows you are here. You have a choice. Do you understand?'

Adelaide Trevingey's eyes widened, glittering in dread. Unable to struggle against him, she kept a tense silence. Then her voice came harsh and bitter. 'If I don't go away quietly I won't leave here at all. Is that it?'

'If you do not leave here quietly, what other course would I have?'

She studied the hard grim face above her. 'I'm not scared of your threats! But I will cooperate with you. Take me to my sister. I want every farthing of the hundred pounds he promised me!'

'We'll get you away after dark. No doubt that was how you arrived here. So be it.'

'Let me sit up,' Adelaide demanded, sulky and indignant.

'I'm glad you're seeing reason, Adelaide. I've brought you something to eat.' Josiah was smiling now. He took a small cloth-wrapped parcel out of his pocket.

Rafe pulled Adelaide up to sit against the damp wall of the shed. He untied her hands, took the parcel from Josiah and tossed it to her. She flexed her aching limbs then opened the parcel with scrabbling fingers, biting into the bread and cheese.

'Could the child be traced to you?' Rafe whispered to Josiah.

'No. Mordecai took it away and left it outside a church.'

Suddenly there was a shrill scream and Josiah was hurled to the ground. In her rage, Adelaide had found the strength to get up and she was kicking at him, shrieking threats and obscenities. Rafe got an arm round her throat, cutting off her cries. She fainted. He dragged her to the blankets, located the gag and tied it tightly round her mouth. Then he trussed her up. His face was harsh. Josiah joined him, brushing dirt off his coat.

'She was given the chance to start a new life,' Rafe said without emotion. Josiah was gazing down on her in the same manner. 'She's a heartless creature. She'll cause us much trouble if she's allowed to leave. She deserves her fate. Mordecai Lambourne will do anything for the right reward. I'll speak to him. She will leave here after dark but via the old disused shaft. Now, let us get out of here and attend to more pleasant things.'

A short time later, while on his way to Marazion, Josiah was attending to something much more pleasant. Something that made him forget the worries about his personal debts, and about how he was going to juggle the money left in the estate's business accounts to pay off, at least, the Pengarron sums, and the real reason why he did not want to be heir to Chenhalls, something he would once have prized beyond all things. He came across a stranger, a pretty young woman of lowly birth, who turned out to be more than friendly.

Over the last few days, Luke had lingered in the coffee shops and hotels of Helston, Marazion and Penzance. He had lingered at gaming tables and had even made discreet, expensive enquiries in the brothels where the clientele was select. He had been everywhere that gentlemen gathered and might lay claim to their mistresses, but so far his search for information on the likely whereabouts of Adelaide Trevingey had been unsuccessful.

'I'm afraid I've again encountered no one who has a close acquaintance of someone bearing Adelaide's description.' He delivered his latest report to Sophie in her parlour. Sophie had shown him a miniature of Adelaide. She bore similarities to Sophie, but her hair was darker, her figure fuller and she had a touch of commonness in her audacious features. From the evidence of her flirtatious pout, she was not a lady in any sense. Luke, however, thanked heaven for her existence and her character, and Sophie's anxiety over her. It had brought Sophie to ask graciously for his help. She was grateful, truly grateful, for all his time-consuming efforts, and she seemed to depend on him now and even to respect him a little. Pray to God, she would soon come to like him.

'What shall we do now? What *can* we do?' Sophie rose from her chair, twisting her hands together.

Luke followed the movements of those soft pale hands. He followed everything she did, down to the tiniest grimace. 'Try not to worry, Mrs Carew. We shall look further abroad. There are certain people being watchful for me. Tonight I am invited to stay at Chenhalls. I shall have a careful word there. It's possible one of the Tremaynes is or was linked to Adelaide.'

'No, Mr Pengarron, I would rather you say nothing to the Tremaynes. I do not trust them. Do give Kelynen my best regards. I miss her very much.'

'Mrs Carew.' Luke frowned. 'I should be interested as to why you don't trust the family. Sir Rafe has requested that Kelynen stay on until his nephew is fully recuperated. I have her welfare to consider.'

'I suppose I may be speaking out of turn.' Nonetheless, Sophie outlined her beliefs about Sir Rafe and Josiah Tremayne.

Luke gazed at her with sympathy and compassion. 'Mrs Carew . . .'

'You have something to tell me?' Sophie had come to find herself interested in anything he had to say. Albeit reluctantly, she enjoyed his company, and was even beginning to like this meeker side of him, which, to her pride, she felt her virtues and frankness had drawn out of him. People would have to take notice of how she, an impoverished widow of no standing, had somewhat tamed the irrepressible Luke Pengarron, heir to a title and a fortune. If only he was interested in her for the right reasons. She could never forget she was vulnerable to cunning, callous men and must not drop her guard. Grateful for his help, she was, but he had done nothing yet to lead her to trust him.

'Yes, I have. I feel this is something you need to know. I've always kept up with the affairs of the Mount, you see. Apparently, your husband long ago sold his shares in the Wheal Lowen to Sir Rafe Tremayne for a fair price. He sold jewellery, below its true value, it was rumoured, to others. Mrs Carew, I am sorry. Mr Carew was a kindly gentleman, but he was incurring gambling debts even before your marriage.'

Sophie fell down in her chair, drained of colour, staring ahead. 'Then he was a laughing stock! And me also. All this time I have ridden a high moral horse, and yet I am to be pitied.'

Luke went to her. 'I don't pity you. I . . . I hold you in the highest regard.'

She had no pride left and could not lift her head to meet his eyes. She wanted to run away, to weep in shame and remorse. As always, fate had yet another hole for her to fall in. Every time she climbed out of one there was another waiting not far ahead.

Luke swallowed hard, his insides turned to liquid. Should he keep his peace, remain a concerned friend at this careful distance, or should he find courage and state his heart? Courage. He might never get a better opportunity. Sophie

119

might respond favourably in her present misery and then she would be unlikely, when she felt her honour restored, to spurn him – he hoped. He hoped and prayed and crossed his fingers.

'Mrs Carew. May I call you Sophie? Sophie ... pray, do not be offended at what I'm about to say. The fact is – the truth is I swear that I feel much more than regard for you. I would have you know that you are the finest and the most wonderful person I have had the privilege to meet. I love you. I never thought I would ever fall in love, but I have, with you, and I swear on my soul that nothing else in the world matters to me. I wish to make you my wife, Sophie. Do not say no straight away, I beg you. Please take a little time to consider my proposal.'

Gradually, slowly, throughout his impassioned speech, Sophie had lifted her head. It seemed she really had wrought a humble change in this once conceited man. There were even tears in his handsome dark eyes. Such an excellent figure he was, even with the slight misalignment of his shoulders, his clothes fitting him well now the weight brought about by greedy living had gone. And he had wealth, property, position. And he was offering to share it with her. But he had forgotten the complication in the shape of little Betty. Again Sophie wanted to run away and weep over the unfairness of fate. She had just received a once in a lifetime offer but it would soon be taken back. She opened her mouth to speak.

Fearing she was about to thrust wretchedness again upon his soul, he added, 'Before you say anything, Sophie, please let me also tell you that I'd like nothing more than to take on your sister's child as ours. We could adopt her. I would settle a large dowry on her. Young Betty's future would be assured. Sophie, I will agree to any condition you care to put on me. I love you. I love you with all my strength. I wish only to secure you and make you happy.'

She was shocked and speechless, but she wasn't about

to turn down such a marvellous offer – infinitely better than Wilmot Carew's – for herself and Betty. She held out her hand and Luke took it at once and helped her to rise. Somewhere from within her turmoil she found the means to warm up a smile for him.

'Does this mean yes, Sophie? The answer is yes? You will have me?' Luke exclaimed.

'I will.' Her voice emerged rusty and weary yet steeped with the relief from all her worries, except for Adelaide. And now she never need feel lonely again. 'I would be greatly honoured to become your wife, Luke.'

New tears glistened in his eyes, tears of pure joy. He kissed the back of her hand, then delicately leaned forward and kissed her lips, for just a moment.

Sophie closed her eyes. This was what she had always dreamed of – a presentable young man of means declaring he loved her and offering her the respectability of marriage. She was pleased to allow Luke to gather her in and to make her feel safe at last.

Kelynen was wandering the cliffs with Rex, enjoying simply being alone with him. Digory had deserted Rex for a new friend – Gabriel. He was guarding Gabriel now while he rested in the summer house. Discovering the joys of the Romanesque building during one of the short walks Kelynen had taken him on, Gabriel now preferred to shut himself away in this lighter environment – a healthier replacement for the tower, of which everyone approved. And as if suddenly becoming aware of the delights of canine company, Gabriel encouraged Digory to his side, and Digory was a willing participant in the nightly sneak up to Gabriel's bedchamber.

Having left Gabriel in the care of Jacob Glynn, Kelynen felt good to be free, to have uninterrupted time in which to think about Rafe, to relive his embraces, his gentle touches and loving kisses, to go back over his every word, which held many a hint of promise. 'I'm so looking forward to meeting your brother,' he had said at breakfast. *Please God, let Luke approve of Rafe.*

She picked her way along the path, which rose and fell gently, past blossoming gorse and banks of infantile ferns. In a few weeks the landscape would burst with patches of colour – towering tapering foxgloves, thrift, white clover, vetch, heather and a great many other wild flowers would appear, most bearing tiny delicate petals of blue, yellow, white or pink. Long grasses would snatch at a traveller's feet then, but for now the ground was mostly quietly barren.

Many feet tread this path – she had no doubt of that – moving stealthily during the night, slipping down into one of the many little coves and inlets she could see. Men from the mine and the local farms and hamlets, there to meet the rowing boats and fishing luggers bringing goods in off a ship that weighed anchor as close to shore as it dared, its crew nervously watchful for treacherous underwater rocks and Revenue cutters; the goods perhaps from Cherbourg or the Channel Islands.

Such a thing had happened last night. There had been a certain tension in the house. She had overheard Jacob Glynn tell another servant, 'Mr Josiah's bound to make himself scarce tonight. He's got no stomach for the trade.' Rafe had dined with a strange, taut politeness, with a suppressed energy, as if ready to spring to his feet at any moment and dash outside. He had bid Kelynen not to leave the house after dark or to let Rex outside, and to keep her curtains closed in her room, and not to secrete herself away up in the attic library, their trysting place. She understood the dangers of candlelight shining out from so high up in the building like some pre-arranged signal. Doubtless, Rafe bribed the coastguard, the Riding Officer and anyone else he thought necessary to turn a blind eye to his illicit activities. It was almost unheard of for a Cornish gentleman to be arrested and found guilty of smuggling contraband into the country, but she had not slept until a slight tap sounded on her door and she knew Rafe was home safe.

A small stretch of land, too small to be considered a headland, meandered out into the sea. Rex dashed off to investigate a jumble of huge, granite, lichen-dressed rocks sitting haphazardly near the edge. He disappeared, and she climbed over the rocks and found him in the centre of them, on a large patch of springy grass. 'What a perfect place to hide,' she laughed. She would come back and linger here another time, but today she was determined to explore one of the coves.

Jacob Glynn had mentioned that Sir Rafe did not approve of his servants wandering this area. This would be due to the smuggling, of course, but it was also likely it was somewhere about here that his second wife had drowned. Ruth had been the provider of the tragic details, gleaned from a chambermaid. The second Lady Tremayne had been wading among the rocks, unaware that the tide was fast about to cut her off. There were few places to climb up and down safely and before she could be rescued she had drowned. Kelynen felt Rafe would not be happy about her intentions, but she would be careful on an unfamiliar beach.

She left the jumble of rocks, Rex bounding on ahead. Here and there the cliff fell all the way down to the waters in proud dramatic drops; in other places it seemed to be bowing gracefully down to the sea. She thought she must soon come upon a place where the path would make a graduated descent, perhaps curving back on itself three or four times and fashioned by man, where she could scramble down on to a beach. She went on and on, but there was nowhere like that. Disappointed, she turned back. Called to Rex to come to her. He ran past her and then suddenly he was not there.

'Rex! Rex! Where are you?' Her heart thundering in fear, she ran to the cliff edge, terrified he had plunged over.

Then she saw the clever act of nature. What looked like

the edge actually concealed a lower grassy ridge where there was a series of several small drops, almost like steps in the granite. Moments later there was an excited barking and she saw Rex about seventy feet below on the pale golden sand, running towards the shore. She was later to learn that this place was known as Rocky Cove.

It was by no means a safe passage down, and at times she found it necessary to cling to roots or jutting rocks, or to ease herself down on her bottom, but she made it to the base in triumph. If this was a smuggler's cove, how did the men make safe journeys up and down in the dark? Robust colleagues stationed at the top keeping a rope secured for them to hold on to, she guessed. With a sense of awe she gazed about as one who had discovered a secret. She felt like a trespasser, part of her wanting to find signs of last night's smuggling run to confirm her suspicions, a greater part wanting to find everything bare and undisturbed for the safety of Rafe and his men.

The entire shore was fronted by rocks and she was curious to find that here slate rock met up with the granite. She leapt nimbly from rock to rock, standing on the highest to watch the tide riding up in ecstatic frothy splashes and gushing back into the sea in tiny rivers. The tide was on the turn but she had plenty of time to climb safely back up to the cliff top.

Again, Rex had disappeared. She called to him and was intrigued to see him coming out of an opening at the foot of the cliff. She hurried to the opening. A cave! It was a cave. Could it possibly be a hide? She felt a lurch of excitement, then a spark of guilt, for she shouldn't be here. Rafe, of course, had unlimited places to hide his contraband. There was the crypt of his church – a false tomb, perhaps, among his ancestors in the little graveyard, or a false floor in one or more of his cellars. It would not be difficult to conceal it in the workings of Wheal Lowen. Even though it was rarely locked, one obvious place was the tower. Although

Gabriel's claim of a ghost there had partly been put down to his morbid state of health at the time, she had asked Rafe if it was haunted. 'In a manner of speaking,' Rafe had replied in confidential tones, lowering his eyes as if amused.

Kelynen went into the cave. It was disappointingly shallow. She felt about the walls, hoping to find the shallowness was only an optical illusion, but discovered nothing deeper in the rough, damp rock. She was coming out when Rex growled deep in his throat. Instinct made her drag him back, sink down beside him and clamp her hands over his muzzle. A thrill of fear rode up her spine. She heard voices. Rough voices. Two men. Who must have been in the cove all the time! But where had they been? Another, deeper cave was the most likely explanation. Thank goodness she was not still up on the rocks facing the sea. The crunch of their feet over the pebbles was getting closer.

''Twas a good 'aul we 'ad last night.'

'Sir Rafe was pleased.'

'He said we're to watch out even more next time.'

'Wonder why.'

'Probably 'cause of that wild rabble up near Gunwalloe. Well, they'd be looking to get in on what we've got going here. They've done it afore in other places. Cost two men their lives round at Newlyn, 'tis reckoned.'

'Then 'tis best not spoken of at all.'

'Right then, we've made sure everything did get stashed safely away. We've checked the beach, made sure there's no sign of what went on.'

'Ais, we'd better be getting on.'

Kelynen held her breath. The men would soon reach her. If they looked into the cave they would see her. She flattened herself as much as possible behind Rex's black body. The men passed by. The glimpse she had of their clothing indicated they were fishermen, most likely from Porthleven, about two miles away. If they had crab pots near the shore here, no one would question their presence. It was likely

125

they had a boat pulled up and hidden not far away. After a minute she let out a heavy sigh. Presumably they had looked in her hiding place on their arrival in the cove. If discovered, her obvious breeding and her pleading that she was Sir Rafe's guest should save her from danger, but she could not be sure. There were stories of those who had stumbled on smugglers' hides being put to death, and these men had just spoken of others' treachery.

It seemed an age before the cove fell silent and she could reasonably be sure the men had gone. She let Rex go. His reaction would tell her if all was clear on the beach. Rex tore off, barking loudly, on the offence after the long confinement and his mistress's alarm. Kelynen waited, praying the men had rowed away, or left the cliff top if they had walked here, and would not take issue with a straying dog.

Rex came back to where she was crouching and licked her face in a snuffling, friendly fashion. The fright was over. Within minutes she had scrambled back up on to land, reproaching herself for her foolishness at coming this way so soon after a smuggling run. Rafe would be furious with her and rightly so. And she must look a mess. Her dress was creased and grubby. She wiped at her face with her handkerchief in case it was grimy. She would hate to look like an urchin in front of him. On a thought, she shook the hems of her dress and petticoat to remove all traces of sand, then took off her shoes and emptied them out, cleaned them, and brushed off her white silk stockings. No one would know she had been down in the cove.

She hurried on. A time of quiet inside the circle of rocks would calm her, somewhere pleasant where she could think about Rafe and her hopes for a future with him. It had seemed strange at first, wanting to live away from Pengarron Manor, but not now. She wanted only to be with Rafe.

Then she saw him. Coming towards her. Waving. Calling her name.

And she ran to him, full of joy and love and wonderful expectation, straight into his arms.

After a long stream of kisses, he said, 'You are prettily flushed, beloved.'

'I am a little unkempt.' She frowned.

'Do not apologize for that. I love the part of you that is still a child.'

He took her to the rocks, helped her to climb over them, and they sat in the shade from the hot sun, closely entwined. He took off her milkmaid hat. 'Let me look at you.' Slowly, thoughtfully, with a fingertip, he traced the contours of her face. 'You are so tender, so lovely, and so very much mine. Beloved, I intend to speak privately with Luke tonight. To ask him to write to your father, and if all is agreed – and I do so hope that it is, and quickly – then I shall meet you in my little chapel and bind you to me forever. Say it's what you want too.' He kissed her fiercely before she could answer. 'Say it.'

Her every pulse racing, her every emotion soaring high, she breathed against his lips, 'I want nothing more, Rafe.'

Almost before the last word trembled off her tongue, he kissed her with unrestrained enthusiasm. He filled her with excitement and a little fear at the passions that lay in store for her as his wife. When her breath had almost gone, he took his mouth away and gazed at her, gazed all the way down to her feet, peeping out from her petticoat. Back came his eyes, stopping at her throat, which he kissed, probing with his lips and the tip of his tongue. In the same way he had outlined her face, he felt along the neckline of her bodice, and suddenly pulled it down off her shoulders, which he covered with tumultuous kisses. Kelynen felt herself ever more melting to him. There was a strange rising within her, something that escalated and fanned out, that climbed and then fell and climbed again as if seeking to reach some undefined but supreme crest.

Rafe reached down and pulled off her shoes. 'I knew

you'd have perfect, delicious feet, beloved.' He massaged each foot gently, pushing his fingers between the silk of her stockings, dividing her toes. Kelynen enjoyed the sensations but felt this was somehow wicked, overtly personal, and she was wanton in allowing him to continue. But how could she stop him? At that moment she had no power to do anything against Rafe's will. He was in control of her, as if he was already her husband. With a thrill of trepidation and exhilaration, she knew he was not going to wait to become her husband. She forbade it in her mind, yet knew the thought would not ultimately win.

'Am I frightening you?' Rafe whispered into her ear.

'A little.'

'Never be frightened of me, beloved. I know how to give pleasure without the risk.'

She did not know what risk he was talking about, other than pregnancy – she knew that much after a frank talk with her mother – but she felt she did not know very much about what actually happened during intimacy. All she knew now was that she trusted him.

He was gazing at her deeply. He gentled her down, asking her if she was comfortable, telling her again not to be afraid. His hands were tender, moving over her, creeping over her, gradually and relentlessly invading her. It was as if he was finding regions of her that had not existed before.

She opened her eyes and found him watching her. 'I'm about to make you mine, Kelynen. I shall be your first and your last love.'

She was lost to him. And then suddenly she was lost altogether. She would do anything for him. Give him anything. What more could she give him than herself? This was her life now. Rafe was her life.

Fifteen

Sir Rafe's guests were travelling to Chenhalls together in a Pengarron carriage along with another person whom Luke had taken the liberty of bringing along. Sophie.

Sophie had at first complained that her clothes were hopelessly unfashionable for the occasion, but it had taken little persuasion on Luke's part to get her to come. After the demurrals and doubts she had expressed to Kelynen about entering a second marriage, she wanted Kelynen to be one of the first to learn of her betrothal, and, in recompense over her wrongful beliefs about the Tremaynes, she was eager to present a sociable front to them. Also, it was the perfect opportunity to inform the Reverend Lanyon of Betty's true identity.

'After we leave Chenhalls tomorrow, Luke and I are to go straightway to Vellanoweth and make the arrangements to take Betty to my house,' she said, sitting opposite Luke for the shaky journey over the rough roads – and serenely, for she now had much to be serene about, returning his frequent fulsome smiles.

'Kane and Jessica will be pleased, as we all are, that Betty will know you, her aunt, and her family roots, but they'll also be greatly disappointed to have to give her up. They dote on her,' Timothy said, displeased that Sophie Carew had kept this vital information from him. Did she not respect his calling? She should have trusted him.

'Kane and Jessica can see her as often as they like,' Luke said in soft, generous tones. 'Betty – or rather, Elizabeth,

as we have decided to have her baptized – will be a
Pengarron. Her adoption will keep her in a close bond to
Kane.'

Livvy, sitting next to her intended sister-in-law, had been
astonished at the betrothal. She did not consider Sophie
Carew a suitable wife for Luke. However, she included
Timothy, aloof and critical, in her comments, hoping he'd
see them as intelligent and compassionate. 'I do hope you
find your sister, Mrs Carew. There are many reasons why
she may not have been in touch with you. She may have felt
it best to go away and start a new life. She may have
felt too ashamed to face you, but she'd have known that
leaving her baby where she did, it would have been well
cared for. By the evidence of the silk Betty was wrapped
in, Miss Trevingey obviously intended for you to discover
the baby's identity.'

'Thank you for your kind assertions, Mrs Lanyon. I do
not think badly of Adelaide.' With her own and her niece's
futures now assured, Sophie had come to similar conclu-
sions about her wayward sister. She hoped Adelaide was
faring well, and Adelaide's deviousness likely ensured she
was, but now she had no particular wish to see her again.
Adelaide might threaten her new position.

'You have forgiven her.' Livvy aimed the words in
Timothy's direction. 'Yes, I admire that. One must forgive.
It's what our Lord has commanded us to do and for very
good reason. It is what gives us peace of mind.'

Timothy pulled in a long, deep breath. He had just had
a piece of his last sermon quoted at him.

In the banqueting hall, Josiah stood at a distance from his
uncle and intended bride, seemingly happy for them, but
in reality anxious at the development.

Kelynen Pengarron, with her astuteness and her adoration of his uncle and her love for Chenhalls, was a danger
to him. His uncle might be content to allow him free reign

with estate business, but the fawning young thing hanging on to his arm might start to pry where she should not. His only hope was that the marriage would go ahead quickly and his uncle would take his bride away on an immediate prolonged honeymoon. He couldn't rely on his uncle's goodwill after the inevitable discovery that his spendthrift ways had led to him forging his uncle's signature at the bank, to the effect that he had already been allowed his inheritance, and that he had subsequently drawn heavily on the Chenhalls accounts.

He needed to make some money fast. Therefore he had put his own house, near Porthleven – a small but comfortable property, convenient for privacy with his mistresses – up for sale. Checking his appearance, a frequent habit of his, in a silver, scroll-framed, cut-glass mirror, he fussed with his white, human-hair wig and was reminded that he had sent the mirror home from Florence while on the grand tour. The house held many of his acquirements. They belonged to him. He would claim them and sell them. And there were many forgotten treasures in the many unused rooms, an easy and stealthy way to build up some funds so he could take himself off somewhere. Then he'd find a wealthy mistress, one who would keep him for a change. And, hopefully, one day his uncle would forgive him. He didn't really care much for the man who had reared him, but his uncle's willing benefaction had always made him feel safe.

His reflection blurred and the pounding headache he'd been suffering for the last few hours almost made him pass out. Thankfully, his uncle and his bothersome new love were too besotted with each other to notice him clutching the sideboard. That woman he had encountered on the road had done something to him, and Josiah was also anxious about that. Everything about the time they'd spent together behind some bushes was hazy. He couldn't remember her name; she probably didn't offer it. He supposed that after

131

a little preliminary flirting they must have started kissing. He wasn't sure how far she had let him go but he remembered her showing him her shoulders and bare legs. What did she look like? If his memory served him right she was fairly ordinary, quite small and comely, with black hair, but there were many local females of that description.

She'd had a basket with her, had offered him something to drink from it. Like a fool he had accepted, and from the dreadful way he was now feeling – quite unlike being hungover – it must have contained an opiate. She had stolen the watch on his waist tab and all his money, but that was no surprise. But she had talked a lot. Asked him a lot of questions. Why? Perhaps she had wanted to know his routine and was planning to rob him again. He would stay here for a few days and hope never to come across her again. Certainly he would never trust another wayside stranger.

Before the greetings were over, Luke, unable to contain himself, had passed on his good news. Kelynen threw her arms round his neck. 'That's marvellous! I won't ask you how you won Sophie, and so quickly, but I'm delighted you have.' She kissed Sophie's cheek, aware once more of her friend's stiffness when receiving affection. Like Gabriel, Sophie had never known a loving family, and Kelynen put her aloofness down to this. 'I couldn't wish to have anyone else become my sister-in-law.'

'Sir Rafe, you do not mind me bringing Mrs Carew, I hope? I couldn't bear to be parted from her so soon,' Luke said, a keen stare on his host. He had only a passing acquaintance with the baronet, but had observed how he had a penchant for women, was uncommonly skilful at the gaming tables, could drink all night with little ill effect, was usually good-humoured, and had, until recently, paid his business accounts on time. From these observations, there was nothing to dislike in his character, but Sophie had harboured suspicions about him, and Luke had a tendency towards caution.

'I'm delighted to welcome Mrs Carew into my house, Mr Pengarron,' Rafe replied with all his charm. 'I shall order a room to be prepared for her immediately. Mrs Carew, may I suggest that after you have rested from the journey you take a turn round the gardens? Of course, they aren't at their best until the summer months, but I'm sure you'll find many spring blooms to take pleasure in.'

Kelynen watched as Rafe's charisma did its beguiling work on the company. Luke relaxed. Sophie seemed comfortable. Was her betrothal, wanting to be with Luke, the reason for her apparent friendliness towards Rafe and Josiah? The strain marking Timothy and Livvy as they had entered the hall had dissipated a little. Timothy was even laughing. Perhaps this short stay would be beneficial to their marriage, somewhere away from home on neutral ground, where they could drink and admire the cats.

Lady Portia shuffled creakily in. Two steps behind her was Jayna Hayes, carrying her dogs. 'Come along all of you.' The old lady clapped her brown-speckled hands. 'It's time for the viewing.'

'Viewing, milady?' Timothy smiled graciously at her quivering, purple-clad form.

Lady Portia closed her parchment fan with an indignant snap. 'Young man, I am talking about your wife's portrait of my brother. What else? Come along. You may help me up the stairs to the gallery. Then I want you to give Mrs Lanyon a time of release so she may start on my portrait.'

'You didn't like it, did you?' Livvy asked Timothy. They were alone in their room at the back of the house, which overlooked the sunken garden, the trees and the turrets of the tower. She followed his gaze to the enormous four-poster. Was he planning to sleep beside her tonight? Suddenly she missed the nearness of him in bed.

'Like what?' Folding his arms, he propped himself against a window ledge. He was shutting out much of the light,

133

while the light behind him gave a golden sheen to his earth-brown hair. Wearing non-clerical clothes with a touch of colour, he cut a first-rate figure.

Knowing he was simmering with malcontent towards her, and having expected this sort of challenging, derisory answer, Livvy wanted to swipe away his self-righteous, intransigent expression, and she wanted to weep. She wept a lot nowadays, which she hated, having before considered easily distressed females as tiresome and pathetic. 'It doesn't matter. I'm going out for a walk,' she said.

'You asked me a question, and now you can't be bothered to stay and talk.' He muttered under his breath. 'Now isn't that typical.'

'Timothy, you do not wish to talk to me! You answered my question with a question. That was rude and insulting.'

'If you're referring to Rafe's portrait, I thought it had a certain . . .' He rubbed his chin.

'Yes?' She came close to him. There had been many exclamations of admiration over the portrait, especially about her blend of colours, brighter than the usual mode, but she most wanted to have Timothy's verdict. Somehow it was imperative to have his approval, his appreciation, so she could feel justified at the amount of time spent working away from home.

'You've definitely picked up Rafe's flamboyant character.'

'Anything else?'

He made a face and looked away. 'I liked it, Olivia.'

The contemptuous dismissal cut into her deep. He made her feel as if she was no more than an irritation to him. 'You wretch!'

'I beg your pardon?' His dark eyes whipped back to her, twinkling dangerously.

'Don't you pretend indignation. You infernal hypocrite! Stop treating me with such cold disdain. I won't tolerate it. Do you understand? Be very careful, Timothy, or you will make me hate you, and I shall remove myself and the children and go to live at the manor.'

He straightened up and loomed over her. 'I'll not allow you to take my children away from me! Never!'

'But you'd have no care if I were to leave you, is that what you're saying? It is you who hates. I'm sorry I upset you over the matter of Betty's refuge. I'm sorry for neglecting you. If you can't forgive me – and you must acknowledge I've been willing of late to fall in with your wishes – then we are truly lost and our marriage is over. And I am beginning not to care!' She ran from the room, leaving him to crumple back down on the window ledge.

Rafe was on his way to Luke's room to present his case for Kelynen's hand in marriage when he saw Livvy hurtling down the corridor ahead of him. He went in to Timothy. 'My young friend, it seems you are having a little marital trouble.'

'No, Rafe, verily, a large amount of trouble.' Timothy remained bent over, as if in pain. He was in great emotional pain.

'One of you has fallen out of love?'

'I will always love Livvy. She tired of me long ago.'

'You think she has a lover?'

The direct question, delivered matter-of-factly, made Timothy look up. 'No! No, I am sure she has not.'

'How can you be sure? It's the usual step in a loveless marriage, for one or both partners.'

'But the only thing Livvy does away from the house is paint. Of late, she's been busy making plans for alterations to the nursery.'

'The nursery, you say? Then she is a woman who loves her home and children. If she has not looked elsewhere yet, don't you think you are fortunate?' Rafe moved closer to him, where he got a better view of his wounded face. 'It's not unknown for clergymen to indulge in extramartial activities. I take it you aren't considering this?'

'Of course I'm not!' Timothy was on his feet, horrified at the suggestion.

'And it's more to do with your love for dear Livvy than moral values,' Rafe stated. 'The solution then is simple. Go after her.'

'What?'

'Timothy, Livvy is not the sort of woman who can be brought to heel like a dog. Talk over your troubles with her. Root out all your feelings, and hers. It might not be easy, it might initiate further battles, but something worth having is always worth fighting for, don't you think? I did not love either of my wives. One was highly strung, the other dull and unsatisfying. Just recently I think I might actually be falling in love.' Rafe's thoughts swept over Kelynen's pretty face and soft yielding body, her kind, trusting nature, the way she eagerly responded to him in all things, her interest in all things. She would be a mate to enrich him, not reduce him. 'Yes, it's been a surprise to me. I'll do anything, and I mean anything, to secure and keep her.'

'Who is this lady?' Timothy was distracted from his woes by Rafe's enthusiasm.

'You shall hear soon enough. Now be gone, Timothy. Go to Livvy. I want to see two happier faces at my table tonight.'

His head a whirl of confusion of advice and emotions, Timothy turned to the window. He saw Livvy half walking, half running, shoulders down, her beautiful red hair tossed about, heading towards the trees. He went after her.

There was no sign of Livvy at all in the grounds, and the last place in which to look was the tower. He tried the arched door. It was unlocked. He went inside and shut the door behind him, shrinking back from the darkness and oppressive atmosphere.

On the second storey he found her, scrunched up on the cold stone floor of an almost bare bedroom, likely the one used by the ailing nephew. She was weeping into her hands.

'Livvy . . .'

'Go away. Leave me in peace!'

'Livvy, please listen to me. I'm sorry for my belliger-
ence. We must talk. Come and sit on a chair. I promise I
won't take a high-handed stance. Please, beloved, I want
us to put things right.'

She raised her head. A large tear rolled down her cheek,
making Timothy want to take her in his arms and promise
her anything. He held out a hand to help her up.

She ignored it, dried her eyes on her handkerchief and rose
on her own. 'I'll talk, but only for Hugh and Julia's sakes.'

He formed a smile, put all his love for her into it. 'Well,
that's a start. It's cold in here – bleak, don't you find? Why
don't we talk outside?'

'I'd rather stay here.'

'As you wish. Oh, Livvy, I hate us being torn apart like
this!' Suddenly he hauled her in against him, clamping her
tight.

Her arms were trapped, but rather than being offended
by this impulsive rush, she was delighted. It felt romantic,
ardent, and she wanted to hold on to him. 'I was wrong
and I was selfish, I see that now, Timothy. I can't stand
you not being close to me any more. Even at night. I miss
you wanting me.'

Timothy let her go, downcast and distraught. 'You've
never enjoyed intimacy with me, have you, Livvy?
You've never actually given yourself to me and I've
never felt I should take from you. There's a difficulty.
You indicated it just now. Even at night, you said, *even*,
Livvy. I think love-making may be our biggest problem.
I've tried always to be restrained because I thought I
should be, but have I been a dull lover to you?'

'Timothy, what nearly happened to me before we married
was a long time ago. I'm not nervous any more, haven't
been for years. I should have told you.'

'Then tell me this, do you love me?' He was afraid to receive a thoughtful pause and then a sorrowful explanation of how she had grown away from him, that they were not really suited and should never have married. He had never had anything of consequence to offer her and he had often wondered if she resented it.

She said at once, reaching for him, 'Yes. I love you. I've never stopped loving you.'

'Oh, darling.' He lifted her face and kissed her mouth, not with his usual gentleness but with vigour, letting loose some of the passion he had held back for so long.

Livvy enjoyed the shocking roughness of it. She felt she was being kissed for the first time and kissed him back with equal force. Confident with her at last, feeling her body throbbing against his, Timothy pulled her towards the bed. They fell down on it. He was lifting her skirts, pushing them impatiently out of his way. His desperate urgency, his rush of power, was flooding her with desire and she was straining for him. She met his insistence with demands of her own. Both were discovering the devastating newness of love and want. Reality and presumptions were left behind in glories beyond all imagination.

His voice emerged strangled, raw. 'I'm sorry, Livvy, darling, if that was awful for you. I couldn't help myself from wanting you so much. I was almost out of control.'

'I know. It was all right, beloved.' She extended a finger and ran it through the sweat on his face. He was so hot. It excited her. Everything about this encounter excited her – making love in a strange place, the small chance of them being discovered. She had not reached fulfilment – she knew there was more yet to be experienced – but she had enjoyed enormously being taken by his power, being under his governance. This was the one aspect of her life with him where she wanted him to be dominant. She wanted him to be a thrusting, virile man. When she was confident in the ways of making love, she would sometimes take supremacy over him, do things he'd enjoy, and their love-making would always be wonderful.

From his heavy breathing, the energy agitating and building up inside him, she was shot through with new and more intense thrills, knowing he was about to start all over again.

Sixteen

Kelynen was trying to coax Gabriel into allowing her to bring the overnight guests to his room.

'I'm sure your family are interesting and charming, but please, Kelynen, allow me my privacy.' With Caterina's shawl round his shoulders, he was sitting at his dressing table, the grooming items pushed aside, where he was writing music, his violin resting on his lap. Digory was snoozing on the bed.

She was pleased he had not ordered the curtains to be drawn, shutting out the fading evening light. He seemed to be gaining in strength by the hour, able to eat more with each meal. His bearing was firmer, his voice was stronger and he was no longer so strangely colourless. She had feared he had ruined his health permanently, would always remain weak, but it seemed he had a tough constitution and a quiet determination.

'Please reconsider. Luke and Livvy would so like to meet you. Luke has brought his newly acquired fiancée with him. Sophie Carew and my brother-in-law, the Reverend Timothy Lanyon, are wholly considerate. No one will overwhelm you, you have my word.'

'Please, I'd rather not be disturbed.'

'Of course.' His threatened posture visibly relaxed and she felt bad for pressing him. Gabriel had that effect. He was so pleasant, grateful and uncomplaining, so peaceful at times, and he also gave peace. She felt guilty for leaving him for so long that afternoon and apologized.

'I take no issue with you, Kelynen. You are entitled to your freedom.'

'Freedom is very important to you. Are you enjoying being back here among your family?'

'I don't remember my previous time here at all.' His answer was offhand.

'Don't you like Chenhalls?'

He met her enquiring gaze with one of resignation. 'No one likes living here.'

'No one?' She couldn't see how anyone could remain unaffected by the house's splendour and sense of history, the beauty and peace of the sunken garden, the wildness of the coast. 'I find that hard to believe.'

'Kelynen, I hate it here. Only your companionship makes it bearable. Josiah cannot wait to leave for good. In fact he's going away very soon. There's no future for him here. I've asked him to travel with me to Vienna and live with me awhile, but he says he has his own plans. My uncle never wanted Chenhalls. He finds the responsibilities stultifying. He's always wished my father were the elder brother. He only finds it tolerable here when he's involved in a smuggling run or some similar excitement. It's the curse of the Tremaynes to never feel settled, to never find lasting happiness. It's the madness we are said to possess.'

Something in his direct, fathomless gaze made her shiver. 'I don't understand why anyone is not charmed by Chenhalls. I have a great fondness for it. Perhaps the isolation is a factor in this disturbance you say is felt, but it isn't the case that one has to live here all the time. Sir Rafe spends time at his town house in Truro. He travels regularly up to London, and further abroad when he can.'

Gabriel's expression became apologetic. 'I fear I've disappointed, or perhaps even offended you, Kelynen.'

'Of course I'm not offended. I'm honoured that you feel you can share your thoughts and feelings with me.'

'You are a good friend to me, Kelynen.'

'Perhaps before you leave, when you are completely well, you might consider meeting all of my family. I'd like that so much.'

He smiled and his eyes shone a brilliant blue. 'Then I think I'd like that too, perhaps soon. When I look more presentable. I took my first look in a mirror today. I was horrified to see how close I must have come to starvation. I was a ghoul. How horrified you must have felt at our first encounter.'

He laughed at his own humour, a pleasant, husky sound, and Kelynen smiled and looked at him closely. His looks were improving. She was pleased for him. He had a fine, kind face to go with his fine, kind personality. When he returned to Vienna he should surely find someone new to love. Perhaps before he left he would confide in her about his lost love; she had not changed her mind about the reason for his illness. Perhaps she and Rafe could visit him there. She would like to keep in touch with Gabriel, and she would like to travel. 'Promise me you'll always take care of yourself, Gabriel.'

'I gladly give you my word, Kelynen. I owe you that. Enjoy the evening. You look beautiful, by the way. Stunning. You always do. And if I may say so, you look different. Vivacious and full of joy.'

Like someone in love, with hopes for the future, he pondered after she had gone. He had agreed with Josiah a little earlier about having reservations over the proposed match between Kelynen and their uncle, but as she was so impressed by Chenhalls, hopefully, if it went ahead, it would be a happy union.

He looked down at the score sheet. His mind had remained clear all day and he had made good progress. By the time he was fully recovered the ballet should be finished. He had thought to look for a suitable dancer to perform it, but Caterina would have hated that. It was hers and should remain hers alone. Instead he would bury the music in the grounds of their apartment as an act of tribute to her, the last thing he would do for her. Then he would continue with his life, perhaps move away, start anew, something he felt he might actually be able to do now, thanks to the tender-hearted young woman who had not only saved his life, but saved him from himself.

Kelynen checked her appearance before going downstairs. She stared at her reflection in the mirror and saw what Gabriel had seen. Her fair hair, golden in the candlelight, was carefully dressed under a silk, jewelled turban, and her figure was feminine and perfect in duck-egg-blue satin and white encrusted lace. Her dark eyes were shining, her complexion soft and pretty.

How had she managed to hide from Gabriel her state of agitation? Rafe had not yet had the chance to talk to Luke. Luke had spent only enough time in his room to change out of his travelling clothes before hurrying to Sophie, to walk with her round the gardens, and afterward he had not left her side. Rafe had decided to talk to Luke after supper. It would afford a better opportunity, he had said, after Luke had seen what he and Chenhalls could offer her, after Luke had feasted and drunk a good deal of fine wines, when he would be satiated, content.

There should be – she crossed her fingers – no problems in Rafe securing agreement from Luke over his intentions and in getting Luke to write to their father, recommending him. But she was worried about something else, something fearfully personal.

When Livvy and Timothy had finally reappeared for afternoon tea, it had been obvious from their glowing eyes, rosy faces and affectionate interactions that they had become reconciled and had been intimate. Kelynen now stared into the glass and touched her face – her cheeks were burning. Would the others be able to tell she had done the very same thing that morning? While Timothy had led Livvy to a chair, his chest thrust out manfully, their fingers reluctant to relinquish their touch, Rafe and Josiah had exchanged knowing looks. Luke, abandoning his adoration of Sophie for an instant, had grinned to himself. Sophie had glanced down demurely. They all knew about love-making – although Kelynen wasn't sure if Sophie, having had an elderly husband, was much experienced – and they were all able to pick up evidence of a sexual encounter.

But this was silly. Surely she was being anxious for nothing. If Luke had thought for a moment she had been seduced he would have raged at Rafe, perhaps even challenged him to a duel, and he would have dragged her out of Chenhalls. On the other hand, he would have to demand that Rafe do the decent thing and marry her. So she could not lose. She had allowed Rafe to have his way, sweeping aside her former belief that a woman should only succumb on her wedding night. Her mother, Livvy, Jessica and Sophie, she presumed, had been virgins until then. It had never occurred to her that if she married she would not be pure. Rafe's demands had shocked her and delighted her, overwhelming her in mind, body and soul. She was no longer spotless, but it didn't matter. Marriage would bring her back into a state of grace. If Rafe made intimate approaches to her again, she would ask him to wait until after the wedding ceremony. And he would happily comply, of that she was sure. She knew Rafe and trusted him. He was a loving, attentive, physical-minded man, but also wonderfully considerate.

She would soon be married, so there was no need to stay here cogitating and worrying and feeling guilty. After all, there were as many women who gave themselves to the men they loved, or merely to seek pleasure, as were those who did not. Swaying in front of the mirror, confident she was looking her best – indeed, quite stunning, as Gabriel had said – she picked up her fan and went downstairs, slowly, sedately. The mistress of the house. The future Lady Tremayne.

The meal went well around the great banqueting table. Everyone was in good spirits and for once Lady Portia stayed down until ten o'clock, amusing the company with her frank banter. Most of the conversation centred on Luke's forthcoming nuptials.

'Where will you live?' Lady Portia asked, vigorously employing a toothpick between her few yellowed teeth. 'Pengarron Manor or your own property? Poltissey, you say?'

'Polgissey, milady,' Luke replied. 'We intend to reside there until I come into my inheritance. It will be the perfect place for our little ward to grow up in.'

'Ward?' Rafe raised his brows after glancing at Josiah.

'We are to adopt a child,' Luke said.

'A child?' Lady Portia had not heard the facts clearly. 'Already? Then you had better make haste in taking her to the church, young man!'

Luke smiled graciously at the old lady, and Livvy, who had consumed an enormous amount of wine, giggled behind her hand. Sophie blushed and drew in her lips. 'It's my sister's child,' she explained tightly. 'Mr Pengarron and I are to adopt her.'

'Oh, an orphan.' Lady Portia nodded, finally dislodging a piece of minted lamb from a lower back tooth. 'Very noble of you, I must say, young lady. Mrs Carew, that's your name, isn't it? Carew . . . Carew . . . Are you the young thing that was wed to old Wilmot? That old fool! Good lord. No children of your own, I'll warrant. Wilmot Carew was hardly capable of mounting a crippled pony!'

Sophie gasped, her colour deepening. Livvy rammed a fist to her mouth in an unsuccessful bid to stop laughing aloud. Timothy shushed her but was too happy to take the indiscretion seriously. Kelynen stared at Rafe, willing him to do something before Luke was offended and declared he and Sophie were leaving, but Rafe was already signalling to Jayna Hayes to escort his sister away.

'Really, m'dear,' he said jovially, 'it's long past your time to retire.'

After Lady Portia's removal he looked with chivalry at Sophie. 'Mrs Carew, I do beg your forgiveness. My sister is getting quite senile.' To the whole company, he said, 'Now we are finished eating, may I suggest we move off to the summer parlour where we may play cards or pursue other entertainments. Mr Pengarron, would you be kind enough to allow me a private word?'

Nettled over Sophie's embarrassment, while secretly rejoicing over the hint that she may still be a virgin, Luke was gazing protectively at her. 'I really have no wish to talk business tonight, Sir Rafe. Could we not delay until tomorrow? I hear you have a splendid music room. Mrs Carew is much accomplished on the spinet. She has already agreed to play something for us, and Kelynen has a sweet voice. Perhaps a musical end to the evening?'

'As you please,' Rafe capitulated graciously. He took Kelynen's arm, mouthing to her, 'Worry not, beloved. We shall prevail,' and led the way.

The music room had plain walls and long windows and an unusually high ceiling, even for a grand house, to aid the acoustics. As if a recital might be given at any moment, comfortable chairs were set around three sides of a raised polished wood dais, on which were set a number of gleaming instruments.

'It's a pity you couldn't persuade your nephew to play something for us, Rafe,' Timothy said. He was keeping Livvy close at his side. 'I'd be most interested to meet him.'

'Gabriel is still too weak for such an occasion and unfortunately tempting him into a social life is a lost cause. I don't think even dear Kelynen could accomplish that.'

The windows were open, and suddenly music – beautiful, lyrical, redolent of winter shores and of tempestuous seas – rose and spun through the dark spring air. Just prior to that, Kelynen had dragged Luke away from Sophie and

146

asked him, 'Well, what do you think of Chenhalls? Is it not splendid?' But now they, like the others, were transfixed, not moving and hardly breathing until several moments after the last lingering, haunting note.

'Gabriel Tremayne is indeed a master of the violin,' Luke said. 'I would like to hear more of his music.'

'He's played for the King, you know. Now he plays and composes for Emperor Joseph.' Kelynen smiled, blessing Gabriel. This could only help her and Rafe's cause.

'It's a good thing you were here to save the destruction of so great a talent. The house? It is somewhat portentous. You look exceptionally well, little sister. The air here agrees with you, or is it perhaps that you've found something or someone even more pleasing? I've not noticed a rapport between you and Josiah, I'm pleased to say; the fellow has nothing to recommend him. Does Gabriel mean something to you? Is that why you're so keen to stay on and see him fully recuperated?'

'Gabriel has a certain charm but he does not move me in that way. Luke, could you not speak to Rafe tonight?'

'Kelynen, dearheart, don't tell me you're becoming concerned in the business affairs of this estate? No, that could not be so. The Tremaynes don't allow women such an indulgence. In fact, they positively abhor it, from what I know about them. Now, Sophie and I, in view of her widowhood, are planning a small private wedding, but she wants you to be her maid of honour. I've given no mind to weddings before. I've written to Father and Mama, of course, but they won't be home in time to help with the arrangements. You'll have to tell me what I should know. I don't want to appear brash.'

Kelynen hoped to be able to talk about her own future tomorrow. Her parents might be interrupting their stay in the fashionable spa town to attend two weddings. She was disappointed to have Rafe's own declaration reinforced that he did not approve of women being involved with business, but that could be said for almost every husband, and there were many other things she could do – charities she could set up and the like.

His headache now at unbearable proportions, Josiah longed to retire. But he was anxious to discover if Sophie Carew was worried over the whereabouts of her sister and was making enquiries, and so he invited her to take her place at the spinet. 'If I may say so, it's noble of you to take on your sister's child, Mrs Carew,' he whispered, his speech slurred.

Sophie had only just comprehended his words. She did not like him standing so close. His breath smelled odd, and although he had imbibed little at the table, he appeared to be inebriated. Sir Rafe was passing him hard looks and was, she hoped, about to dismiss another of his wretched relatives. 'She will be a blessing to Mr Pengarron and me, Mr Tremayne.'

'It is my own sad experience to be orphaned so young. I take it this is the case?'

'It is not.' Sophie stepped back with music sheets in her hand. 'Misfortune has decreed my sister is unable to bring up the child herself.'

'Misfortune? What sort of misfortune?' Pray God, this hard, frigid woman was not suspicious over Adelaide's safety.

Sophie was disturbed by the insistence in his tone. Throughout the evening she had been aware of the strange covert looks he had given her. The man was a degenerate reprobate if he was seeking to pursue her in the presence of her fiancé. 'Mr Tremayne, why all this interest in my sister and her child?' She glared at him and his eyes narrowed as bright colour flowed up his face. 'Unless . . . unless you are my sister's lover. Are you?'

Fear made him shoot out a hand and he gripped her arm, hurting her. 'You'd be unwise to utter another word on similar lines.'

Luke looked across to see if Sophie was ready to begin playing. He saw her grimace of pain. Saw Josiah Tremayne sullying her with his hand. He shot to her rescue, thrusting the culprit aside viciously. 'How dare you, Tremayne! I'll call you out at dawn for this.'

Rafe was there in an instant. 'What's going on? Josiah?'

'I'll tell you what happened, Sir Rafe. Your damnable nephew was making approaches to Mrs Carew. I'll tear his heart out! Sophie, beloved.' Luke encircled her trembling body in his arms.

'I'm sure we can settle this without further unpleasantness,' Rafe said, firm and apologetic. He glared at Josiah with a look that conveyed he must be careful what he said. 'Josiah, would you care to explain?'

Holding her breath, Kelynen stared at Sophie with something akin to hostility. Why did Luke have to bring her here? Surely, in her stuffiness, Sophie had been mistaken? Josiah had been quiet all evening, and he had never as much as breathed wrongly while in her own presence. If there were trouble, Luke would not be receptive to Rafe's request for her hand.

'It's him, Luke,' Sophie whimpered.

'What do you mean, Sophie?'

'He's the father of Adelaide's child. He was asking me questions, lots of questions, and when I became suspicious he threatened me.'

Josiah was finding it difficult to stand up now. It was an effort to speak in his usual calm and polite manner. 'Yes, I admit it was I who sired Adelaide Trevingey's baby, but I've not seen her for months. She went out of my house one day and I haven't seen her since. I believe she was already interested in another man. I'm ashamed of my conduct towards you, Mrs Carew. Madam, you have my full and humblest apologies. I was taken by surprise by your frank question. Before, I was only concerned about the child and Adelaide. I take it she is well?'

'Adelaide has disappeared.' Luke still looked as if he wanted to place angry hands on the other man. 'Can you shed any light on that for us?'

'Oh dear, then she really did do what she had always intended. To venture to one of the big cities, without informing her sister of her whereabouts. I can only hope she has settled.' A gifted, convincing liar, Josiah had long ago thought up this explanation. If Adelaide's murder was ever discovered, Mordecai Lambourne could take sole blame. The mine captain was known as being habitually rough with women and his word was unlikely to be believed against any evidence supplied by himself and Sir Rafe.

'You can only hope that I never take stronger issue with you, Tremayne!'

'Now, please, Mr Pengarron, Luke, I plead with you and Mrs Carew for your forgiveness,' Rafe appealed with upraised hands. 'Josiah has owned up to the paternity of the child. The way he went about things was foolish and inept. You and Mrs Carew are to adopt the child. Miss Trevingey has started a new life. Surely no more need be said on the unfortunate matter?'

'I agree, for now at least, but I cannot go on accepting your hospitality, Sir Rafe, nor allow my sister to remain under your roof with such a bluff rake.'

'I shall remove myself from the house immediately,' Josiah said, holding his burning head and glancing red-faced at his uncle.

Luke ignored Kelynen's horrified expression. He would not change his mind, not with the way Sophie was trembling against him. She had suffered enough, first at the supper table and now in this room. It would have been a shock as much as a relief to her to learn of Adelaide's fate. 'Kelynen, go at once and order Ruth to pack your things. Sir Rafe, I ask you one favour, that you permit us a runner to light the way ahead for our carriage. We shall leave within the hour.'

'No, Luke!' Kelynen cried. 'Leave with Sophie if you feel you must, but allow me to stay. Mr Gabriel Tremayne needs my presence here. He may have a relapse.'

'He is not your responsibility, Kelynen. Do as I say, at once. Livvy, go with her. I'm only doing what I'm sure Father would order if he were here to do so.'

Transferring her anguished gaze to Rafe, she received a quiet nod from him. He was unperturbed. His words of a little earlier returned to her. *We shall prevail.*

Indeed, they would. Even a command from her beloved father would not tear her away permanently from Rafe.

Seventeen

'Would you like to take a rest, sir?'

'It's only a few miles ride along the bay, Jacob.' Gabriel looked across from his mount to his manservant, who was riding beside him. Digory was with them, enthusiastically sniffing and marking new territory. 'And you've just said that we've reached Pengarron land and will soon be at our destination.'

'Aye, that I did, Mr Gabriel, but I promised Sir Rafe I'd take good care of you.' Jacob Glynn studied his young master's face, searching, taking his time, pleased to see no signs of exhaustion yet in the pale, marble-like skin. He liked Mr Gabriel, who made few demands and didn't fuss over trifling things or easily lose his temper or behave in a superior manner, and who wasn't above sharing a bottle or two of spirits with him. Jacob hoped to keep his present position. It involved little skivvying, but he was artful at pretending it did. He hoped to be given the opportunity to travel overseas – Mr Gabriel would need a manservant on the long journey to Vienna – so he was trying to prove he was loyal, caring and indispensable.

'You'd make an excellent nursemaid.' Gabriel twisted his face wryly, and then grinned. He was wearing Caterina's shawl under his riding coat but still he was cold. The clouds were low and grey and the wind was keen. It was not a good day to pick to make his first excursion from Chenhalls. 'I'm sorry I disappointed you by refusing to pause for refreshment at Marazion. I'd never enter a busy tavern.

Perhaps this would be a good place to stop and take a swallow of my uncle's untaxed rum. I've noticed how often your eyes stray to the flask.'

After they reined in, Jacob poured rum from the leather-covered flask into a small silver cup and passed it to Gabriel. Gabriel quaffed it in one toss, handed the cup back to Jacob to help himself, and then he gazed over the small divisions of land that made up the Pengarron tenant farms. The fields were ploughed and planted, many down to the cliff edge, some crops showing green shoots. They looked healthy. As they had journeyed, Jacob had told him some of the names of the towns and little fishing villages of Mount's Bay, quizzically strange names some of them had, inventive and charming: Newlyn, Mousehole – pronounced Mouzel – and Penzance, meaning holy head. All steeped in history and legend, Jacob assured him, from the torching of property by landing parties from the Spanish Armada and the routing of that enemy two centuries ago, to giants and the 'small people'.

Looking back the way they had travelled, Gabriel's attention was captured mostly by St Michael's Mount. It was a marvellous, beguiling sight with the castle on its summit, its church and village below. A three-masted ship was heading towards the little harbour to join two others already moored there. Rowing boats bobbed inside the harbour while, with the tide in and covering the pedestrian causeway, another boat was making for the shore, perhaps to fetch supplies for the St Aubyns, the titled family who owned the Mount.

'The castle is a pleasing prospect from any angle. I suppose it's haunted; a great many places in this county are reputed to be.'

'Bound to be. 'Twas a giant what built the Mount. Cormoran was his name, and evil he was too, and he was bravely slain by a local boy named Jack. Jack dug a deep pit about halfway up the Mount and when the sun came up he blew a horn. Woke Cormoran up, he did, and Jack stood where the sun would be in the giant's eyes, so into the pit Cormoran fell. The pit's a well now. We belong round here,' Jacob ended proudly. 'You beginning to like it here, sir? I mean, Cornwall?'

'I can see it has its charms.' Quietness was one of them. Gabriel wondered now why he had chosen to live in a busy foreign city, where he had found it necessary to shut himself away much of the time. 'I like the sea. It's soothing.'

'You should spent some time closer to it. I can show you some easy places to get down on the shore. Reckon it'd be a good place to write music.'

'I'm sure you're right, Jacob.' Gabriel suddenly massaged his brow.

'You all right, sir? You look to me like you're getting a headache.'

Gabriel continued to press at the tightness there. 'I am getting a little weary and it is foolish to linger. I haven't ridden for months. I shall ache in all places after I dismount.'

Man and servant journeyed on, shortly to trot on to the manor parkland. Longing now to rest, Gabriel was looking forward to seeing Kelynen again after nearly a week. He was hoping Luke Pengarron would not be there. Pengarron had replied to a letter from his uncle, stating he was too preoccupied with his forthcoming nuptials to attend on Sir Rafe, as requested, at the Sealeys Hotel in Marazion. On hearing of Gabriel's intended visit to Kelynen, Rafe had charged him to discover the date of Sir Oliver's return home. His uncle intended to speak to Sir Oliver direct.

Kelynen stretched her arms out for the dressmaker and obediently, although not patiently, allowed the final adjustments to the dress she was to wear as Sophie's maid of honour. 'How much longer, Miss Gluyas?'

'Pray, just one more minute, Miss Pengarron.' Eulaliah Gluyas's fingers worked nimbly with the final pins. She stood back and surveyed her work, a subdued creation at Sophie's request. 'Perfect. This oyster pink suits you well.'

'Don't you like it, Kelynen?' Sophie asked bluntly. Her own gown was to be more lavish, in deference to her bridegroom's position, the tight bodice encrusted with pearls. They were in Lady Pengarron's sitting room instead of an upstairs dressing room, so that Beatrice could view the fitting. 'I'm beginning to get the impression you have little interest in the wedding. Are you sulking still because Luke ordered you away from Chenhalls?'

'I am not sulking!' Kelynen pulled at the skirt, causing Eulaliah Gluyas to gasp over escaping pins. 'I never sulk.'

'Ahem.' Beatrice cleared her phlegm-coated throat and gave Kelynen a look of warning.

Kelynen was immediately sorry over her pique. 'Forgive me, Sophie. I adore the dress, honestly I do. And yours is truly beautiful. It's a pity the wedding is to be quiet. The whole county should have the opportunity to witness how gorgeous you'll look. Miss Gluyas' mother created my mother's wedding gown, did you know?'

'Miss Gluyas mentioned it during the first fitting. Thank you, Miss Gluyas. I think we are finished for the day.'

Sophie's soft, superior tone made Kelynen, to her annoyance, sound as if she had been deliberately difficult. Could no one understand how upset she was to have been ripped away from Chenhalls? She was not a juvenile. She was not stupid and incapable of looking after herself. Why were her feelings so unimportant? Luke's love for Sophie was making him overlook everyone else's needs.

Eulaliah Gluyas helped Kelynen to change before taking her leave. She had left a collection of accessories for Sophie to choose from, for herself and her maid of honour. Sophie rang for tea and then looked over the gloves, fans, garters, hose and silk flowers. A milliner had also called that morning and left an array of hats – as a widow, Sophie did not intend to wear a veil. 'I'm sorry you are feeling stifled to be kept

155

at home, Kelynen, but Luke is right in his belief that it's wise for young Elizabeth and me to reside here to avoid unwanted intrusion before the wedding. And, of course, it would be inappropriate without your presence until after the ceremony.'

'I don't mind being requested to do something, Sophie. I object to being ordered about and then not being listened to.' Kelynen retreated to Beatrice's side. Beatrice was as smelly as ever, but Kelynen, like all the Pengarrons, seemed immune to it. She was humming and hawing, as always, but apart from admiring the dresses, was staying unusually passive.

Sophie surveyed Kelynen coolly. 'I'd have thought your brother's wedding, his happiness, would be your priority.'

Kelynen stared back into her sharp eyes. Since her betrothal, Sophie's future status seemed to have swelled her head. She behaved as if she was the lady of the manor. She sought to discuss the menus with Esther King. Yesterday she had sat in on the interviews for a new housemaid with Polly O'Flynn. The lady's maid she had acquired for herself and the nursery maid for Elizabeth rivalled Elgan for efficiency and snobbish aloofness. Elizabeth was under a strict regime and was rarely brought downstairs. Things in the manor were running smoothly, as usual, but there was much less laughter and sometimes a boring hush. Kelynen felt the sense of anxiety in the servants to perform their tasks well and on time. Polgissey would be run like clockwork. Kelynen couldn't see herself visiting there often. It was as if she and Sophie had never been close friends. Well, no matter, when she was Rafe's wife she'd have her own household to occupy her.

'Luke could have agreed to speak to Rafe,' Kelynen said severely.

'Ah, here's the tea.'

How dare you ignore me! Kelynen's eyes constricted as Sophie sat down in her mother's chair. *How dare you disapprove of Rafe's and my desire to marry!*

Kelynen had exchanged angry words with Luke on the way home from Chenhalls, the confines of the carriage a crush with the addition of herself and Ruth King. 'You've no right to take this high-handed attitude with Rafe. It wasn't him who upset Sophie. He had something of the utmost importance to speak to you about and it didn't involve business.'

'I make no apologies for my actions. The matter is closed,' he had bit back, squeezed in beside her.

'No, it isn't!'

'What is this matter of great concern then?'

A hush had fallen inside the rocking, creaking, lantern-lit conveyance, the others all straining to hear her explanation. 'Rafe and I are in love. He wanted to talk to you, to ask you to recommend him to Father.'

Astonished looks had been passed back and forth. Sophie had given a little cry, as if the news distressed her, then she had let out a snort of derision.

'That's ridiculous,' Luke had cried. 'You're just a child. You don't know anything about love.'

'A child, am I? You were ordering me to find myself a husband not many weeks ago. Sir Rafe is eminently suitable, no one can deny that.'

'Whether this would make a good marriage for you or not, it can wait. Father and Mama will decide. Trouble me not with it again.'

And Luke had resolutely ensured she did not trouble him about it again, offending and infuriating her by declaring she was merely infatuated with Sir Rafe Tremayne. Doubtless, Sophie's renewed bitterness against the family was holding his mind closed. In a couple of days her parents were due home and she was longing to set up a meeting between them and Rafe so he could put their case to them.

The tea was drunk in a frosty atmosphere, and then Sophie excused herself. Unsurprisingly, Luke was waiting for her beyond the door. Kelynen glanced out of the windows. The weather was growing increasingly miserable and so was the mood inside the house. She rested her head on Beatrice's fat shoulder, and as on every day since her return home, she appealed to the old nursemaid. 'I do love him, Bea. I think of Rafe every minute of the day and night.'

Beatrice patted her hand. 'I d'know, cheeil.'

'Luke and Sophie are being beastly.'

'They'll soon have nothin' to crow about.'

'What do you mean?' Kelynen gazed into Beatrice's piggy eyes.

'That there woman's not for Luke. She's as cold as mine water. Poor boy, he's happy now but it won't last.'

'But he's in love with her. He'll be happy for the rest of his life just knowing she's his wife.'

'Think about it, my handsome. Luke's been adored all his life. He'll not be long in wanting she to treat him the same. It'll matter to him that she won't. Oh, she'll be a good wife, I'll give 'ee that, but he'll grow to resent her lack of love and start looking for what he wants elsewhere, and she'll resent it and grow colder. If they'm as unlucky as I fear, they'll end up hating one another.'

Kelynen buried her face into Beatrice's shoulder again. 'That would never happen to Rafe and me.'

'No, don't s'pose it would, if you're as willing to honour him always and he's as kind as you reckon he is. But, cheeil . . .'

'But what?' Kelynen looked up at Beatrice, for her last words had been delivered mournfully.

'Oh, nothing.' Beatrice stared into her eyes and stroked her chin. 'Just remember I'm always here for 'ee, Kelynen.'

After escorting Beatrice to her room, Kelynen decided to put on her cape and take a walk with Rex. He was restless after being cooped up away from the dress fittings. She'd find a solitary spot and think of Rafe. Read again the note he had placed into her hand last week before she had been hurried out of his house. *Meet me at Tinner's*

Leap, the day after tomorrow. She had told Rafe about all her regular haunts on her father's property. How clever of Rafe to arrange a meeting where they could easily and secretly meet.

She had met him there, a little place on the cliff close to Trelynne Cove, where a broken-hearted young tin miner was said to have leapt to his death. There was a huddle of tall rocks, similar to those on Rafe's land where they had made love.

She had found him waiting for her and she drew her pony alongside his proud aristocratic mount. At once he leaned across and kissed her lips. 'I don't like us having to meet like this, beloved.' The regret was clear in his strong voice. 'But I wasn't prepared to wait until I've spoken to Sir Oliver. I've missed you dreadfully. How are you?'

'Missing you too, Rafe, so very much,' she replied, eager to be in his arms. 'It is romantic, meeting secretly like this.'

'Yes, it is, but in this case it's unnecessary. Come.'

'Where are we going?'

'To a quiet little place I know.'

They rode away from Tinner's Leap until they reached the main thoroughfare leading towards Marazion. Rafe led the way across it and headed inland along a narrow rough track until he stopped at a tiny cottage. It was well kept, with tidy gardens at the back and front inside low granite walls. There was a little wooden gate and at either side of the front door were stone benches. Hens were pecking at the ground and a large pink-and-grey pig was snuffling contentedly in a sty at the back. A white cat dozed on the wall on one side. Pretty patterned curtains were up at the windows. While Rex shot off to examine the surroundings, Kelynen took pleasure in all that she saw.

'I don't know this place. Who lives here?'

'One of my former servants; he was a gamekeeper. I call on him occasionally.'

'And he will be discreet about us being here together?'

'Kelynen.' Rafe gave her a long meaningful look. 'He's not here presently and he won't be home for some time.'

Inside the two-up two-down cottage, two small tankards and a flagon half-filled with porter were set on a small square table. Kelynen liked the surroundings. 'He's very tidy, this old gamekeeper. He must spend hours cleaning his brasses.'

'Before he worked for me, Joel Jackson was a soldier. He likes order and precision. Shall we take a drink?'

'I'll pour it.'

Before Kelynen reached the table Rafe encompassed her in his arms and kissed her as though feasting on her. 'It's been hard waiting to be with you again.'

Pressing into him, holding on to him tightly, she was happy, and thought she could never become happier. 'I know. I've prayed every minute that we'll soon be able to be together forever.'

'You take the tankards, beloved, and I'll carry the flagon.'

'Where?'

'Upstairs.' He smiled blatantly into her eyes. Once more he was melting her into him but she had resolved not to risk intimacy with him again.

'But Rafe, can't we simply spend time together? I don't think we should . . . go so far again, not until we're married.'

'Kelynen, darling.' He clasped her hands, kissed them, and gazed into her eyes. 'You're not going to be cruel to me, are you?'

'Well, I think we should be sensible, don't you?'

'We are in love. I love you.' He kissed her hands again. Kissed her lips, her eyes. 'You love me, don't you? You trust me, don't you?'

'Of course I do, Rafe. I love you so much it hurts.'

'You're not a child any more, Kelynen,' he said, even though she had just sounded young and vulnerable. 'You're a woman, and I'm the man who loves you and wants you – all of you. Now.'

She was fighting with herself. She didn't want to deny Rafe anything. She didn't want to deny herself, either. After the initial hurting, uncomfortable moments of his love-making, she had enjoyed the ultimate closeness of him, the intense sensations, the glorious culmination. 'Well, I . . .'

'Beloved, I knew you wouldn't disappoint me.'

She couldn't remember making her way up to the old gamekeeper's bedroom with him, but her senses became focussed while she'd sat on the lumpy bed, sipping porter. She was clutching the tankard long after Rafe, sitting close, had emptied his and began to unfasten the laces and hooks of her dress. She edged away from him, pleading shyness.

'Darling.' He came after her, smilingly placing his head at an encouraging angle. 'You'll only feel the shyness once. Why not get it over with? Enjoy being with me. Do you not think that I, too, am a little shy? It's important to me that you find me pleasing.'

'Are you really shy?' she asked, her nervousness shooting to an alarming rate as he pulled the tankard out of her hands.

'I am, because it's you. I want our life together to be perfect. Kelynen, I love you. I've never told that to anyone before.'

This last affirmation swept away all her reservations. Soon she was completely exposed to him, and he to her, and it seemed natural. It was wonderful lying entwined with him on the bed. Gently he made her his and then did so again, with passion, showing her, teaching her, adding ever more and more to the delight and pleasure.

'I think I could happily spend the rest of my life here like this with you,' he said at length, holding her close, keeping on with his caresses.

'You say wonderful things, Rafe.' She could quite happily die together with him here, at this moment, and go to eternity with him. The sky was getting ever darker, filling the little scarcely furnished room with shadows, and she knew she would be feeling cold if not for the warm aftermath of making love and the warmth of Rafe's body.

'You, beloved, do wonderful things to me. I shall take you to many towns and cities before we finally settle down. I'll be proud to show you off to whomever we meet. Would you like that?'

'Yes. I'll be happy anywhere as long as I'm with you.' She raised herself up and leaned over his chest, gazing into his strong handsome face. 'I'd like to give you a son, Rafe. Would you like a son?'

He took her hand and kissed the fingertips. 'Indeed I would. With Tremayne and Pengarron blood in him he would be a very special child, and Sir Oliver and your mama will adore him and be as proud of him as we will be. We shall be married, Kelynen, and soon, that I swear. Now, no more talk. I want you to make love to me.'

Now, with Rex walking at her side, she relived all the wonderful moments spent in Joel Jackson's cottage on that afternoon and a subsequent occasion. She was to send word to Rafe the instant her parents arrived home, and he intended to ride over the next day and request an interview with them.

Suddenly Rex shot off, barking excitedly. She took no notice, assuming he had smelled a rabbit or something, until there came a familiar answering bark. She halted, frowned in puzzlement, then smiled and ran after Rex. Digory! Digory was here. Rafe had got fed up with waiting and was here to speak to Luke. It wouldn't help matters but it would be wonderful to see him.

She ran to the front of the house, past the two dogs as they playfully nuzzled and fought, until she reached the steps. She stopped dead, disappointed, but even so, able to be delighted. 'Gabriel! Is it really you? You look so different. How well you must be feeling to actually venture out. Hello, Jacob.'

Jacob Glynn had already helped his master to dismount.

After touching his forelock to Kelynen, he led the horses round the back of the house.

Gabriel came forward on stiff legs. 'It's good to see you again, Kelynen. Forgive the unannounced visit. I had a sudden urge to spread my wings and I wanted to show you that I've kept my word in continuing towards good health.'

Rafe had been right. Now Gabriel's face had fleshed out he was indeed fine-looking. If she had seen him like this on her first visit to Chenhalls she would have harboured hopes for him rather than his devious, rotten half-brother. 'You are very welcome, Gabriel. Come inside. Let me take your arm. You look a little weary.'

Slowly, they mounted the steps. Puffing now, Gabriel's climb grew more laboured. 'I fear the journey has tired me. Before we go inside I need to inform you that my uncle sends you his affection. He wishes to know when your father is due home.'

Kelynen told him. 'You approve of your uncle's and my intentions then?'

Gabriel still wasn't sure how he felt about it but he said, 'I shall be proud to stand beside him in the family chapel.'

Kelynen squeezed his arm. 'I hope you will find the happiness you deserve again, Gabriel. Forgive me, but although we've never spoken of it, I am sure you have suffered a sorrowed heart.'

Breathless, Gabriel paused on the top step. 'Caterina . . .'

'That was her name?'

'Yes. I suppose it would have helped if I'd spoken about her.'

'She left you?'

'No. She died. I'll tell you and Uncle Rafe all about her before I leave Chenhalls, to let her rest in peace, and then I shall find peace too. Now, is your brother at home? I confess I am a little nervous at meeting him.'

The great double doors of the house were opened and

next moment Luke was there. 'Kelynen, have you not noticed there is about to be a heavy rainfall? Pray, bring your guest inside.'

When sister and brother and newcomer were facing each other in the great hall, Kelynen stepped slightly in front of Gabriel. Her eyes shone with a threat. 'Luke, this is Mr Gabriel Tremayne. Gabriel, my brother Luke.'

Luke gazed for long thoughtful seconds at the other man. He held out his hand. 'I am pleased to meet you, sir.'

'Likewise, Mr Pengarron.'

Kelynen silently implored Gabriel to say something else, but it seemed he had retreated into his habitual guarded quietness.

'Um, well, this is a surprise, isn't it, Kelynen?' Luke said. With nothing more forthcoming from the visitor, he was thrown. Then he suddenly rushed forward. 'Quick, Sister, he's about to faint!'

Eighteen

'He's an exceptionally quiet fellow, just as you've remarked, Kelynen.' Sitting at the head of the dining table, Luke was referring to Gabriel.

'He's terribly embarrassed at being overcome like that,' Kelynen replied. 'I'm grateful to you, Luke, for allowing him a room to rest in.'

'Well, he has his man to attend him. Perhaps an hour or two of sleep and later a hot meal will revive him. I'd be most interested to hear about his life in Vienna and his music. I shall never forget how he played that night.'

'One thing is certain,' Sophie said, across the table from Kelynen. 'Mr Tremayne should not sally forth again today in these inclement conditions, not in his present state of health. Luke, do you not think a letter should be sent to Chenhalls, stating that Mr Tremayne will be under Pengarron hospitality until the weather has broken and he has recovered enough to travel? It might even be for two or three days.'

'Of course, my dear.' Luke smiled at her.

Kelynen felt she might just as well not be there, although she appreciated Sophie showing no objections to Gabriel's presence. It would be good to have him stay. 'I'll write the letter,' she said, intending to add for Rafe the time and date of her parents' expected arrival. Suddenly, she was longing to see them again.

Gabriel joined them after supper. Dark shadows were smudged under his deep-blue eyes but he held himself straight and his voice was firm and unwearied. He smiled at Kelynen in a deep way and kissed her hand, leading her to think he had a good measure of the same sort of charm as Rafe. When introduced to Sophie, Kelynen watched her reaction to him. Sophie received him with politeness and an obvious instant approval. Gabriel had that effect on people, and Kelynen was grateful to him for deciding to pay this unexpected visit. He might calm the ill feelings caused by the wretched Josiah Tremayne's outrageous conduct.

'You're not intruding at all, Mr Tremayne,' Luke assured Gabriel after he had apologized for the inconvenience he was sure he must have caused. 'You are welcome here. I was perhaps a little hasty in rushing my family out of your uncle's house. Blame should rest only on the blameworthy.' He smiled warmly at Kelynen, thinking this should please her and hopefully put an end to the bickering in the house. Then perhaps his sister would settle down and stop her jealous behaviour towards Sophie and take a proper interest in the wedding. Sophie had been a little stiff after the dressmaker had left. He did not need to be told why; he had overheard the strained comments, and a little soothsaying from Beatrice had put him on guard. He wanted nothing to mar his nuptials. 'You oughta understand, boy,' Beatrice had breathily deliberated. 'The maid's in love and ye snatched her away from him. Can't spect her to be 'thusiastic over another's similar delight, can 'ee?'

Luke now continued. 'Mr Tremayne, I don't suppose I could press upon you to . . . No, it's presumptuous of me and you need to rest.'

'You would like me to play something, Mr Pengarron?' Gabriel said. Having not yet taken a seat, his gaze filtered into the next room where he spied a harpsichord. 'I'd be delighted to. Kelynen, I think it's time we performed a duet. Shall we?'

She enjoyed sitting next to Gabriel, spinning out a country

air. He added his own intricate interpretation, while she laughingly tried to match his flashing fingers. Luke clapped loudly. Sophie forgot to be a demure hostess and was on her feet, tapping them and swaying. She declared, 'I've never heard the piece performed like that before! It's a raucous tune, but you, Mr Tremayne, made it sound heavenly in a lively kind of way.'

'I beg you to play something beautifully sad like you did the other night,' Luke said. 'I'll fetch a violin.'

Kelynen saw that Gabriel was happy to be persuaded again, and while he played something of his own – after explaining it was one of his earliest compositions and his uncle's favourite – she sank into assuming he would soon be performing the music for her and Rafe in the little chapel at Chenhalls.

Rafe was with Mordecai Lambourne and the rest of his smuggling team down in Rocky Cove. Under a pale moon, which gave everything a ghostly outline through the lightly falling rain, upwards of thirty men had already carried much of the haul up to the cliff top. It would soon be taken away by mules and farm beasts, their hooves muffled to lessen the noise of their passage, their manes and tails greased to stall easy capture by skulking Revenue or Preventive men. Firearms had replaced staffs and cudgels as means of defence, for the haul tonight did not consist of the usual brandy, rum, tea, lace or spices. The stakes were higher and more dangerous. The men had not been told what the contraband was, but they speculated it was precious metal from the heavy, unyielding weight of each casket.

The ship lowering the stolen goods over its side was a privateer, offloading gold bullion stolen from a French naval vessel out in the Channel. Rafe had joined the ship the night before at St Michael's Mount and had taken part in the piracy, an act involving some bloodshed on the French side.

'Another hour and we'll be done here, Lambourne,' Rafe whispered to the lander. Rafe had come ashore in a Porthleven fishing boat, and, together with Lambourne, was heaving and hefting one of the last caskets over the rocks. The two big strong men were struggling under its weight but determination and the adrenalin racing through their veins – and sometimes brute force – lent them a power higher than usual.

During necessary brief respites the men whispered to each other. 'Your share tonight will make you a rich man, Lambourne. Does this mean I'm to lose a mine captain?'

''Fraid it will, sir. Got plans, I have.'

'And so have I. I've languished long enough in this dull place. I intend to live out my days far away from here.'

'Good fortune to 'ee, sir,' Lambourne panted as they tied rope, dropped down from above, to aid the casket's passage up the cliff. The two men climbed up with the casket, using another rope to help keep their balance, Lambourne in front of it, Rafe behind, to keep it from snagging or swaying.

Grunting with the effort, Lambourne disappeared over the top. Rafe put his shoulder in under the casket to launch it clear of the overhang, to steady it, and then he pushed it up the last arduous inches to land. The hide in the cove, which featured a cleverly concealed tunnel entrance that led all the way to a secret chamber under the tower folly, was not to be used tonight. This particular haul was to be met by closely guarded waggoners on the coast road and taken, under the guise of cloth merchandise, to Falmouth, where a ship was awaiting sail to Bristol, and would be met there by the agents of a consortium of buyers.

With that done, Rafe gasped in some much-needed air. The muscles of his upper body were aching unmercifully, his lungs working almost beyond their capacity. His heart was thrashing in excitement, as if about to leap out of his chest. But he was never happier than when in the throes of risk and peril, and an operation of this kind offered many dangers, from apprehension by the law, discovery and theft by those outside of it, and – in view of the origins of tonight's booty – diplomatic outrage. The stakes were high but the reward phenomenal. His present income paid for the needs of Chenhalls, his other household, and many a luxury, but this would fund his new life with Kelynen. He wanted to build a far larger estate, somewhere more exciting than this quiet county of his birth. Portia could live out her days at Chenhalls, as was her wish, and then he would sell it. It was time the Tremaynes broke away from the place where so much tragedy had beset them, the place that seemed to cling to them and seek to bring them down. It would please his nephews. Gabriel could initiate his own theatre company and orchestra if he desired, and Josiah could spend his days in idle contentment.

He was greatly looking forward to the future with the bride he was determined to have – the sweet, adoring young woman he felt he actually loved, who would give him a healthy heir. He felt he would find peace at last and wish for nothing more.

Strange muffled noises came from above. Rafe swore silently to himself. *Lambourne, order the men up there to keep quiet!*

He made to peer out over the overhang but suddenly something big, dark and heavy dropped past him. An instant later and his head would have been exposed and he too would have been sent crashing down. *Hell and damnation, they'd dropped the casket!*

But it wasn't the sound of splintering wood and spitting metal he was to hear, but a sickening thump and a terrible cracking. Although he couldn't see clearly down to the beach, from where gasps of horror now came from the last men waiting to come up, Rafe knew it was a man who had plunged past him. Mordecai Lambourne. How could he have been so bloody careless?

Yet almost at once he knew it wasn't a fateful step that

had led to Lambourne's death. Something was horribly wrong. He heard shouts and gunshots and screams above him and below. The operation had been betrayed! His men were being killed. Others had concealed themselves on the cliff top tonight and other boats must have stolen round to the cove. Rafe pulled out the pistol in the belt around his coat. He raised himself up to the cliff top to help fight off whoever the enemy was. He wasn't afraid; he was furious at the betrayal and in the mood for slaughter.

When his face cleared the overhang he saw nothing but confusion. He didn't get the chance to see who was annihilating his men or to pull himself up to defend his plunder. A violent kick between the eyes sent him plummeting down after his mine captain.

'Right, then,' a hard voice hissed after all those loyal to Sir Rafe had been dealt with. 'Let's get this lot away. My maid did us a good job getting the right information out of the younger Tremayne. Pity he weren't here tonight too.'

'Be trouble for us, do 'ee reckon?' came another rough voice.

'Not he. Too soft, too stupid, and too damned shifty himself. He won't have much to say; he won't want the law looking into his affairs. We've as good as got away with it already.'

Nineteen

Early next morning, Josiah Tremayne arrived at Pengarron Manor. He was relieved of his dripping wet travelling clothes and shown into the parlour, and his half-brother was asked to join him there.

'What does he want, Luke?' Kelynen tried to peep into the room, but Luke pulled her away. 'Is he concerned about Gabriel? Come to escort him home? Sophie won't be pleased to learn he's here.'

'Sophie is presently occupied with Elizabeth. Hopefully, Tremayne will take himself off before she comes down. Gabriel doesn't have to leave. He's welcome to stay for as long as it pleases him.'

'I'm so pleased you like Gabriel.'

'He's a man of honour, talented and somehow fascinating. When will you ask about his tragedy? It might well make an excellent plot for a play. He could write the music for it. We could co-write an opera. That does appeal to me.'

'He'll be returning to Vienna soon, and your idea wouldn't appeal to him anyway. Gabriel's far too private a person.'

'It's a pity he's leaving Cornwall. And it's a pity Gabriel doesn't appeal to you.' Luke's black eyes surveyed her with impatient meaning behind their intensity. 'You'd still become mistress of Chenhalls. Gabriel would make you a worthy husband. I think Father and Mama would approve of him.'

'I'm in love with Rafe!' Kelynen was stung by his disregard over what she really wanted. 'When will you allow me my heart and stop insisting it's infatuation I feel? Can you not accept that my feelings for him are the same as yours are for Sophie? How would you like it if I suggested you jilted her? She doesn't love you and has nothing to offer you.'

Afraid Sophie would come downstairs and overhear a quarrel in which her name would be unkindly bandied, Luke dragged Kelynen away to the study. 'Take back what you just said! It was vicious.'

'No, I will not. You have no care for my feelings so why should I care for yours? Get your hands off me or I'll call Rex and set him on you.'

'Yet again, Sister, you show your immaturity. Has it not occurred to you that this is what Rafe Tremayne admires in you? His former brides were very young. As for Sophie, she is everything I want. She doesn't behave like a moody brat! What have you against her? You were friends.'

Kelynen issued a long, exasperated sigh. She had not wanted to get involved in another petty argument with Luke. 'I've nothing against her. I was merely trying to point out that you are about to marry the one you love, so why shouldn't I? Why can't you be happy for me, Luke?'

'I don't know.' Luke was suddenly thoughtful. 'Kelynen, are you sure your attraction to Sir Rafe isn't simply a wish to marry someone who reminds you of Father? Livvy, Kane and I are all aware of how much you've missed him. Surely you can't think this man measures up to him in any way?'

Kelynen wasn't one for slapping faces but now she treated Luke to one that resounded round the room. 'How dare you? I am not a fool. I know what I feel in my heart. Where I differ from you, Luke, and perhaps you are jealous of this because here I can outdo you, is that the person whom I love, loves me back. I shall know passion with Rafe. Can you say that about your bride?'

Luke rubbed his stinging face. She had touched the raw spot in his otherwise happy heart. 'Damn you, Kelynen!'

172

There was a nervous knock on the door. Polly O'Flynn's voice, subdued and apologetic, stole through the storm. 'Excuse me, sir. Miss Kelynen, Mr Gabriel Tremayne requests your presence in the parlour.'

Kelynen stalked past Luke and the housekeeper, who had her eyes aimed at the floor.

'Any idea what's going on, Mrs O'Flynn?' Luke asked, wheeling his stiff shoulder, the tension making it ache. 'Do you think something's amiss?'

'I fear so, Mr Luke. Mr Josiah Tremayne has already left to return to Chenhalls, and Mr Gabriel whispered to me that Beatrice and Mrs Carew should be brought to attend on Miss Kelynen.'

Luke sighed. 'Go, then, and fetch them please.'

Luke stationed himself outside the parlour. Apprehension caught at his nerves. Sir Rafe Tremayne was as much a womanizer as his nephew Josiah was – as he himself had been until he'd fallen in love with Sophie. Had Sir Rafe sent word that he had a new mistress and was no longer considering remarriage, or was even planning to take a different wife? Luke couldn't think what else could have warranted the visitation of the odious Josiah Tremayne. He was unprepared for the sudden terrible, anguished scream from Kelynen.

Sophie had nearly reached him but he didn't see her as he shot through the parlour door. Kelynen was bawling in a state of collapse in Gabriel's arms, and he was crying too.

'What is it?' Luke skidded to a halt.

Doing nothing to prevent his tears, Gabriel explained in a stricken voice, 'There was a smuggling run on Chenhalls property last night. It was betrayed. A gang of cut-throats, believed to come from near Gunwalloe, fought against my uncle's men. Uncle Rafe was hurled off the cliff. He died shortly afterwards.'

A fresh outbreak of weeping came from Kelynen. She

clung to Gabriel, her body shaking and retching. 'No! No!' she cried.

Luke glanced at Sophie. Her eyes were large and shocked in her lovely face. She advanced towards Kelynen. 'My dear, I'm so very sorry.'

Luke grasped Kelynen's shoulders. 'Beloved, come to me. I'll send for Livvy and Timothy. I'm sure you'll want Livvy here until Mama arrives home, and Timothy can give you spiritual comfort. I'll also send word to Kane and Jessica. Take heart, you'll soon have all your family with you.'

Kelynen thrust his hands off her. 'Leave me! Go away! I don't want any of you. I just want Rafe! I want Rafe, oh God help me, I want Rafe.'

'I think it best we leave her awhile with Mr Tremayne,' Sophie said, grabbing at Luke, for he was determined to wrench Kelynen away and clasp her to himself.

Beatrice waddled in through the doorway on Polly's arm. Luke glanced despairingly at the old nursemaid for advice.

'Missus Carew's right. Give 'em a few minutes,' she rasped, her raddled eyes wet over Kelynen's distress.

Luke withdrew, taking Sophie with him. 'You have my deepest sympathy, Gabriel.'

Gabriel nodded and wrapped Kelynen in tighter to him.

On the other side of the door Luke pulled his face down in torment. 'Oh, Lord, I was only quarrelling with her minutes ago about Rafe Tremayne. She really loved him and I couldn't accept it. What's she going to do?'

'The young gen'leman'll be her best hope fer now,' Beatrice deliberated. 'Oh! The poor little soul. If only Sir Oliver was here – and a maid needs her mother at a time like this.'

Alone with Luke shortly afterwards in his mother's sitting room, Sophie said, 'Do you think we ought to postpone the wedding?'

He took her into his arms, feeling the need for the comfort

of bodily warmth as Kelynen's lamenting went on and on. 'No. I mean, I don't want that. Do you? I'll talk to my father. It's going to be a quiet ceremony anyway. We could go ahead but forsake the celebration.'

'Yes, I think that will do. Poor, dear Kelynen. She doesn't deserve this heartbreak.' Sophie nestled her face against his neck. To witness love and tragedy in all its extremity had left her shaken.

Her lashes caressed his skin and her breath warmed him. Luke shivered in delight, then looked down on her lips. They were slightly parted, unwittingly inviting. Her eyes were closed, so he knew she was at ease in his embrace. He kissed her, not in his usual controlled way, but with steady force. Relieved it was not herself who was bereaved of her bridegroom, she roped her arms round his neck.

Desire flamed in Luke and he wondered if she would allow any liberties. He wanted to disprove the impression others had of her that she was interested in him only for his wealth and position. Did she find him attractive? Did she have any affection for him? He took his mouth from hers and placed it over the delicious hollow of her neck, pressing into her softness, tasting her, wanting to know her. It was hardly the time to be making sensuous approaches towards Sophie, with his sister perhaps needing him any moment, but he couldn't keep restraint. He edged her to the side of the door so that if anyone opened it and entered they would remain unseen. Sophie leaned against the panelled wall, her head touching one of Livvy's family portraits, her eyes boring into his.

She went on staring at him, her breathing coming fast, her bosom heaving. Luke swept his gaze down to the upper swells of her breasts just in sight above a muslin fichu – such an exquisite creamy place of beauty and promise. He knew her shape was perfect and longed to see more. He stepped even closer to her, gazing into her eyes again. Sophie swallowed. Then, in a gesture rare to her, she reached up and gentled away a loose strand of black hair from his face. Taking this as her permission – and that she was even daring him to take advantage of her during this time alone – Luke kissed her fiercely, one hand gripping the back of her neck, the other over a firm, tender breast, exploring.

He kissed her fully, holding nothing back. Receiving no dissent from Sophie, he was delighted at the knowledge that she was not a prude, as he had taken to fearing, but a warm-blooded, sensual being. He was to be married in a few days, and he had every hope that before then he would know his beautiful bride entirely.

Livvy and Timothy arrived. Livvy spent a few minutes in Kelynen's bedchamber, where she had been taken, and then she sought out Luke, finding him in Beatrice's room.

'Is she resting?' Luke asked. 'Beatrice sent up a concoction of valerian for her to take.'

Livvy shook her head. 'Luke, she's leaving for Chenhalls now with Gabriel Tremayne. Nothing I said would dissuade her. I pleaded with her to wait for the funeral but she says she has to see Sir Rafe. Shall I go with her? She insists she can cope with just Gabriel Tremayne and Ruth.'

Luke looked at Beatrice. 'What do you think, Bea?'

'I hate to think of her all alone without any of we, but p'raps this is something she needs to do alone. The maid's a growed woman.'

And so Kelynen left in the same Pengarron carriage that she had been forced to travel home in a week ago. Gabriel was inside with her, his horse led home by Jacob Glynn.

'I hope she doesn't blame me,' Luke said to Sophie, Livvy and Timothy on the doorstep.

'Why should she do that?' Timothy asked. Kelynen had allowed him to pray for the repose of Sir Rafe's soul – he too was grieving for his friend – and then to ask the Almighty to give her strength to face the days ahead, but after all her weeping, the quiet dignity Kelynen had displayed had touched him deeply.

'People tend to think strange things when bereaved. They look for someone to blame for the tragedy. I forced Kelynen to come home against her will. She might come to the conclusion that if she had still been at Chenhalls it would somehow have made a vital difference, perhaps something she might have said or done would have prevented Sir Rafe's death.'

'He was a good man,' Livvy said sorrowfully. 'I shall miss him.'

'Do you think he loved Kelynen?' Luke asked as he hugged the elder of his two sisters.

'He was fond of her. We'll never know for sure.'

Sophie gazed after the rapidly disappearing carriage. 'Gabriel Tremayne is Sir Gabriel now. I wonder what he will do with Chenhalls . . .'

Twenty

Three weeks had passed since the interment of Rafe's body in the Tremayne tomb, which was on the outer flank of the chapel at Chenhalls, and Kelynen's ritual there never varied. She ensured fresh flowers were in the urns on either side of the great stone door. She put her hand on the huge iron ring of the latch and knocked gently, as if to convey to Rafe that she was there paying homage to him, remembering him, still loving him. The door was kept locked or she would have gone inside and stood before the coffin on its lonely dark shelf. Finally, whatever the weather, she sat on the long ornate stone seat at the side of the tomb, where she could see the sea. There she relived every precious memory of Rafe, sometimes numb, sometimes crying, sometimes silent. Sitting alone – Rex always waited for her at a respectful, mournful distance – until someone, usually Gabriel, came and persuaded her to come away.

Often she walked to Rocky Cove and stared down on the beach where Rafe had died. The tricky climb down had been destroyed in the murderous fight, the overhang trampled off. The bodies on the beach had been taken away by boat. She had thought to get someone to sail her round to the cove but had felt, even in her extremity of grief, that it was too morbid. She had consulted the miner who had lifted Rafe into his arms and watched him expire. The young man – his life saved after his moments of selflessness by smothering his head in another's blood and pretending to be dead

– had stood nervously, having made a vain effort to be clean and tidy, in the banqueting hall.

'Did Sir Rafe say any last words?'

'No, miss, sorry. He was knocked clean out. I thought he was already gone when I lifted him, then I heard . . . his last breath escaping. Don't believe he suffered none.'

'That's a comfort to us, thank you.' Gabriel had been there, also wanting to glean information about the outrage that was rapidly becoming an inevitably romantic and exaggerated part of Cornish folklore. His offer of a generous reward for the apprehension of his uncle's murderers had brought a quick response and the authorities had a number of men, mainly ruffians, awaiting the September Assizes at Launceston. How had the robbers known about the gold, which had been recovered from the ship at Falmouth, but which was unlikely to be restored to its rightful government and would find its way into the national treasury? No one knew for certain, but common opinion had it that the gang regularly sent out spies along the coast, and then they would plot how to steal off smuggling runs when they were at their most vulnerable. Gabriel had paid the young miner handsomely for his trouble and before dismissing him had expressed his condolences to him. Many a miner, fisherman and Chenhalls servant had lost his life that night, and the youth's own father had been shot and killed.

Kelynen had stared into space, picturing the violence enacted upon Rafe, his fall off the cliff and his last moments.

Gabriel had gently touched her. 'Did you find that a comfort, Kelynen?'

'It's as if Rafe just left.'

'What do you mean?' he had asked, trying to warm her cold hands in his.

'I can't help thinking there should have been a last word for me.' Frozen inside, her eyes watering as they did so many times a day, she appealed to Gabriel. 'There's been nothing.'

'Kelynen, my dear love, I don't understand. Uncle Rafe had no time to think of such a thing.'

'But I can't help feeling there should be something. Anything. I've searched his room. There's not a note, not a reference to me. I know he didn't mean to, but it's as if he just went away and left me.'

'I know how empty you are. You feel that you never said goodbye to him. That you've been cruelly cut off.'

She settled her gaze on his pale, caring face. 'Is that what happened to you?'

He nodded. 'I understand everything you're going through, Kelynen. My grief almost finished me. I always thought there was nothing higher, nothing purer than being in love, and then love itself betrayed me. You saved me, Kelynen. I shall stay for as long as you need me.'

'Some day you must tell me . . .'

Sometimes, as she kept vigil close to Rafe, her mind drifted to Gabriel's heartbreak and she took small comfort in knowing he understood exactly her suffering, and she wondered who the woman had been, whose death had nearly destroyed him.

'Kelynen, my love . . .' said a voice.

It wasn't Gabriel who had come for her today. It was a woman with auburn hair and compassionate eyes of grey-green, who was as beautiful as the sea. Her mother. Come to her again, as she did, with her father, every few days, to shower her with love and solace and to beg her to return home.

'Mama . . .'

Kerensa, Lady Pengarron, bent forward and kissed her, sat down beside her and held her hand. She never tried to hurry Kelynen away from here. She had a soft voice, the accent pointing to her humble origins. 'Your father is talking to Sir Gabriel. They enjoy one another's company. We are all to share a meal quite soon.'

Kelynen had no appetite but she always ate a little of

each meal for Gabriel's sake, not wanting him to worry that she would starve herself as he had. 'Have Luke and Sophie gone to live at Polgissey yet?'

'They left the manor for Polgissey last week, remember?' Kerensa rubbed her daughter's chilled fingers, wishing, praying there was something she could do to ease her anguish. Her parchment-white face and great, soulful eyes made Kerensa want to cry for her. She was going to add how empty the manor house now felt, how lost she and Oliver felt at Kelynen's unaccustomed absence, but that would have been insensitive. 'Elizabeth's thriving. She's a dear child. Your father is hoping to hear news of another grandchild before the year's end.'

'Yes. Luke would like a son. Has he forgiven me yet for not attending his wedding?'

'Oh, Kelynen, beloved, Luke never felt that. He was more anxious that you would understand about him not delaying the ceremony.'

'I wish I'd married Rafe.'

'Of course you do.'

'You didn't know him, did you, Mama?'

'I only saw him socially once or twice.' Kerensa indulged Kelynen, repeating what she had said before. 'He was a handsome man, witty and full of charm.'

'Father would have given his permission for us to marry, wouldn't he?' Kelynen was always anxious about this.

'I'm sure he would have.' How could she tell the truth? That on hearing about Rafe Tremayne's intentions for Kelynen, his favourite child, Oliver had cried that the man was far from suitable, that he would have used all his power to block any such union. In the illogical way of one hurting over a loved one's pain, he blamed himself for Kelynen's distress, believing he should have insisted she come to Bath with them. 'Your father's only concern would have been that you'd be happy.'

'Rafe and I would have had a wonderful life together.'

'It's something to cling to, Kelynen.'

'I do, Mama. I shall cling to everything concerning Rafe for the rest of my life.'

Kerensa was disturbed by that affirmation. She hoped Kelynen would find love again, not spend her life entrenched in this terrible grief. 'We've brought Samuel and Tamara with us today. Are you ready to come inside and see your young brother and niece? You'll be amazed how they've grown.'

The tall, commanding figure of her father appeared round the side of the tomb, bringing Rex with him. Kelynen sprang up and ran into his arms. Sir Oliver Pengarron held her tight, tighter, worrying about how insubstantial she looked and felt in his embrace. He had another name for her, which was a derivative of Michelle, the French name he had given her. 'Shelley, beloved, Rex and I are eager for your company.'

Kerensa left them alone. Her greatest hope was that in her father, Kelynen would find the degree of comfort she needed to finally bring her home and get on with her life.

Oliver led Kelynen away from the tomb, hating the unhealthy amount of time she spent here. They were on the path towards the sunken garden.

'This was where I first saw Rafe,' she said. 'Where Livvy painted him.'

He bit back an impatient sigh. What could he do to get this man out of her head? Kelynen stared up at Rafe Tremayne's portrait several times a day. If only he could utter what he really thought about the man, make his usually sensible daughter see Tremayne for what he'd been – a philanderer, who thought more of adventure than duty; an opportunist, who didn't stop at free-trading but had taken part in the slaughter of innocent foreign sailors. Matthias Renfree had reminded him that the Tremayne accounts were long overdue. It was time to demand that Kelynen come home. But Beatrice had warned against it, declaring it would only make the dead man's hold over her even stronger.

'Your mama and I are hoping to hold a family dinner soon.'

Kelynen looked at her father and loved him even more for this latest act of loving attention. He was proud and aristocratic, his black hair – silvered at the temples – swept back by the sharp wind coming in off the sea. Rafe had been like him, strong and noble. She had witnessed her mother gripping his hand, fearing, Kelynen thought, how she could never bear to lose him. A world without her father too made Kelynen shudder.

'Beloved, you're getting cold. I'm taking you inside. I long to take you home. When will you come home, Shelley? If it's what you want, Gabriel can come too, and stay as long as he likes. I get the impression he doesn't care for the estate he has inherited.'

'He doesn't,' she said, as her father hastened them towards the house. 'But he feels he must stay, at least for the mourning period, before he departs for Vienna and leaves Chenhalls in Josiah's care.'

'An unwise decision.' Oliver did not explain his remark, and Kelynen took it to be in reference to Gabriel's intended return home; concern had been expressed that he might sink back into a decline when faced with the location of his grief. 'What do you want to do, sweeting?'

'I know you and Mama are worried about me. But I can't leave Rafe yet. I can't! Please try to understand.'

'At least come home for a day. I promise we won't try to force you to stay. Think about it. Please, Shelley, say you'll think about it.'

But she couldn't even think that far ahead and said nothing in reply.

'When is she to take her leave?' Josiah asked, his tone hard and disapproving. He had joined Gabriel at an upstairs corridor window, where his half-brother was watching Kelynen and Sir Oliver approaching the house.

Gabriel did not take his gaze from Kelynen's fair form. Swamped by the imposing figure of her father, she looked lost and pitiful. He ached to find a way to ease her pain. Kelynen was the gentlest, most compassionate person he had met. Even in her anguish she had insisted on riding with him to the mine, farms and villages to offer her sympathy and practical help to the others involved in the tragedy. And she had been a comfort to Aunt Portia, who was taking her brother's death hard. Kelynen did not deserve this heartbreak. Gabriel found Josiah's demand offensive. 'You despise her presence here?'

'Not as such, but we can't get on with our own lives with her weeping all over the place,' Josiah whined. 'It's hardly doing her good. Her father should take her home. Today. He's softer than his son, Luke. I couldn't see *him* allowing the girl to languish here. She'll go mad. Throw herself off the tower or something.'

'She will not! Despite what the rest of you think, I know Kelynen is already facing up to life without Uncle Rafe. She is not selfish and she is not a coward. I'm confident that in a little while she'll come to terms with her loss. You are being too harsh and—'

Gabriel was forced to stop and reach out a hand to Josiah, who was suddenly sobbing and reaching for a handkerchief in the inside pocket of his fashionable black coat. Josiah blubbered like an infant over their uncle's death nearly every day. 'I'm sorry. Forgive me. I forget how close you were to Uncle Rafe.'

Josiah moved away, head bent over, his shoulders shaking as he wept. 'I–I don't feel secure any more.'

'Is there something I should know?' Gabriel had not considered his half-brother's character much before, but saw him now as something of a snivelling dandy. The day Josiah had informed him of their uncle's death he had also

184

complained that life wasn't fair, that his latest mistress had cruelly thrown him over. As he watched Josiah hastily mopping his face and checking his appearance in a mirror, he wondered how he was coping with the business concerns of Chenhalls. The lawyers had repeatedly requested a reading of his uncle's will, but Gabriel had been in no mood for that. His new position would be legal and final and he'd feel trapped. 'You need time to clear your mind. I'll go to the mine tomorrow. And I must ride over to Marazion to consult with the lawyers. You have your inheritance, Josiah. You may do whatever you wish now.'

'No! Don't do anything, Gabriel, I beg you. I wouldn't dream of dispensing with the responsibilities entrusted to me until a more appropriate time.' Josiah pinched his cheeks and turned round to Gabriel. With a half smile, he added, 'Put your energies into comforting Miss Pengarron. I beg you also to take of yourself, Brother. You are still very pale.'

'Concern yourself not about me, Josiah. I feel well and strong and indeed I am always inclined towards paleness.' It could be seen in Gabriel's firm smile that he was speaking the truth. 'Now, let us go downstairs and ensure none of the cats are about for the sake of Sir Oliver's comfort, and preside at our uncle's table.' Gabriel did not think of the house as his own yet.

Late at night, unable to sleep, Kelynen stole up to the little library in the attic. Snuffing out the candle, she sat in the darkness and recalled the first kiss shared here with Rafe, and imagined him being with her now. 'I love you,' she whispered, hearing his voice deep in her mind, saying it back.

She dozed and woke to find not Rafe on her mind but, strangely, Luke. She had dreamed of Beatrice, drunk on gin and weeping over and over again, 'Poor boy, poor boy'. Kelynen felt guilty about the pleasure she had felt over

Beatrice's declaration that Luke was destined to become miserable in his marriage. She prayed for Luke to have a son and heir. And lots more children. Luke would like that, sons and daughters and his adopted daughter, all loving him and looking up to him. She would make amends to Luke for her grouchy behaviour, and make firm friends again with Sophie. And she would support them both. That should help to keep their marriage strong. She hoped Sophie was able to be as loving and giving towards Luke as she, herself, had been with Rafe. She didn't regret making love with Rafe. She had given all of herself to him and he had given all of himself to her.

She had a thought that was awesome and wicked, but if it were real, such pleasure it would give her – something to take with her into the future. If only she was having Rafe's baby. Then she would always have something precious of his, part of him to love, and they would never totally be parted. She made a calculation, then sat up ramrod straight. Nature was late in paying a monthly call on her. And Ruth, just lately, had taken to checking Kelynen's underclothing in a most odd fashion, followed by expressions grave and worried.

She laid a hand over her tummy and tears of joy and delight streamed down her face. She left the tears unchecked, and, although it was wicked, she thanked God out loud. 'Oh, Rafe, part of you still lives, here inside me.'

A glow appeared under the door and grew stronger and brighter. For one crazy, love-filled moment she thought it was Rafe, or a sign from him, come to share this most special of moments with her. The door was opened. She let out a cry of bliss.

'Kelynen, my dear friend, are you all right?'

It was Gabriel. She didn't give him time to put down his candlestick before rushing to hug him. 'I'm fine. I'm happy. Oh, Gabriel, I'm so happy! I'll be happy now for the rest of my life.'

Twenty-One

A s if in a playful mood, fingers of light crept into the little attic room, highlighting the gold print on some of the books. Kelynen saw it as pinpricks of promise. The flame of Gabriel's candle had flickered out long ago. They had stayed up all night talking but neither were the least bit tired.

'Thank you for telling me all about Caterina,' Kelynen said. Sitting side by side, he was holding her hand and she was resting her face against his upper arm, as she did when seeking comfort or counsel from Beatrice. 'How long do you think it will be before you finish the ballet?'

'Not long, although . . .'

'Yes?'

'I've recently come to the conclusion that I should never finish it. Caterina's life was suddenly snuffed out. An unfinished ballet to her memory would appeal to her love of drama. She'd have been bound to want – to demand – the end be rewritten several times anyway. Caterina was like that, full of her own ideas, always wanting total control, but not always knowing what she wanted. The end of the ballet could be anything. I feel that it's not, even for me, to say exactly what it should be.'

'Few people who create something would feel that way. Caterina was a fortunate woman to have known your love. You're such a selfless man, Gabriel. I couldn't have got through these last weeks without you.' Kelynen thought that the fiery Austrian had not deserved his love. Strange to think that if she had not died, then the intense feelings and wild life they had shared would almost certainly have destroyed him, and she hated that thought. Without consideration – for it was as natural to her as breathing – she nestled into him, and he brought his arms round to enfold her.

He gently stroked her hair. 'We have much in common, Kelynen.'

'Yes, we do. We have had those whom we loved cruelly ripped away from us. And fate has decreed that we should be available to bring each other through the darkness. I can go home now. You can return to where you long to be; I have held you back long enough. I would not wish to stay away from Chenhalls. I shall call regularly on Lady Portia and write to you of her welfare. I shall ensure that Livvy paints her portrait. And one day my child and I will visit you in Vienna and you can show us all the wonderful places you have spoken of. St Stephen's Cathedral and all its fine spires and statues; the Lindenallee in the Augarten – and the other park, the Lusthaus in the Prater, where we might see the Emperor in his carriage.'

Gabriel unwrapped her from his arms and looked directly into her eyes. His expression was serious. 'Kelynen, my dear, do you not see that neither of us can simply do what you've just said. You are having a baby.'

'I know. My parents will be disappointed but they will not disown me. I shall be content with my child. It will prevent a marriage but after Rafe there is none I could ever wish to marry.'

'You are not considering what the life before you and your child will truly be like. Your present happiness will not stay intact. Your child will be shunned, and by all levels of society, and that will make you feel selfish. I could not return to Vienna and leave you in a fix. Indeed, I would not dream of it. There is nothing for it, Kelynen, but for us to marry.'

'What?' Kelynen's heart drifted downwards as she acknowledged the dire truths put before her, yet somehow she could not help a weak smile. 'But, Gabriel, it's not what you want. I would not dream of asking such a noble gesture of you.'

'You did not ask me, I offered. I know I've spoken as if I could not bear to ever marry anyone after Caterina, but if I married at all I could only consider you. Think about it, Kelynen. Uncle Rafe wanted an heir. As my wife, with me taking the child as mine, that's what it would be. It would have its father's name. And you love Chenhalls. Sir Oliver, I think, has a liking for me. It's the perfect solution.'

She was struck silent for some moments, her gaze growing more and more animated at the prospect. 'Yes, it would be the perfect solution. And Josiah could go away as he desires. I certainly don't wish him here. But Gabriel.' She frowned. 'Are you sure you could stand living here? You hate Chenhalls. Of course, I would not wish to bind you to my side. You could still go to Vienna at any time you please.'

'I would not do that. I know how disadvantageous it is to grow up without a father. Your child, Uncle Rafe's child, will know a contented family life. Few people will guess the truth of its paternity – indeed many will not doubt that I am responsible as we have spent much time alone together. Kelynen, if you agree, let us take a hasty breakfast and then ride to Pengarron Manor. I think Sir Oliver and Lady Pengarron will be cautiously pleased to receive us.'

Twenty-Two

'Lady Portia, may I come in?' Kelynen waited just inside the old lady's stuffy darkened bedchamber.

Although it was a bright summer day, a coal fire burned determinedly in the great serpentine fireplace and all the windows were closed. There was a sickly combined smell of stale flesh, a potent earthy perfume, and dogs. Cosmo and Hartley had just been taken outside by Jayna Hayes, but it was plain they had performed many a 'naughty-naughty', as Lady Portia called their constant marking of furniture legs. Kelynen took a long, bracing sniff at the posy of flowers she carried.

'Come closer, child. I can't see a bit of you.' If Lady Portia's voice had been a pen it would have made a wobbly scrawl all over the paper.

Kelynen went to the bed – a box-shaped affair, hung with brocaded curtains that had perhaps once been a dark purple – which looked older than its incumbent. Struck frail in bereavement, Lady Portia, propped up by a jumble of pillows, in her nightgown, a fluffy wool shawl and sleeping cap, was like an ugly, wrinkled, shrinking child. 'I've brought these roses for you,' said Kelynen.

'What? Find me my spectacles, girl. Can't see a damned thing! I'm sure I'm going blind.'

'You'd feel stronger, milady, if you ate a little more.' Kelynen located the spectacles and placed them on Lady Portia's long nose.

'How you do like to see people filled up with food. Should

190

follow your own advice! Roses, you say? Hold them up. Let me see. Oh, how pretty. How sweet of you. You've even put ribbons round them. You look rather pretty yourself. Why?' Kelynen received a shaky, accusing pointed finger. 'Is something going on? Not stopped grieving for Rafe already, have you? I thought there was a growing attraction between you. Fine little wife you'd have made him if he'd had the sense to see it, instead of playing reckless games and getting himself killed.'

'There was an attraction between us, milady, much more than that.' Kelynen would never hide the truth about whom she had loved. 'I'll never stop grieving for Rafe. I'm wearing the gown I was to have worn at my brother's wedding, and also my mother's bridal veil. I married Gabriel a short while ago. The roses I carried in the chapel.'

Lady Portia stared at her. Her baggy eyes flickered and closed, as if her brain was clicking over what she had heard and was trying to understand it. 'Yes. I remember now. Hold my hand, Kelynen.' Kelynen put the posy down, sat on the bed and did as she was bid. 'Can't tell you, m'dear, how pleased I am to have you permanently in the house. You've wed quick because you're with child, I remember you telling me that too. It's Rafe child, I suppose?'

Kelynen nodded. 'I'm glad it's Rafe's. I'm not ashamed.'

Lady Portia chuckled and seemed more her usual feisty self. 'Of course you shouldn't be ashamed! Any woman should be proud to conceive a Tremayne brat. Rafe would have been tickled. If it's a male child it might have tamed him at last. A worthy wife you'd have made him, but Gabriel will make a better father. I like Gabriel. He's a strange boy though, a bit too quiet. He won't be fun like Rafe was.' Now she was spilling tears. 'Oh! How I shall miss bickering with Rafe. We quarrelled nearly every day, but really I adored him. I know Rafe loved me. He loved everyone. But Gabriel will bring stability to Chenhalls. At my age I'll be grateful for that. And you, little bud, you'll bring so much more. Chenhalls likes you. It needs you. I need you.'

'I'll always ensure you're well cared for, Lady Portia. I don't want you to worry about anything.'

'You must call me aunt from now on.' Lady Portia suddenly sat up and muttered in a hushed, almost nervous tone. 'I want you to take a word of warning. Watch out for Josiah. Rafe doted on him, but I find him a loathsome toad. He's a wastrel, a whoremonger, not worthy of the Tremayne name. His charm hides a rotten soul. Now, you've endured enough of an old woman's prattling. I take it your family is here. Go down to them, make the most of your wedding day, Kelynen, which has united two great ancient families.'

Lady Portia had given Kelynen much to think about. She was pleased at some of the things she had heard, delighted at others – concerned too – but pushed it all aside for now, including Josiah's noticeable resentment of her marriage – he was shunning the quiet reception in the banqueting hall. She rejoined her husband and their guests.

Disappointed and angry though they were over Sir Rafe's seduction of their daughter and her pregnancy, Oliver and Kerensa had been persuaded that marriage to Gabriel was preferable to her locking herself and her child away in shame. They watched their younger daughter wend her way smilingly through the guests, mainly Pengarrons and Lanyons, including the children, to her bridegroom. Their new son-in-law, stationed in front of the fireplace, smiled down at Kelynen and she smiled up at him.

'Thank God the time she spent nursing him bred a mutual affection,' Oliver said drily. He was finding this day hard, losing his favourite child so suddenly. If Rafe Tremayne were not already dead he would have wished it on him – would have given him a thrashing at least.

'I wish she had never met Sir Rafe, and certainly that she was not having his baby,' Kerensa replied. 'But it's not

192

entirely a bad thing. It's kept Gabriel here. I doubt she would've married another and would've spent her life mourning her loss. Kelynen is determined to make the best of the situation.'

'I only pray she will be happy, but I fear she's ruined her life.'

'There's a chance she'll find happiness, Oliver. We did and who'd have once thought it?'

Oliver, always free in giving public affection to Kerensa, lifted her hand and kissed it warmly. 'Let's hope they don't suffer as many rough patches as we did at the beginning.'

Luke was quiet, drinking little, and as soon as he got the chance he ushered Kelynen aside to talk to her privately. 'I feel responsible for this. I should never have agreed to you staying here. Gabriel's a good fellow but can you possibly be content with him?'

Kelynen glanced at Gabriel. He was talking to Kane, whom he had not met before. She felt warmed. Gabriel was finding so many people and the bustle and noise a strain, but he was genuinely interested in all of his new in-laws. 'I'm certain I shall be as content as anyone can be in my situation, Luke. I even consider fate has been kind to me. Now do not blame yourself for anything that has happened to me. Father blamed himself, you know, and I have put him right. I take full responsibility, and happily so, for the life of my baby. You and I and our spouses must get together often. We must not allow our new concerns to let us drift apart. Sophie looks beautiful.' And she did, dressed richly, her pearl-blonde hair immaculately styled under a wide feathered hat. She shone, she floated, and she brightened the house that had been so recently plunged into the depths of gloom. 'You are a fortunate man.'

'Thank you, Sister dear. I must say, your attitude cheers me.' He signalled to a footman carrying a tray of wine and took two glasses for himself, unaware of Sophie's disapproving gaze.

'It's a pity you didn't bring young Betty with you,' Jessica suddenly boomed close to Sophie's ear. 'I was so looking forward to seeing her.'

Offended by the approach, which she saw as a piece of common behaviour from this lowly farmer's daughter, Sophie retorted, 'Elizabeth fares well. She is settling into her new nursery. I was not about to distress her with an unnecessary journey and a stay overnight in a strange place.' Her eyes shot to her five-year-old brother-in-law, Samuel Pengarron, who was tearing about unchecked with his dark-skinned toddling cousin, Tamara Drannock; obviously the child's mother was a native of some kind. Thank goodness that Kelynen, who had made many a friendly overture to her today, had married an equal. Lady Pengarron, beautiful and agreeable though she may be, was formerly of the lower orders. The Pengarrons were in danger of becoming a mongrel breed.

Oliver had noticed the tension between his two daughters-in-law, and their differences. He bent his great dark head to Kerensa. 'It was a shame Luke couldn't have found someone delightful like Jessica, or someone kinder like Gabriel.'

'You think Sophie unkind, darling?'

'She's definitely lacking in something.' Indeed, Oliver felt that out of his two children most recently married, Kelynen had the greater chance of happiness. At least he could take comfort from the new loving manner between Livvy and Timothy.

The day ended with a short concert given by Gabriel in the music room. He played light soothing music on the violin, cello and spinet, avoiding anything lively, for it would have been out of place while the house still mourned, or anything sad, because he did not want to create a morbid atmosphere. This set, as he intended, a sleepy, relaxed tone and the guests made their way light-heartedly early to their beds. He and Kelynen disallowed the tradition of the bride and groom being escorted first up to the marriage chamber, and finally they were alone. A hush settled over the music room.

'Are you tired?' he asked, settling next to her in the front row of chairs, where she had sat between her parents.

'I am, a little. Are you?'

'Not tired, but relieved to find peace. Kelynen, you are used to having many people around you and I am used to privacy. Before we arrive at any problems, could we agree to compromise?'

Kelynen found herself smiling at him. 'Well, I could only see my family at the manor and you could spend most of each day in the tower.'

He returned the smile and lifted her hand. 'I didn't mean quite such extremes, my dear love. When we socialize, if I am allowed a quiet corner that will do me well. I like your family. I should not want you to cut yourself off from them. They must come here any time they choose and not wait for an invitation.'

'You are good to me, Gabriel.'

'And you to me. We shall be good companions, Kelynen. It's the first time in my life I've desired to have one. Shall we go up? The servants are waiting to retire.'

They climbed the stairs hand in hand to the master bedchamber, where Jacob Glynn, and Kelynen's new maid, Hettie Hayes, a cousin of Jayna's, had moved all their things. Kelynen was going to miss Ruth King, but it would have been unfair to deprive her of the manor, her home for over thirty years, and the closeness of her family at Perranbarvah. Sorrowful that soon she would be sleeping in Rafe's bed, but not with Rafe, Kelynen tried desperately not to think about it.

Gabriel too was finding this strange and awkward. He sought an everyday subject. 'I know you rise early for Rex. Would you mind if I continue to breakfast in my room – well, our room?'

195

'Of course I won't. Let us agree that we will not change our usual routines.'

On the first floor, past the picture gallery, they arrived at a pair of decorated double doors. Jacob and Hettie, who favoured Jayna in competent, ruddy looks, were stationed either side, wearing suitably nondescript faces. They opened the doors and the couple stepped inside. The confines were three times larger than any other Chenhalls bedroom, and much more lavish. Rafe had tried to coax her into this room, telling her of the great four-poster bed that took dominance, of how much he wanted to make love to her on it, but she had refused, fearing Ruth would soon know of the indiscretion. Part of her was sorry she'd had no previous contact with the opulent, rambling, exotically draped monster, but part of her was glad she had not, for the memories would have been too painful. Couches and chaise longues abounded on the deep, golden-red Turkish carpet – so many places where passion and love could have flowed unchecked. The ornamentation rivalled that of a cathedral's, all in gold gilt. All ostentatious and rather awful, Kelynen thought at a second gaze.

She allowed Hettie to take her to her new dressing room. Kelynen had given no thought to wedding-night clothes, but her mother had. She returned to the chamber wearing sinuous white silk. Gabriel was there, in a brocaded dressing gown. His pale blond hair was lying newly brushed on his shoulders. How different to Rafe he was, his near starvation taking away any broadness of build he might have had. While Rafe's eyes had leapt with merriment and wickedness, Gabriel's were quiet and kind. Beatrice had, years ago, counselled her and Livvy about men. 'A maid shouldn't trouble herself for looks or wealth in a husband. Marry thee a kind man and ye'll never know a moment of foreboding, my handsomes.' No one could ever fear Gabriel or dislike him.

He came forward with a glass of champagne in each

hand. Kelynen had observed that he often enjoyed more than a fair amount of spirits, but he had kept restraint today. The few times she had thought him noisy was when laughing, intoxicated, in Jacob's company. 'I feel we ought to share a toast, but to what?'

Kelynen took a glass and considered. To toast their future together seemed out of place – theirs was a marriage of convenience. There was no point in toasting Chenhalls, as Gabriel hated it and it was, in truth, a tragic place for the Tremaynes. Rafe was the latest to have met a tragic end on its land. Kelynen shivered, suddenly fearful for her baby. Perhaps she should get away from here – past events decreed the child was unlikely to thrive here. No! Even if there were a curse of some sort she would change that. The human spirit was stronger than superstition. And Gabriel had broken the curse. He had nearly died here but had survived. Soon he would be at his strongest, and in the sultry glow of the candlelight she saw his good looks. And she saw that he was desirable – desirable enough to have made a beautiful, headstrong Austrian cling on to him.

Gabriel broke into her silence by gently touching her face. 'Let's toast the baby. Wish it well. Ask God to bless it.'

Suddenly emotional, she could only nod.

He clinked his glass against hers. 'To the new life growing inside you. My cousin, who is now to be my child, and to you, Kelynen.'

After the first sip, Kelynen said, 'And to you, Gabriel.'

They discarded their dressing gowns, snuffed out the candles, except for one on Gabriel's bedside, and got into the ridiculous bed. Kelynen lay still, waiting for Gabriel to make his first move at consummating their union. It was his right. She would not deny him that. And she did not mind too much. She trusted him to be considerate. Propped up on his arm, he gazed down on her. He stroked her face and whispered, 'You are tired. Go to sleep.' He blew out the last light.

Grateful for his sensitivity, she said goodnight and turned away, able now to settle her thoughts on Rafe, and how it should be he at her side. She wept silent tears long into the night. When Gabriel put his arm lightly over her, for no other reason than to give her comfort, she clasped hold of his hand.

Twenty-Three

Encouraged by Sophie, Luke had returned to writing his play and he was also newly inspired by Gabriel's promise to score some accompanying music.

'This new departure could prove greatly successful for both of us,' Luke said over the supper table one night to Sophie at Polgissey. Eager to show Sophie that she took priority in his life he was careful not to get carried away as of old, when he had written endlessly, missed meals, and had often not bothered to retire to bed. Nowadays he was always eager for bedtime. He couldn't have enough of Sophie's fragrant, tender body.

'Respectable landed gentlemen who are gifted at the arts make for a fascinating combination,' Sophie said from the other end of the table. 'You and Sir Gabriel are already greatly admired locally.' While not wishing her father-in-law, of whom she was in awe, the end of his life, she was looking forward to the day when Luke would inherit his title and she would become Lady Pengarron. She would not wear her title with the disregard that Kelynen did hers. 'Did you finish the final scene in Act Four today, dear?'

'Not quite.' Luke smiled. He loved Sophie all the more for being interested in what a lot of wives would see as an unnecessary pastime, and who would urge him only into stretching his wealth by expanding his business interests.

'You must apply yourself or Gabriel will be ahead of you again. How quickly music comes to him. How exciting, that now His Majesty has heard of his presence in the country

199

he has invited him to perform at Court again. Perhaps one day we shall be given the chance to accompany him.'

'Yes, my beloved. I would like to show you around all the meet places of the capital. Mind you, it will be a hard task to get Gabriel to go up to London; at present he is pleading his bereavement to keep him quietly at Chenhalls.'

'But he will have to go eventually. One cannot ignore a command from the King. Fortunate for Kelynen, to be presented to Royalty.' Sophie tried to sound offhand. 'But then she too probably doesn't welcome the honour in the same way as most people would.'

Luke looked at her curiously. He had not forgotten she was much given to sarcasm, and could be blunt and even cruel, but it was something of a surprise to realize that Sophie harboured jealousies. Before, she had always pleaded contentment with her humble life. His joy at securing her meant he would do anything to please her. 'When Kelynen and Gabriel finally do go to London, likely now not until after the child is delivered, we shall journey up with them. My connection to Gabriel should ensure us a visit at Court.'

Placated, Sophie brightened. 'I shall look forward to it.'

'And I'm looking forward to having you to myself after this.' He gave her an enduring smile.

Sophie smiled back graciously and then hid a maddened expression behind her wine glass. Polgissey was on the opposite coast of Cornwall to Mount's Bay – the wilder, rugged North Cliffs. She wished Luke up in the tower room, his study, which overlooked the surging Atlantic Ocean. When not at a distance of more than a few inches from her, he was altogether too attentive, touching her and kissing her, plying her with endearments. Then as soon as they were ready for bed he sought to perform the act of love, although she could never think of it as such. It was a ludicrous procedure that was uncomfortable and embarrassing. She found it impossible to believe women actually enjoyed it. How could Kelynen have allowed Sir Rafe to seduce her, to become with child by him? Sophie was horrified both at Kelynen's joyful anticipation of the birth of her bastard child and Gabriel's calm acceptance of it. Kelynen was little better than Adelaide in that respect. Neither had any shame.

'Oh, I'd nearly forgotten. I've invited Mr and Mrs Rosevear to join us after our repast, to play cards,' Sophie said. She did not approve of Luke's steward, one of his closest friends and a former Pengarron groom, and his wife, a squire's daughter who had once been the mistress of a young lord who had been sordidly murdered, but their presence would stave off Luke's pawing for an hour or two.

'I'm pleased you care for Jack and Alicia,' Luke said, eating the last morsel of plum pudding before reaching for the port. He ignored Sophie's frown. Sometimes she complained of alcohol on his breath but he was careful not to overindulge. He missed, however, the fun of getting riotously drunk.

'I like to compare notes with Mrs Rosevear on Elizabeth's and her child Mary Caroline's progress.'

'Mary Caroline is three years the older but the girls should grow up as good friends. Jack is disappointed there have been no more children as of yet. I hope we shall soon be able to give the news that we're expecting a happy event, beloved.' He gazed at her over a full measure of port, with half lowered eyes.

Sophie hated that look, which spoke of his intention of making another assault on her to further his desire for an heir. She wished she were pregnant. It would help in her excuses to deny Luke his pleasure. 'I wish with all my heart that blessing will not be far off.'

She kept on with the cards as late as possible, and after the Rosevears had left she picked up her embroidery – anything to keep Luke at bay.

From behind her chair in the parlour, Luke massaged her shoulders. 'D'you know I'd never have taken you for a

201

night body. Are you not tired though? You seem to be tense.'

Sophie tossed aside the petticoat she was making for Elizabeth, trying not to show her irritation, her disgust. Luke, apart from his energies in the bedchamber, was good to her, showering her with devotion, and she would never forget how much she owed him.

While Luke waited, naked, in bed for her, she brushed her hair and then applied lavender-rich salve, a speciality of Beatrice's, to her hands. She could see Luke's reflection, watching her, anticipating her. She imagined him licking his lips as if he were a cat about to get yet another large helping of cream. Why did he want sex so often? It was every night that she was not indisposed. Kelynen did not get the curse now she was with child, but on the two occasions she and Gabriel had stayed overnight in the next room there had been no sounds of disturbance on the mattresses. If only she could gain the courage to ask Kelynen to have a word with her brother, to implore him to be as thoughtful a husband as Gabriel seemed to be. Sophie was reminded of how the Bible said that Joseph knew not the Virgin Mary until after the Lord's birth. How fortunate for Kelynen if she was sharing the same consideration.

Patient in his waiting, Luke's thoughts turned to his sister. Kelynen's life seemed to be working out better than anyone had imagined. Once a week she rode over to Pengarron Manor to spend the day there, and sometimes Gabriel went with her. Once a week she and Gabriel together called either at Polgissey, or at Vellanoweth to see Kane and Jessica, or to dine with Livvy and Timothy. Lady Portia doted on Kelynen, and had gained sufficient strength and energy under her care to allow Livvy to be halfway through her portrait. Sometimes Luke and Sophie and other members of the family visited Chenhalls. For the time being, Kelynen was shunning a social life and this suited Gabriel. As far as Luke could see, it was a time of unusual peace and harmony for all the Pengarrons. It amused and satisfied him, however, that when he had children of his own, he'd have a lot of exciting and perilous tales – not least about his own youthful exploits – to tell about the family, its history stretching back to the French aristocrat who had come across the Channel with William I.

His stiff arm suddenly began to trouble him. 'Come and ease this for me please, darling,' he said, knowing Sophie had witnessed his discomfort in the mirror.

She delayed another full minute before coming towards him. 'Turn to the side then.' From behind him, she began a forceful manipulation of his shoulder.

'Ow! Pray, be careful, Sophie. You are no good at relieving my pain.'

'I've told you this often enough, Luke. I have not the touch for this sort of thing.' Suddenly she was appalled with herself, for she had been tempted to hurt him so he would have had to leave the room and resort to Elgan's ministrations. She gentled her massage. She braced herself for what would happen soon. He would turn to her and bring her into the bed and start the kissing and fondling, asking her what she liked, telling her that he wanted only to please her. She should not have let herself show enthusiasm that day in his mother's sitting room or allowed him to be free with her body. She had immediately made it plain that there would be no more impure happenings before their wedding night, but Luke, virile man that he was, had thought she had enjoyed it. She had, but only for a moment, before a sick, ashamed feeling had taken over. Now she was too good at fooling him that she enjoyed full conjugal rights.

Minutes later, Luke took her by surprise by stopping. 'Are you tired, darling? Are you not well?'

She opened her tightly closed eyes and saw him staring down on her. 'Well, I . . .'

She was pleased to have been given the opportunity of

making an excuse, until he exclaimed, 'Lordsakes, you are grimacing. Was I hurting you?'

'No. Of course you weren't, Luke.' She gently pulled on his long black hair, hoping it would pass as a gesture of loving.

Luke lay down on his back. In an instant some of his happiness drained away. Sophie was not the most affectionate of women, she never made the initial move towards intimacy, but he had considered this to be natural shyness. He had stayed too deep in his delight at discovering, as he had hoped after Lady Portia's insensitive declaration, that he had indeed married a virgin. Thinking back now over their numerous couplings, an awful suspicion niggled at him. 'You don't hate being with me, do you?'

'Please don't think that, my dear.' She forced herself to reach out a hand and drop it on his chest, which was still hot and heaving from his exercise. 'I am tired, I swear. I've been very busy today and I was foolish to have stayed up so late.'

He thought this through. Since they had moved here Sophie had worked tirelessly putting her own mark on Polgissey. Every room had new fabrics or frescos or furnishings, all influenced by the Italian villa style. She had commissioned paintings – not from Livvy, not liking her carefree style – of horses and hunting and heroes of ancient Rome. He was pleased that his home showed modern flair, but he was not reassured that she welcomed his approaches. 'You would tell me if anything was wrong? If I . . . if I did anything you didn't like. It's important to me that you are perfectly content.'

There would never be a more ideal time to ask him for less frequent intimacy, but they had only been married a few weeks and it was commonplace, so she understood, for a young couple to resort to their bedchamber often. Glancing at his expression, already steeped in hurt and rejection, she was afraid to risk killing off his feelings for her. He might grow distant and then resort to a mistress and she would hate that. If only Wilmot Carew hadn't tried that one time to . . . Then perhaps she wouldn't find the whole thing so disgusting.

She turned on her side and pressed herself in tight against him. She stroked his face and kissed his mouth. 'I'm sorry, darling Luke. Forgive me. I'll ensure that I never allow myself to get so weary in future. Living alone for so many months I got into the habit of filling every hour with activity so I wouldn't feel lonely and to help me sleep. I love you and I do enjoy being a wife to you.'

Her enthusiasm made his heart bounce with joy. She had not mentioned before that she loved him. She had not taken off her nightgown before, indeed had almost clung to it, but now she was untying the ribbons down its front, exposing a beautiful, smooth marble-white shoulder and more. He kissed her there. She kissed his throat, his face and his neck. His desire returned, greatly intensified. Always she had lain beneath him, warding off anything different. Tentatively he tried joining them together as they lay. She did not object and he went ahead and enjoyed several moments of slow easy union. Luke kept everything gentle and broke off for a while before going on to a climax.

He pulled her nightgown up to cover her body and held her a while, before telling her one last time he loved her. Then he retreated at a distance, feeling she would appreciate the space.

Sophie did. And she lay thinking that hopefully he would not bother her so often now. But nonetheless she was capable of ruthlessly pursuing and enduring anything to ensure her security.

With Gabriel and Lady Portia being late risers, and Josiah shunning her company, Kelynen always ate alone in the breakfast room at Chenhalls. She did not mind this. It enabled her to imagine Rafe was with her. Sometimes she spoke to him in her mind and talked about their baby, suggesting names and the possibilities of its future.

Its adoptive father is to be presented to the King, Rafe. Aren't you proud? Of course, Gabriel would rather not go, but I'll be there to encourage him. He'll make us both proud. He's good to me, such a comfort, and do you know, I believe he has some of your slightly wicked humour. I hope the baby has all of yours and Gabriel's good qualities.

After walking with Rex, she would then most days hold a short conference with the chef and housekeeper, Mrs Barton, to agree on menus and plan the smooth running of the house. She found it also fell to her to talk to the head gardener, the head groom and to sort out just about everything else concerning Chenhalls. She had thought Gabriel might start showing some interest in his inheritance, but he, having been assured by Jacob that his uncle had allowed Josiah and his loyal and efficient staff to run the household, was content to let the arrangements rest. He ensured he was with Kelynen for some hours each day. He strolled with her, rode with her, played music to her, and the rest of the time he shut himself away to compose for Luke's play and an anthem for his audience with the King. He confided that while he was always keen to perform in public, it was the socializing before and afterwards he hated.

He had looked at her from under his fair brows. 'I suppose you'll want to take a look about the city?'

She had smiled back teasingly. 'I can hardly wait. I shall order my dressmaker to prepare a whole new wardrobe. I want to attend every ball, visit every theatre and historic building. It's fashionable to view the prisons and asylums, and we might get the chance of many a public hanging.'

Gabriel had paced the banqueting hall, his head down, hands gripped behind his back. He had given a downcast, questioning look. 'My dear, you are joking?'

Finding his horror amusing, she had playfully tossed a cushion at him. 'Dolt! Of course I was exaggerating. But it won't hurt you to attend a few of the quieter occasions. There's no point in being in London without taking advantage of some its delights.'

Gabriel had caught the cushion with an element of shock and surprise. Puzzled at first, he finally let out a loud laugh. 'I'm not used to such behaviour from another. I've not had brothers and sisters to grow up with, to spar with and share entertainments. I suppose a large family has its advantages. Do you miss yours?'

'Sometimes. I couldn't imagine the lonely life you must have led.'

'There you are wrong.' Looking into her eyes, he had reached out and touched her ear lobe with his fingertips, something he did often, a simple act of affection she liked him to do. 'Not ever having had much company, I don't miss it. I never feel lonely.'

'You must have felt lonely after Caterina died.' She had straightened his neckcloth. He had the habit of loosening it and it always ended up twisted to the side.

'That was different to craving for just anyone to be there.'

'I suppose it was.'

He had then suggested they sit with his aunt in the summer house, always ensuring he gave Lady Portia at least a few minutes of his time each day. Kelynen had agreed, and it wasn't until much later that she realized it was the first morning she had not gone to Rafe's resting place.

And so, as she started on the long, often crushing journey of coming to terms with losing Rafe, the days spun along with reasonable ease, until the afternoon she clashed with Josiah.

She was passing the library, the only room Josiah entered for any length of time on the few occasions he was at Chenhalls. One of the double doors was ajar and she reached out to close it, but something made her want to enter the room, which was kept darkened in the daytime to protect the priceless collections of books and artefacts. Rex grumbled, demanding the walk he was about to be taken on, but Kelynen dragged him inside by the collar. 'Shh. This will only delay us a minute or two. I want to take a look around.'

So close was she to her dog she fancied she knew his thoughts, and as if he had asked the question 'Why?' she said, 'I don't know. As mistress of this house it's my duty to ensure everything is in order in all of the rooms.'

Her eyes shot straightway to the heavy desk at the foot of the stairs. It was in disarray. The drawers were pulled open with papers scattered about and stacked on chairs. Was this how Josiah left things now his uncle was not here? She thought not. Josiah was too meticulous in all his habits. And Mrs Barton always pointed out any disturbance in the rooms; she would have mentioned it if the library was given over to ill use. So Josiah had been here recently. Probably last evening when she and Gabriel had been occupied in the music room. She was pleased he had sold his house, ready for his proposed plan to move away, and spent most of his time at temporary lodgings in Marazion.

Rex grew restless so she pulled aside a curtain and opened one of the long windows to allow him to jump outside.

She spied a set of small brass keys, presumably to the desk drawers, on top of some documents and picked them up, then lifted the documents and began to read them. They concerned the Wheal Lowen mine, the dates going back two and three years. Everything seemed straightforward. She had an invoice book in her hands when she was startled by a sudden loud voice. 'You are trespassing here, Lady Tremayne.'

She was facing the doors so Josiah must have climbed in through the window. 'I'm tidying up, Josiah,' she replied lightly, as if she did not care for his opinion or his hostility.

He reached her quickly, pulled the invoice book away

from her and closed it. 'I will do that. You need not concern yourself with anything in here.'

Kelynen would not be turned out. She stared at him, cool, uncompromising.

The handsome dark eyes of Josiah glittered inside constricted lids. 'I'm sure you have some sewing or something similar to attend to.'

She ignored his derision. She didn't trust Josiah in any regard and chose her next words carefully, watching him. 'It's time Gabriel showed an interest in the business affairs of the estate, especially the Wheal Lowen. It isn't fair to allow you to continue with the burden alone.' For several long moments he stared at her and she knew he neither liked nor respected her. A primitive unease caught at her gut. Josiah might seem weak and even pathetic at times, and he often whined like a spoiled child – a lost child now there was no doting uncle to indulge him – but now she recognized there was something even more negative than Aunt Portia's opinion of him, something strongly insidious and deep-rooted, and perhaps even dangerous.

'My brother and I have spoken about the estate. It is his wish that I maintain sole charge. Ma'am, I will have you know that I am moving out of Chenhalls for good. Hence,' he motioned at the strewn papers, 'I'm about to remove what I need to take with me. If you'll excuse me, I'm too busy to linger and talk. A servant will be here shortly to carry out the things to the carriage.'

'I wish you well, Josiah,' she said without sincerity.

'And I wish Gabriel and your good self a successful marriage. It's what my uncle would have wished.' He was now pure sarcasm. 'A contented environment for his child.'

'You can be assured that is precisely what his child will have,' Kelynen replied, unruffled. 'Sir Rafe would have been proud to know his greatest wish will come to pass, that a child of his will one day inherit Chenhalls.'

Josiah leaned unacceptably close to her. 'I'm not sure

that my uncle intended to keep Chenhalls. As for Gabriel, he may feel happy to acknowledge another's child, but he may feel differently when you produce a brat of his own one day.'

'Whatever Sir Rafe may have intended, Gabriel has already decreed that the child I am carrying will remain heir to the estate.' Kelynen stood her ground. She would not allow this insufferable man to unnerve her. However, there was much she wanted to say to Gabriel about this disagreeable encounter.

Jacob Glynn helped Gabriel along to the master bedchamber, although anyone witnessing their unsteady passage, their chuckling and shushing, would have decided that the valet was the more intoxicated of the two.

'I'd no idea my uncle kept such a splendid wine cellar, leaving aside its smuggled contents,' Gabriel explained to Kelynen when he finally lurched up to the bed.

'Is that where you've been all evening?' She glanced up from the novel she was reading. 'Did you not receive my message? I wished to speak with you.'

Holding on to a bedpost, he chewed his lower lip. 'I think I did. Yes, your maid sought us out, didn't she? Jacob took the message. I don't think he quite understood what she said. My apologies, forgive me. Wasn't anything urgent, I hope.'

'I have concerns about Josiah, but they can wait until tomorrow when you have a clearer head.' Climbing across the bed and getting out on Gabriel's side, Kelynen held out her hand to him. 'Come along.'

He grinned. He was always incorrigible when he had taken too much drink. 'Trouble yourself not, my dear love. I c–can manage.'

'You are slipping to the floor.'

'I am?' He crumpled in a heap and lay on the thick carpet, laughing. When she reached him, he used the bedcovers to haul himself to sit up and then wound his arms around her legs. 'I love the way you never get angry with me. Caterina would have bawled my head off for this. She probably would have kicked me and declared if I fell and broke my neck it would have served me right.'

Kelynen found it hard to understand how he could have loved the dead woman so much. She lowered herself down to him. 'Was she different at the beginning?'

'No. I was always aware of her violent temper. People warned me about her. She had destroyed many a poor man's heart. But she fascinated me, as she had done all the others. She was ten years older than me, you know. I was lost the instant I saw her. I was drawn to her sophistication and her wiles.'

After she had helped him take off his dressing gown and get into bed, his head resting sleepily against the pillows, she found herself curious. 'Do you find me lacklustre in comparison to her?'

He snapped his eyes open. 'Good heavens, no! You're refreshing and stimulating, and the very best of company. I'm writing some of my best music now because of you. I'm confident Luke will be pleased with what I've created to complement his play, and also that the King will approve of the anthem I've written for him.'

Kelynen was surprised at how much it mattered to her that Gabriel thought highly of her. Each day she felt she was growing closer to him, could delve a little deeper into his mysteries. 'Why did you and Caterina not marry?'

'I would have married her in an instant but she hated the thought of being tied to one person. She would have thrown me over eventually.' Energized now, he sat up and looked down on her. 'I think I like being married to you. It was a good thing we were friends first, each respecting the other's needs.'

'We do have a connection,' she said. Her forgotten book fell to the floor. She bent over the bed, picked it up and placed it on the bedside cabinet. When she turned back, Gabriel had moved in close. She thought back to the time when she had edged away from him, repulsed by his appearance. There was nothing in his fine pale looks to make her want to do so now. She did not mind being close to him. Every night she found comfort in his nearness. Throughout every day she reassured herself he wasn't far away.

'Yes, I agree, Kelynen.' He was gazing directly into eyes.

Kelynen gazed steadily back. She could smell the rum on his breath but it wasn't offensive. Nothing about him was. There was everything to like. She had often marvelled how fate had kept him waiting in the background to save her from disgrace, to provide her with everything she could need. She owed him much and was willing to give him much. He was her husband and had the right to her body. One day he would choose to seek that right, and she did not find the thought in any way daunting.

Gabriel put a hand through her hair, combing it tenderly with his fingers. His eyes were on her mouth. He swallowed. He wanted her. Curled up close to her every night, he had wanted her for some time. Trying to judge when the time was right for her. It had to be before the child made her big and cumbersome. But was it too soon? He'd hate to offend her, to lose the respect of this dear, lovely young woman who had saved his life. Made his life worth living. Kelynen did not need any sort of observances played out to her. He could ask her outright. He just needed the courage.

'Can I be with you?' he whispered.

A short time ago it would have been unthinkable, giving herself to another man. But she nodded.

'Please don't feel pressured into agreeing,' he said. 'Don't let it be something you just want to get over – the first time with me.'

He looked at her in a way that declared how high his hopes were that she wouldn't accept the way out he'd offered her. She couldn't speak, but, as if they had a will of their own, her hands reached up to his face, and she closed her eyes and tilted her lips to his.

Gabriel put his hands gently behind her head and the next instant he was kissing her. He was making love to her and she was returning the love, and the pleasure and the passion that rose so naturally in them, with such intensity and durability, was a shock to them both.

Twenty-Four

'I s something wrong?'
'Pardon?'
'Kelynen, you've been distracted all the way through the meal,' Livvy said. The sisters were sharing a quiet luncheon at one end of the banqueting table. Another place had been set for Sophie, but she was unusually late. 'Are you hating being with child? You're fortunate you haven't spread like a mass of blubber as I did both times, and have so far kept an undistorted figure. You are content still with Gabriel?'

'I've hardly noticed my condition and I'm very content with Gabriel.'

Her expression like a hound on a scent, Livvy prevented Kelynen putting a forkful of veal into her mouth by grabbing her arm. 'There was a lot of emphasis on that last remark. You're fond of him, of course. How fond?'

To her annoyance, Kelynen couldn't hold a non-committal gaze and reddened as she brushed off Livvy's hand. She put the fork down, knowing she would choke if she tried to eat.

'So that's it!'
'What?'
'You and he have come together in bed.'
'Livvy!'
'Don't pretend to be coy. Or worried that your servants might overhear. There are none here at present and you can hear an approach on the stone floors. Besides, one might

as well allow servants into the bedchamber – no secret can ever be kept from them.'

'You are greatly changed since you and Timothy have been successful in intimacy,' Kelynen chided.

Livvy giggled wantonly. 'I know you're pleased for me. I only wish I'd discovered the joys of the act of love much earlier. Well? Is the pale and enigmatic Gabriel Tremayne a delight or a bother to you? Has he the strength and vigour to please you?'

'Livvy! You go too far.'

At last Livvy was chastened. 'I'm sorry. He's much different in physique and manner to Rafe. Forgive me for being indelicate.'

Kelynen was quiet for a while. She pushed her plate away. Livvy resumed eating. She ate well now she was happy in her marriage. Gradually the sisters' eyes met. They had always confided a good deal in each other. Kelynen needed someone to talk to and she felt she couldn't mention this to her mother. Livvy finished her wine, knowing she was about to hear something delicately confidential, and she applied a suitable discreet expression. 'What is it? You know it will remain locked in my head forever.'

Kelynen sipped from her water glass and cleared her throat. She glanced at all the doors. 'You've guessed correctly. Gabriel and I are now fully man and wife. He's gentle and understanding, but also . . . what I'm trying to say is . . . well, I was quite prepared to do my duty, but . . . I find it quite alarming that I enjoyed it so much with him.'

Livvy's head was bent close to hers. 'I'm pleased for you. Why are you alarmed? He had a lover. He's probably known several women in that way. It would be awful to face a lifetime of being unfulfilled in marital relations, don't you think?'

'Yes, I suppose so, but . . .' Tears brimming behind Kelynen's eyes began to flow and she left them unchecked.

Livvy got up and hugged her. 'But what, beloved?'

'It's made me feel disloyal to Rafe,' she sobbed. 'If it had been awful, or something to endure, I'd see it as a necessary act in gaining a kind father and rightful position for Rafe's baby. But I didn't mind at all, Livvy, and I found myself a willing participant. Since then I can hardly bring myself to look at Gabriel. He's been quieter than usual. Either I've troubled him or he's feeling the same as I am, in concern of Caterina. Oh, Livvy, I'm so unhappy.'

Livvy laid her head on top of Kelynen's. 'Don't distress yourself. What you and Gabriel need to do is to give each other a little time and then talk about your feelings.'

Livvy got the horrid, cold feeling of being watched by hostile eyes. She glanced up and saw Sophie in the doorway. No one in the family liked this cool, detached woman, whose rapid social climb had turned her into an insufferable grande dame. Sophie stayed put and stared, and Livvy grew angrier by the second. Didn't she realize she was intruding on moments that should be private? Was she insensitive or uncaring? Or both!

'Kelynen, my dear.' Sophie stepped quickly towards her. 'Can I send for someone?'

Livvy shushed her sister-in-law with an impatient flick of her hand. Offended, Sophie turned and marched back outside. Her arrival here had been delayed by an attack of queasy stomach. Hating to be unpunctual, she had fretted at first. Then, wondering if this was a sign that her hopes of giving Luke an heir were to be realized, she had made the journey here in a state of anticipation at sharing the news. Her intention had been spitefully ruined. She was aware that she was not accepted as readily by the superior Pengarrons as Sir Gabriel was, but then she did not have land or a title. She was a lowly widow, with an illegitimate niece to rear. Who did this upstart family think they were? They had far more scandal in their history. Not just a single skeleton in a cupboard, but a whole cryptful of them! One of Sir Rafe's cats pressed itself against her skirt and mewed for attention. She kicked it, sending it squealing across the cobbles of the court.

'I've always felt the same about those loathsome creatures.' It was Josiah Tremayne who had witnessed her cruelty.

'This house is full of such!'

Josiah advanced so quickly it took her by surprise. She shrieked as he pinned her against the arched door. 'I take it I am included in that observation. How is my little girl, Mrs Pengarron?'

Sophie struggled but he was too powerful. He squeezed her arms, hurting her. His strong cologne filled her nostrils, as did the uncommon sweetness of his breath. She felt herself weakening, growing dizzy, but clung on to her determination to protect her niece. 'Are you interested in Elizabeth?'

'I wish the little bitch the same fate as her mother.'

'Get your hands off me!'

'With pleasure.' He let her go abruptly. Dazed and nauseous, Sophie fell to the doorstep. Josiah bent and hissed in her ear. 'I'm sure Luke Pengarron doesn't get the same pleasure out of you as I did from your whore of a sister. You and he deserve one another.'

Once inside the house, aware of what his act of brutality could mean in terms of reprimand from his half-brother and retibution from Luke Pengarron, Josiah hurried up to his aunt's room. He had a particular reason to visit her. He came face to face with Gabriel.

'Ah! Brother! We are well met. I was looking for help. Mrs Luke Pengarron is outside. She has fainted.'

'Why did you not carry her inside?' Gabriel rushed past him towards the stairs.

After Sophie had rested and was safely on her way home under the care of Livvy, Kelynen went to Gabriel in the music room. 'We need to talk about Josiah.'

'I've remonstrated with Josiah,' Gabriel said, rising

respectfully from the pianoforte and score sheets. He sat down again at once, his attention on his work. 'He intends to write a letter of apology to Sophie.'

'You should have ordered him out of the house at once, Gabriel.'

'I could hardly refuse his request to visit Aunt Portia. Josiah's behaviour was that of a spiteful child. You must know how that can occur, coming as you do from a large family.' He carried on writing down the melody that was racing through his head, but was conscious of Kelynen's unyielding demeanour. 'The situation is over. It must be kept in proportion.'

'I'm pleased you're aware of how vile Josiah is. Goodness knows why he wanted to see your aunt. He's never bothered with her before, and she can't bear him. Gabriel, will you please leave that and attend to me. I'm trying to have a serious discussion with you.'

'Kelynen?' She now had his undivided attention. It struck him that until the consummation of their marriage a few nights ago she would have come close to him, perhaps putting a hand on his shoulder, or tidying back a strand of his hair. He preferred that she stay where she was. He liked having her close. He liked it a little too much. It saddened him that the unexpected loving experience had put a barrier between them.

'Gabriel, I don't trust Josiah in any way. I think you should look urgently into all the estate business. I shouldn't be surprised to learn that he's cheating the estate. The more I think about it, the more I'm convinced that the way he was clearing those things out of the library points to him having something to hide. He's also taken a great many things from the house. How do you know they are rightfully his? You should consult the inventories.'

Gabriel did not welcome this complication. 'Surely not.' He glanced down at the music sheets.

Kelynen swept them away. 'You must forget this for now and put your mind to where your priority lies.'

'In your opinion, Chenhalls is my priority?'

'You may not care for it but there are hundreds of people relying on the house, the land and the mine for their livelihood. The anthem for the King is finished; your duty now lies first with your people.'

'My people?' He frowned. 'I have not thought of them as that before.'

'That is what they are to you.'

'And I'm neglecting them, is that what you're saying?'

'Gabriel, how many of the servants do you know?' she asked, not unkindly, nor in challenge.

He got up and paced the length of the room, his hand up to the back of his neck. 'Jacob. Mrs Barton, the housekeeper. I believe your maid is called . . . Hettie.'

'And the chef?'

A long, strained pause, then, 'Damn it, Kelynen!'

She raised her brows.

'Oh, very well, you've made your point.' He shrugged. 'I'll ensure I get to know all the servants. Tomorrow I'll ride to Marazion and consult Uncle Rafe's lawyers, and thereafter I'll go to the Wheal Lowen. I'll take a look at the papers in the library now. See what Josiah has left behind.'

'May I come with you?' Kelynen would try persuasion if he refused.

'I expected that question.'

'And?'

'Of course you may,' he said with a responsive smile.

While pleased that he was not to shut her out of estate affairs, Kelynen did not miss his note of uncertainty. 'With my help you'll soon realize what is necessary and then you'll be able to find as much time as you need for your music.'

On the way to the library, she said, 'I'll meet you at the Wheal Lowen tomorrow and then go on to Trewarras.'

'I'd rather you did not, Kelynen.'

'Why?' She tucked her arm through his, quite forgetting she'd been feeling troubled about him only a short time earlier. 'We've been there together before, to offer comfort over our mutual bereavement.'

With ease, he took hold of her hand. 'There are dangers on the mine face and danger from disease in the village. There is the child to consider.'

'I promise to take the greatest care. It's our duty to ascertain exactly how the miners live so we may improve their lot. I have many ideas. I've noticed a lot of redundant stone lying about; they could use it to rebuild or strengthen their homes, make them less like shanties. We could give each family some hens, or a pig or a goat. And seedlings to encourage those who haven't already done so to clear a little ground for a vegetable garden. And we could supply a beast and ale for an ox roast in belated celebration of our marriage. It will lift their spirits and there will be benefits for everyone.'

He studied her enthusiasm with admiration. 'As you please then, but you must swear to me you will always take care. I'll order the Home Farm manager to procure what's necessary from the farms and markets. I also have an idea. I shall arrange with Luke to have a performance of one his plays somewhere here in the grounds. The Arthurian one would do us well. And we shall also have music and dancing. At the end of the summer will be appropriate, after the grieving period is over.'

'That's a wonderful idea, Gabriel.' Kelynen didn't like the thought of his last sentence. She couldn't envisage a time when she didn't grieve for Rafe, but she squeezed his arm. 'I'd like to start a school for the children. Have a little building put up where the tenant farmers' children may also attend. And I think the mine surgeon should be encouraged to hold regular clinics. I don't like the man currently employed. He's lazy and uncaring. Could we ask Dr Menheniott if he'd consider taking over the position? There's no end of the things we could do, Gabriel.'

220

Gabriel halted and gazed at her. 'I see you know much about the life of Chenhalls. You are amazing. You humble me. Let us get busy then and find out more about our people.' Two housemaids, hanging back with cleaning materials at a respectable distance, exchanged contented glances. Their worries about the future after Sir Rafe's death were gone and they, like all the servants of the great house, were enjoying the peaceful atmosphere, now quite used to their new master and mistress's affectionate ways.

In the library, after drawing back some of the heavy curtains and opening a window to dispel the dry, musty air, Kelynen and Gabriel took everything out of the desk drawers and laid it out on one of the long display tables, which they had cleared of a miscellany of books. Papers and documents were few but there was an interesting bottle of spirit. Gabriel pulled the cork and sniffed the contents. 'Ah. A very nice canary. Would you care for a drop, my dear?'

'Just a sip. Josiah hasn't left anything relating to recent transactions – I find that very suspicious. Perhaps he doesn't want comparisons made with earlier figures. I don't expect we'll find all the books and papers we need to see in the mine office either.'

'Nor do I now. Josiah wasn't at all keen for me to become involved in the running of the estate and mines. I fear my brother isn't going to like these investigations.' He added, 'I intend to go underground tomorrow.'

'Gabriel, surely you don't mean it?' To Kelynen's horror it seemed that he did, for suddenly he was enervated, his blue eyes dazzling and eager.

'Oh, but I do, my dear. Darkness and confined spaces do not bother me. I want to see how everything works.'

Kelynen was filled with a strange, gut-reeling panic. 'You will be careful?'

'I promise. I'm sure I'll be reasonably safe. I understand Uncle Rafe did not stint on protective measures.' Gabriel was now at his most lively, and once again Kelynen was reminded how much like Rafe he was. Rafe had also sought new experiences, shunning risk and danger.

'How can you bear to? The very thought makes me shudder. I'd feel locked away, as if I'd never see daylight again, as if I was dying. You surprise me, Gabriel.'

'I know.'

'You do?'

'You've always thought me soft, Kelynen, haven't you? But I've done many a daring feat. I've climbed church spires. Ridden unbroken horses. I've walked barefoot on hot coals. I've walked across a lake on thin ice as a wager. I enjoy a challenge. I suppose it's why I was attracted to Caterina.'

'Do you see taking control of Chenhalls as a challenge?'

'Yes.'

'Am I?'

'Are you what?'

'A challenge.' She blushed fiercely. What had made her ask that?

Gabriel was staring at her. 'I'm beginning to think so.'

She pulled a group of papers out of a cupboard and plopped them down on the rest. 'Let us see if there are any inventories among this lot,' she said briskly.

'Must we?'

She felt his fingers threading through her hair. His touch made her skin tingle at the neck. She didn't have to look at him to know what he'd meant. The atmosphere in the dark margins of the room was charged with sensual warmth, an intoxicating energy. She wet her bottom lip. 'We've a lot to get through.'

He leaned around her until he was gazing into her eyes. 'It can wait for a while.'

She tried to sound firm, as if uninterested in him, but it was far from the truth. 'And what you have on your mind can wait until tonight, in our chamber.'

'Why then? Why there? Have you no sense of adventure, Kelynen?'

His smile, usually kind and easy, was marked by challenge and wickedness. Kelynen found it – she found *him* – mesmerizing, enticing, irresistible. She made one last attempt at propriety and rightness by taking a step away, but he thwarted this by putting his hands on her. And something, which she could not define, broke inside her, something slipped away, and eagerness, want and need flamed in her for him and she couldn't hold back.

While keeping mindful of her condition, he took her to the exquisite edges of every pleasure, and beyond them. In a blaze of abandon veering on recklessness, he caused her to climb peaks and ride crests and soar to altitudes that left her burning in delight, enthralled and mystified.

Twenty-Five

The lawyer's office was airless, dark and dusty, as if in affinity with the mine workings that Gabriel had come to discuss. Pinpricks of light were dotted in the heavy moth-eaten curtains of some indeterminate cloth, and he mused that it must be the first tiny speck of daylight or lantern light the miners looked for when making the tiring, arduous climb to the surface – the first sign of fresh air and life and some form of hope. He was under no illusion how hard and often wretched the miners' lives were.

Mr Penwood Leggo, a bespectacled, clumsy, creaking presence, wore a faded horsehair wig and smelled alarmingly of menthol and drains, making Gabriel wish the windows were thrown open. Mr Leggo shot off an officious smile every few seconds while he waited for a clerk to bring the particulars of the Tremayne holdings. Gabriel downed the last of the fine-quality port served him, keeping his nose near the pleasingly large glass to offset the ripeness of the aging lawyer.

'Another, Sir Gabriel?' Mr Leggo proffered the crystal decanter in a brownish bony hand. He placed a penetrating gaze on the pale young baronet, whom he had never thought to meet. His persistent requests for an audience about the late Sir Rafe's will had been met with equally persistent indifference. Not understanding why anyone shunned interest in a considerable inheritance, Mr Leggo felt honoured to have this reclusive Tremayne actually in his office. He was also curious about him, as were all the gentry of Mount's Bay. Rumour had it that Sir Gabriel Tremayne had been about to return to Vienna; his uncle's tragic demise had not been expected to prevent this. But then he had suddenly taken himself a bride, the highly favoured Miss Kelynen Pengarron, and more rumours were circulating that he had anticipated the wedding night and already had an heir in the womb. Rumour also had it that Sir Rafe may have even precipitated his nephew on that pleasure and the child was in fact his. Mr Leggo thought not. Miss Pengarron was too sagacious to fall for the wiles of a handsome adventurer. His granddaughters had begged to differ and, in descriptions the staid Mr Leggo did not approve of, had exclaimed Sir Rafe Tremayne had been wholly irresistable.

'I'd be delighted. It has a rich, smooth taste.'

Mr Leggo winked. 'Sir Rafe saw me well. Can I hope that you will be taking up that particular occupation before too long?'

'I haven't thought about it.' Jacob Glynn had recently asked him the same question, pointing out that the ordinary workmen relied on smuggling to supplement their earnings. His uncle's death had brought the regular runs on Tremayne land to an abrupt end. The prospect of participating in a run was exciting but he had Kelynen's feelings to consider. She wouldn't want him risking his life in the same sort of venture that had so recently cost his uncle his. Perhaps when things were more settled . . . In the meantime there was no reason why he should refuse permission for the coves and inlets and hides to be used by others. 'Expect to hear good news in that direction shortly, Mr Leggo.'

'Excellent. May I say how pleased I am that many of those murderous ruffians will in the not too distant future make acquaintance with the hangman's rope?'

'You may. The ringleaders have apparently fled the county and are unlikely to meet their just punishment, but that is all too often the case.'

'Sadly, I'm afraid it is.'

Cost sheets and profit ledgers were brought and a long, stifling hour passed. As Gabriel had expected there was little good news and some of it made him angry, not least with himself for delaying in acquiring this knowledge.

'So my brother has, in effect, already come into his inheritance, siphoning it off in large sums by drawing bills from the bank on the strength of his expected seventy-five thousand. He's sold shares in many of my uncle's concerns – the East India Company, sugar plantations, merchandise. He has been systematically cheating Chenhalls. My wife thought as much. He has recently removed a lot of paperwork from the house. Was my uncle never suspicious?'

'Mr Josiah gave me to understand that all he did was under Sir Rafe's instigation. When I did endeavour to inform Sir Rafe of the volume and gravity of various transactions, I'm afraid Sir Rafe was not altogether concerned. He kept promising to call on me but he did not. The bank may well tell a similar story. I'm afraid your uncle's wealth, as substantial as it is, has been greatly reduced. What will you do, sir? Bring Mr Josiah to book?'

Gabriel had considered all options after Kelynen's speech. 'Most definitely not, Mr Leggo. My brother is sly and shallow, but I will never forget I owe him my life in bringing me to Cornwall from Vienna, and we have a certain bond. Much of his felony would be hard to prove, I should think, and he has not gone as far as raising a loan on the estate, so he has not left me in debt. Josiah's punishment will be his fall from grace. I shall remove him this day from all his duties and permit him a small allowance. It seems to me he spends as wantonly as the Prince of Wales. If he needs more funds he must either seek work or live off the proceeds of the sale of his house. If he's occurred debts he must pay them off himself. Place a sum of a thousand per annum on him, Mr Leggo.'

Mr Leggo's wrinkles gathered in a certain delight round his eyes and mouth. He did not like Josiah Tremayne. A thousand pounds was a meagre sum to settle on such an irresponsible spendthrift. 'In the circumstances, it's most generous of you, Sir Gabriel.'

Gabriel studied the mine ledgers, leafing back through yellowing pages and fading ink before returning to the latest jottings placed in the lawyer's care. 'These figures reflect the current slump in copper prices. My uncle mentioned his concerns but perhaps they did not trouble him enough. A new level has not long been sunk in the Wheal Lowen, and hopefully there will be a reversal of fortunes. I shall speak to the mine captains, use their knowledge and wisdom, and see if investment needs to be made.'

'I wish you every success. May I offer belated congratulations on your marriage? Miss Kelynen Pengarron is a particularly fine young lady, if I may take the liberty of saying so. I am sure she will be a gratifying support to you in your aims.' Mr Penwood Leggo was certain he would enjoy advising this particular client. He poured more port.

'You are correct on both scores, Mr Leggo.' Gabriel winked. 'I propose a toast – in fact two: to never-empty cellars and to my dear, delightful wife.'

Livvy was in her dressmaker's in a quiet side street at Marazion, ordering new clothes to be made up for her children. 'I sent to London for these details,' she told Eulaliah Gluyas. 'I've made illustrations. Do you think you can follow them? I've noted the materials required and added a colour chart.'

Miss Gluyas carefully shuffled through the numerous sketches put before her on the table in her little private room, above the shop. Sounds of industry came from the cutting and sewing room, also on the first floor, and dust from cloth and sewing threads clogged the air. 'How very different, Mrs Lanyon.'

'It's now the fashion for children to be clad in simpler styles rather than as miniature adults. Their clothes are becoming more practical for freer movement. So I want plain linen coats with curved fronts and narrow tails, white lawn shirts and cotton trousers for my son, and light muslin, high-waisted dresses for my daughter. You may add a variety of coloured sashes for Hugh and mob caps for Julia.' Livvy was in a jubilant mood. She had dismissed the miserable Phylida Bevan, who would have disapproved and even fought against her intentions, and now employed a more amiable nursemaid.

'I'll have no trouble following your instructions, Mrs Lanyon. You have them down in admirable detail. How exciting, to be first in the district with the new fashion. I'm sure others will soon follow your lead in regard to their own offspring. May I ask, are these the likenesses of your children?'

'They are. The background incorporates the new friezes that I designed and painted myself in their nursery.'

'They are very well done – and so real-looking. The dear children almost look as if they're actually moving. I'll be most careful with them. Would you like them back when I've finished with them?'

'I hadn't thought about that. Yes, I would. They will be a record of how the children looked at their present ages. More personal than the usual formal poses.'

'I say!' A raucous nasal voice arrived from the doorway. 'I've overheard all that the two of you said. Think it impertinent of me, would you, Livvy, to order similar clothes for my grandchildren? We could be forerunners locally in the new trend.'

Livvy and Eulaliah looked up at another of the establishment's exalted customers. Lady Rachael Beswetherick, whose husband owned neighbouring property to the Pengarrons. The two families were close friends. The aging lady, who was inclined towards extravagant wigs, over-powdering, over-dressing, too many face patches and too much rouge – despite Eulaliah's efforts to persuade her to be more discreet – had innumerable grandchildren and the dressmaker was delighted at a possible large commission.

Livvy liked Lady Rachael because she was fun, witty and kind. 'I wouldn't mind at all. I'm sure Jessica would be interested too. She allows Harry and Charlie to run wild on the farm anyway, so she'd appreciate the looser clothes. She's with child again. I expect Mama has told you.'

'She has.' Lady Rachael put on her spectacles, picked up one of the illustrations and brought her sharp nose down close to it. 'The boy is like Timothy, the girl like you, another red-haired beauty. I do like the way you've portrayed the children. You have a gift, dearheart. You should paint more of them, and I mean other children too. Why don't you? Could open up a whole new avenue. Now, tell me how young Kelynen fares. When is she expected to deliver? I really must go over to Chenhalls to see her. I haven't set foot in the strange old place for many a year, and Kelynen is becoming quite a stranger. Is her husband as fascinating as he sounds? He's surely a lot different to the risqué Sir Rafe. Now *he* was an adorable fellow, such a sad loss to womanhood.'

Livvy spent the next half-hour fielding off questions about Kelynen from both women in case they got too personal. She left, saying she would see herself out, wanting to sink into her thoughts. Lady Rachael's suggestion that she draw more of her children and others was a welcome one. She had nothing arranged after Lady Portia's portrait was finished. She pictured herself down on the beach below the parsonage, sketching and painting the antics of the fishermen's brats, and at Vellanoweth, capturing the scampering Harry and Charlie in the farmyard and fields. And Luke's ward . . . but no, Sophie would insist of formal portrayals of Elizabeth. Livvy smirked as she imagined Sophie's condemnation of the new fashions for children. Poor Elizabeth was destined to stay in restrictive laces, flowing skirts and too many shawls.

The dressmaker's had a small outside landing and stairs and Livvy was preparing to descend to the street below. A gentleman was about to come up but he waited politely for her. Livvy sighed. It was Josiah Tremayne. No doubt he was here to visit his tailor; Eulaliah Gluyas' brother was set up in an annexe and kept a few select customers.

Josiah offered a gloved hand when she reached the bottom pair of steps and she allowed him to help her alight. 'A very good day to you, Mrs Lanyon.' He smiled deeply.

'Mr Tremayne,' she replied loftily. Kelynen had told her of her concerns about this man. And Livvy hadn't forgotten his deplorable actions towards Sophie.

'May I enquire how goes my aunt's portrait?' Josiah was there in the hope of procuring something of his latest wardrobe, despite a heavy mounting bill. But he always had time for this delectable young woman.

'There is some work left yet to do. Your aunt is an excellent subject.' Livvy had no wish to remain in Josiah Tremayne's company, but if she could establish any of his intentions it might be useful to Kelynen. She stared back blatantly into his beautiful brown eyes. 'I trust you are settled in your new abode?'

'How kind of you to ask. I am, indeed. My temporary lodgings are quite comfortable.'

Livvy could see he was eager to keep her engaged. She knew why – he was always on the hunt for conquests. 'I understand you are to leave Cornwall soon.'

'I am, indeed.' He edged nearer her.

'May I enquire to anywhere in particular?'

'I haven't made up my mind yet. I don't intend to settle for some years. Have you had the opportunity to travel much, ma'am?'

'I'm afraid I haven't. I would very much like to.' Livvy knew she should stop. The prolonged conversation could now only be considered as flirtatious. Josiah Tremayne was smiling confidently and leaning a little towards her.

'I was on my way for a fitting with Mr Gluyas, but would it be presumptuous of me to enquire if you would care to take refreshment somewhere?' He raised a beguiling curve to one eyebrow.

'I'm afraid I am occupied today, Mr Tremayne,' Livvy replied briskly, and she walked past him and went on along the narrow cobbled street. She was sure if she glanced round she would find him gazing after her. To do so would give him unnecessary encouragement. But as she reached the corner to turn into the main street she could not help herself. Despite his detestable character, flirting with him – a young man of matchless good looks and immense, although counterfeit, charm – had given her a power she had never experienced before. He was smiling after her, his hat dangling jauntily from his fingers. He was a handsome sight and she made the look she returned last too long, for he raised a hand in a small wave and nodded, as if an understanding had passed between them.

Livvy went on her way with her heart pounding. She had behaved wantonly, her speech and actions untrue to Timothy. If she ever saw Josiah Tremayne again she must make it plain that she wasn't at all interested in him.

Josiah went after her. This was too promising to leave to the vagaries of another chance meeting. Olivia Lanyon was too succulent – he was drooling. He rounded the corner and very nearly collided with someone. 'Oh! Gabriel! How odd to meet you in town. Would you excuse me, I have—'

'I've been searching for you at your regular haunts. I will not excuse you, Josiah. Come with me to the coffee house. At once!'

'Luke! What on earth do you think you're doing? It isn't good for Elizabeth to be out here like this.'

He ignored his wife's chastisement and carried on showing his ward the beauties of the coast. 'Don't fuss so,

Sophie. We are not far from the house and she's covered up against the sun, which is gentle enough today. What *isn't* good for Elizabeth is to be cooped up inside all day long. Children need lots of fresh air to be healthy.'

'But she's too young to understand where she is.'

'I've told her,' Luke said simply, 'that nearby is the village of Porthcarne. I've pointed out St Agnes Beacon, not far inland, and that how up-coast we can see Trevose Head, and down-coast Navax Point. Did you know St Ives is hidden by the point, Sophie?'

'Yes,' she replied, uninterested. 'At least take her back to the garden. You may stumble in a rabbit hole, Luke.' Sophie watched, angry over the opposition to her views, and jealous as the four-month-old baby smiled up at Luke and chuckled while he tickled her. Elizabeth did not respond to her like that.

'You like the cliffs and you like the sea, don't you, sweeting?' Luke kissed the tiny face, which bore a close resemblance to her mother and aunt's. 'I'll teach you all the names of the wild flowers, the thrift and squills, the primroses and foxgloves. But let us away to the garden, or your Aunt Sophie will nag us further.'

He was hoping Sophie would ask to carry the baby but it seemed she had no maternal feelings. She avoided the nursery while the wet nurse was feeding Elizabeth. It was as if she found this most natural procedure disgusting. Luke hoped his own child would not be relegated to the wet nurse. Sophie was certain she was with child. She had all the usual signs, but so far had refused to be examined by the doctor. He longed to take Sophie for a walk along the cliff top, to climb with her down into Doble's Cove, one of his favourite places to write outdoors, and to make love to her in the glorious fresh air, but she would be horrified at the very thought. He sighed.

'Is something wrong?' Sophie asked sharply.

'No. Nothing.'

'Why did you sigh?' she demanded.

'I was just taking a deep cleansing breath of air, my dear. Don't be critical.'

'I was not!'

Luke glared at her. He had learned it was the only way to stop Sophie from complaining. The fright she had suffered at Josiah Tremayne's behest had unsettled her and she was jumpy and argumentative. And she was boring. What had happened to the beguilingly haughty woman he had fallen in love with? She had pleaded with him not to take Tremayne to task, not wanting to be embarrassed. He had intended to thoroughly thrash the unspeakable swine. If he got his hands on him now, nothing would prevent him from doing so.

'Would you like to go out somewhere today?' he said amiably.

'I'm happy to do whatever you wish to do.'

Luke wasn't happy with this answer. Sophie also now tended to hide herself away. He didn't want to visit any of his family. It was fine for a while but he soon got bored. He had no wish to get on with his play. He had no heart in it with things so dull in his marriage. What he needed was fun. Something new. He glanced at Sophie. She was plodding along beside him instead of stepping aloof and proud. Perhaps she needed new horizons too.

'Change for travelling, my dear! Order your maid to pack your best gowns. We will go to Truro, stay at the Red Lion Inn, for a few nights at least. I think it's time we had a honeymoon.' If a whirl of social activity in the county's foremost town didn't cheer her, make her more sociable and, hopefully, properly eager in bed at last, then nothing would.

Twenty-Six

Kelynen worked tirelessly to improve the living conditions of all those who relied on Gabriel for their livelihood. She started by inspecting the servants' living quarters. Many lived in tiny cottages. Their homes were without luxury but she felt Rafe had served them well. Each had proper flooring and sound roofs and access to an outdoor privy. Nonetheless, she supplied them with practical items like pots and pans, buckets and tools. Those who lived-in had draught-free rooms in the servants' hall. Men and boys were segregated from the women and girls, but she fancied a lot of clandestine mixing went on – indeed, one of the kitchen maids was with child, and she had arranged a hasty marriage with one of the stable grooms. She handed out new bedding and Sunday best clothes for all.

The miners and their wives were at first nonplussed by the considerations shown them. Some welcomed it. Some regretted the time it took to make the encouraged improvements to their homes, especially those who had previously not bothered to clear land for garden patches. They were pleased about the monthly doctor's clinic, to be held in the office, but nearly all baulked at mention of a school. In their opinion it was a waste of time and gave the children false hope; too much was against them to obtain a better life, unless it was the eternal kind, and they thought girls didn't need schooling anyway. The tenant farmers and household servants held this same view almost to the individual, and Kelynen knew she'd have to persevere to get a reasonable half-day attendance when the school was built, on the outskirts of Trewarras.

Gabriel remained concerned about her contracting a disease, for she had insisted on visiting every home, but she politely refused to eat or drink anything and never stayed for any length of time.

She worried about Gabriel's persistence in going underground at the mine. Josiah's fury at being dismissed had led to him threatening to sabotage the mine, but Gabriel had passed it off as childish spleen. Josiah had actually burst into violent tears in the coffee house and beaten his fists on the table, causing him to be further humiliated by the curious stares and derisory remarks at his ungentlemanly conduct. Since then he had lurked in bitter mortification at his lodgings. Gabriel had called on him, and Josiah, while at the door but refusing him entrance, had hurled accusations.

'What right have you got to throw me off? You've lived only a short time at Chenhalls. You care nothing for it. You've never waited upon our uncle. He wouldn't have taken such a cruel outrageous stance. You are unfair. An interloper. You are not morally entitled to a penny of Tremayne money. I only took what was rightfully mine. You are loathesome. I shall pay a gipsy to ill wish you. I shall find a witch to cast a spell over you and that self-righteous minnie you've wed. She has no right to Chenhalls either.'

Having arrived expecting tantrums, Gabriel had intended to make many different appeals, pleading that he did not want a permanent estrangement, but Josiah had ducked inside and returned with a heavy ornament to throw at him, and so he had retreated. Later he had declared that he would write after a few days to Josiah, reminding him of the munificent, undeserved allowance he was to receive. Since then, Kelynen had worried that Josiah really would cause trouble.

Her heart flew to her throat to see Gabriel now dressed in miner's garb. He was pressing a hempen candle into the clay at the front of the brim of a hard hat. His pockets bulged with more candles to light his way in the blackness. She would never forget the fear of watching him that first time disappear down the topmost ladder of the main shaft, and the terrible wait for him to re-emerge, soiled and sweaty, over two hours later, with the partially-sighted Sol Rumford, who had been elevated to Mordecai Lambourne's position. The new captain had been shocked at first at his new employer's intention to go underground, but had applauded his brave spirit – even Sir Rafe had never ventured under-grass. She had been thankful and relieved, yet annoyed, to see Gabriel beaming and sparky, fervent over the experi-ence, and more annoyed and anxious at the covert whis-pering that had then gone on between him and Sol Rumford. It had not occurred to her that the conversation with the short, wiry mine captain, with his dirt-ingrained hands and whiskery, sallow face, had been about the reintroduction of smuggling runs on Tremayne land.

'I thought you'd be getting on with your music today,' she said, taking up station in front of the doors of the vestibule, as if to prevent him going out. He filled the rough working clothes splendidly now he had a healthy appetite. The time spent outside meant he had lost the last of his sickly pallor.

'My dear love.' He smiled disarmingly. 'I know your ploy. The music for the celebration we're to have is finished.'

'Then you should be thinking of creating something to sell. The estate needs money from any viable direction.'

'I've already started on an opera for the London theatre company that wrote to me last week. I am not lazy, Kelynen.'

This was not said with impatience. His eyes were twin-kling like stars. Such humour and energy he had. She would never have believed it at their first meeting, which seemed in a different age now. Gabriel was certainly a different man. One she liked enormously. One she liked to touch and kiss her and deluge her with all manner of attention. She was pleased to do the same to him. She pressed her hands on the collar of his coat. 'Stay home.'

He placed his hands over hers, bent his head and kissed her lips. His voice fell low and husky, something else she liked. 'I will, gladly. But I'll still go to the mine. It warms me that you worry about me, but I promise you that I take every care. My first day undergrass I ordered iron ladders instead of the wooden ones for the main shaft. No more falls because of treacherous or missing rungs while the men are climbing, when they are often at their most vulnerable. I want to see if the ladders are all securely in position.'

'Promise one thing more.'

'You are being artful, but I mind not at all.' He was holding her in the way of a man lost in desire.

'Never go down the mine unless you tell me first. I have a special prayer, which I say for you each time. Then I shall be more at ease.'

'You're so good to me, darling. You have my promise. Come to the stables with me?'

The horse was saddled and waiting long before they emerged from a secret corner of the stableyard. She held on to him and whispered her prayer. *Bring him back, blessed Lord, for I could not bear to lose another. And I shall remain always in Your service.* He kissed her one last time and mounted, then blew her a kiss goodbye. Digory trotted off with him.

She stood alone on the cobbles and watched him clatter away. There had been something else she had meant to tell him, concerning Josiah. But it could wait for when he came home. She wanted him to stay blessed by her prayer. Rex bounded up to her. Sensing her quiet mood, he walked solemnly beside her to the tomb.

She touched the big iron ring, said hello to Rafe, and

237

then sat on the stone seat. She was deeply troubled. Since the extent of Josiah's rottenness had come to light she had wondered if he was somehow involved in the treachery that had led to Rafe's death. It was an irrational thought. Josiah had had much to gain from the sale of the gold. Indeed, with his inheritance prematurely spent, he must have been counting on it. But she couldn't get it out of her mind that somehow he might have done or said something, albeit not deliberately or consciously. Josiah was a weasel, a cheat and a liar. The way he had taunted Sophie meant he was also brutal. Gabriel had humiliated and infuriated him. Josiah was a cornered rat and as such could be dangerous. Pray God, he would soon leave Mount's Bay for good, but what was delaying him?

Disturbed and alarmed, she repeated aloud the prayer she had not long said. Memories of Rafe's ruined body lying in his coffin made her fight back anguished tears. She didn't want the same thing to happen to Gabriel, either from an accident in the mine or through another's treachery. She sprang up from the bench. It was no longer a place of peace and homage. Death and gloom seemed all around her. Thoughts of Josiah had made her feel morbid. He was a whining coward but he might well seek revenge. She knew that need. It was something she tried to forget, but she longed for retribution on all those responsible for Rafe's death. Gabriel had forbidden her, when the time came, to attend the hangings at Launceston gaol when those who might be found guilty were rightfully punished. She didn't particularly want to witness them swinging, their legs kicking, their final bodily indignities, but she'd have liked to question each one for clues as to the full truth of the butchery.

Suddenly she was weary. And she felt strange. She had been overtaxing herself and these gruesome thoughts were greatly unsettling. She would be sensible and lie down in her room, and hopefully sleep. When she awoke, Gabriel would be home and they would spend a pleasant evening together.

Gabriel was met with pandemonium at the Wheal Lowen. Work had stopped. Women were weeping and wailing, huddled together with the men who were not on core and those, still work-stained, who had come up early from below. Fretful children were bawled at to keep quiet.

Sol Rumford came hurrying towards him. 'Sir! I was about to send someone to 'ee. There's been a rock fall. At least three men dead, the injured've been carried to the office. Surgeon's been sent for. There's two missing.'

'Which level?' Gabriel threw himself off his horse and tossed the reins to a miner.

'Bottom. Eighty fathoms.'

'But that's newly blasted and dug out. The tunnels were progressing well, you've said. When can we climb down and investigate?'

'When we get word the air's cleared, or there'll be more dead.'

'How long will that take?'

'Could be hours, but in this case 'tis reckoned on two or three.'

'Until we can go down I'll talk to all concerned and see the injured. Anything life-threatening?'

They started off for the office. 'A boy took a mighty blow to the head. Don't reckon on his chances. His mother 'n' father is with him. Sir, with respect . . .'

'What is it?'

'Well, I, um, don't think you should be thinking of going below grass today.'

'Don't worry. I won't get in the way.'

Before a search and rescue party was cleared to climb down to the eighty-fathom level, the boy died. Gabriel was aware that he was out under the sea, with thousands of tons of rock overhead, and although he could not hear the

239

Channel waters thundering and surging and frothing up overhead, he fancied he could, with its unstoppable, timeless rhythm. It was a long, long wait on the platform, where he stayed, as promised, out of the way. The flame from the candle on his hat brim flared and cast his shadow eerily on the man-made walls. He stood and he stamped his feet and he rubbed his chilled hands together. He thought about the dead men. He prayed for their families. He pondered over the cause of the accident, and how fate had had its indeterminate grip on each individual. Tragedy anywhere was not uncommon, nor was death from disease. His uncle had tempted fate by taking a tremendous risk and had paid the cost. But Caterina . . . her death had been totally unforeseen. Childbirth took many women each year. He was suddenly afraid for Kelynen. He couldn't lose her now, he couldn't!

'I love you!' he suddenly blurted out loud in surprise. As the strange echoes of his profound three words seered up the shaft and died away, he sat down on the platform, huddled over, his eyes closed. His voice came soft and emotional. 'Dear God, Kelynen, I really do love you.'

Everything else forgotten, he stayed still. When he opened his eyes he scrambled back in fright, clinging to the bottom rung of the ladder. Caterina's fierce face was before him, her eyes red and accusing and taunting. Then the contorted image vanished as suddenly as it had appeared, but left him shaking. He knew it had only occurred because there was so little oxygen down here, but he couldn't shake off the impression she had come to warn him he must stay true to her.

Hours passed. One by one the three bodies were located and dug out from the rubble and finally pulled up the hundreds of sets of ladders by rope. It would be small comfort to the widows and mothers to be able to bury them in a proper Christian funeral. Another body was found and treated the same way. A fifth man was found, barely alive, his arms badly broken, his back slashed and bleeding from bending over to shield himself. The rock fall had cut him off in a pocket of air and allowed him to breathe. Shocked and disorientated from his injuries and from being so long in total darkness, his passage up to grass was more difficult, but his workmates attended him with every care.

It became necessary for Gabriel to light a second candle. Being down the mine was no longer an exciting quest. The air was old and stale and cold, yet he sweated and burned. Tapping his boots on the platform, he felt the planks were old and soft. There was an overwhelming smell of dank stagnant water. It was costly to be down this deep; the engines had to work harder to pump out the water so the workings did not flood, and the constant boom and pulse of the engines – usually a comfort, for it felt as if something lived down here – began to grate on his nerves. His repect for the miners and their hard lives took on a new meaning. Every other thought, however, included Kelynen, and he pictured her lovely smiling face to offset the discomforts and the morbid apprehension left from Caterina's vengeful image. If he were as superstitious as the Cornish he'd have believed there was trouble in store. He was anxious to leave here and go home to Kelynen. He longed to hold her and he needed her to hold him so very much.

The long wait was at last over, and, shivering and damp, in space only large enough for a worker with head bent over and pushing a wheelbarrow, he edged along the tunnel behind Sol Rumford to take a close look at where the miners had met their deaths. The steady, relentless drippings of slimy green water made footholds precarious, and his eyes were stinging. The fug from his candle, and the cheaper dips the miners used, also stung his eyes. Breathing was laboured, sounding strange, seeming to bounce off the bare rock.

'Any idea what happened yet, Rumford? A blasting accident?'

''Twadn't that, sir. They didn't stand a chance though, God rest 'em.'

Gabriel tilted his head and the light from his candle lighted a piece of jagged timber. With a jackknife he stabbed the wood. It was old and soft, almost porous. 'Why is all the wood so old down here? A consignment of Pengarron timber was ordered specifically for this level. Why use all this rotten stuff? Did the supply run out?'

'There was some new timber. Not much. 'Twas used up after only a few yards of tunnelling, then we made do with whatever we could find.'

'So as far as you're concerned the mine was expecting a far larger consignment? What do you suppose happened to the rest?'

'Well, sir.' Sol Rumford scratched his nose, surprised at the questions, resigned, like the rest of the workforce, to be given what they were given and that was the end of the matter. ''Twadn't for us to wonder on.'

'I'll look into this. And I'll order some more timber to be urgently delivered. I don't want anyone working in unstable conditions, Sol. Make a note of lost wages. I'll make full compensation.'

Kelynen was unable to rest. As the day wore on and evening fell, she fretted at how long Gabriel had been out. She felt ever stranger, in ways she had never experienced before. Worried about the progress of Rafe's baby in her womb, she ordered Hettie Hayes to send for Dr Menheniott.

Twenty-Seven

'A nd you're confident there's nothing wrong with the pregnancy, Dr Menheniott?' Gabriel asked the question again to reassure Kelynen, who was wound up with anxiety.

After climbing up to grass he had become anxious on learning that the doctor had been summoned to the great house. Still in his dirt-encrusted miner's suit, he stood back from the bed and watched Kelynen's whole being sag in relief. Her eyes snapped on him and he knew she was displeased that he had gone down the shaft during the rescue.

'This sort of thing is not uncommon,' the young physician replied matter-of-factly, including them both in his deliberation. 'Her ladyship's body is undergoing a major change. In fact it is being invaded, you might say. Feeling strange is not to be thought of as anything amiss. You should both expect to be parents of a healthy child in five months.'

'Surely you mean three months?' Kelynen frowned at what she saw as a stupid mistake. This day had turned out to be one of the most frustrating of her life.

'No. No. The size of the foetus is conducive with sixteen weeks' gestation.'

'It can't be!' Kelynen went pale. She was overcome with horror. 'Are you sure?'

'Absolutely.' For all his reassurances, Dr Menheniott was confused. He twitched his frizzed wig and put his hand inside his small stand collar. His patient was trembling and

243

Sir Gabriel had hauled in a sharp breath. 'Do you still feel something is wrong?'

'The pregnancy is more advanced, at six months along,' Kelynen insisted, feeling numb, unreal and afraid. 'Is my baby not growing properly inside me?'

'I don't think that's the case. It sounds to me as if you've got your dates wrong, milady.'

'Then this means . . .' Suddenly Kelynen ripped back the bedcovers and leapt out on to the carpet. In her lace-trimmed cotton nightgown she glared at Gabriel with fury and a sort of madness. 'This could only mean . . .'

'I don't understand,' the doctor said, nonplussed, finding it hard in the strangeness of the situation to speak with authority. 'Lady Tremayne, I advise you to get back into bed immediately and rest.'

'Would you leave us alone, Dr Menheniott?' Gabriel said evenly, but with a detectable tremor. 'You'll find refreshment awaiting you in the banqueting hall.'

'Well, if you're sure my services are no longer required.'

'They aren't. Get out!' Kelynen screamed at him. Irrationally, she wanted to hurt him for being the bearer of this terrible news. 'Get out, both of you. I don't want either of you here.'

Dr Menheniott gathered up his bag and left the room, but worried about his patient, he lingered outside the double doors.

'Try to stay calm, Kelynen.' Gabriel came towards her.

'Get away from me! It's your baby I have inside me. I don't want it. I want Rafe's baby. I thought I was with child by him, but I wasn't, and now I've conceived yours. It makes Rafe really dead. There's to be no child of his. There's nothing left of him. He's gone forever.' She rushed at Gabriel, and because she needed to hurt someone, she smashed a hand across his stricken face and started beating her fists on his chest. 'Rafe is dead! I loved him and he's dead! I'll never see him again. His child meant I'd have

244

had a part of him forever. I don't want your baby. I don't want you. Do you hear? Get out! Get away from me. Don't ever come near me again!'

Gradually he managed to still her clawing hands and pin her arms down. He was forced to hold her in his strongest grip. 'Stop it please, Kelynen. You're hysterical.'

For several moments she thrashed and gritted her teeth. And all the time she stared at him from sharded eyes as if she loathed him, as if she blamed him for every part of her distress. Gabriel's heart grew heavy, his every hope lost. Her next words were uttered in contempt, one biting word at a time. 'I want to be alone. Let go of me. Leave. Leave!'

'I'll do as you ask but only if you promise to keep control. Otherwise you'll make yourself ill and I shall call for Dr Menheniott's assistance.'

'I just need to be alone. Can't you understand that?'

Slowly he unfurled his arms from her. She stepped back on tremulous legs, grabbing the bed. She climbed up on it, lay down with her back to him, curled up and became as still as stone. Gabriel looked down on her. 'I'll come back in ten minutes.'

She didn't answer. He knew she had shut herself off from him and her surroundings and was again deep in grief for his uncle. He was fearful that the madness that had robbed her of reason might stay and affect her for some time. When he reached the door he thought he heard something. He listened. It was a strange murmuring. Kelynen was chanting. He went back to her, leaned over her until he could hear what she was saying. Over and over again, she repeated under her breath, 'Rafe's dead. Rafe's dead. Rafe's dead.'

He hastened from the room and was relieved to find Dr Menheniott there. 'Did you hear?'

'I took the liberty of remaining in attendance,' he replied grimly.

'I'm so worried. She seems to have lost all sense of reality.'

Dr Menheniott regained the bedside. 'She needs sedating and someone must stay with her at all times. You should send for her parents. She is very close to her father, I understand. She will need him.'

'I wish she needed me,' Gabriel said, hurt and bewildered.

Dr Menheniott made no answer. The private involvements of his patients were none of his business, but he thought it a pity that the contentment he had previously witnessed in the young couple had just been disastrously destroyed.

Two days later Kelynen came out of her daze and found her father keeping vigil over her. As if not caring about anything at all, in dry, lifeless words, she insisted she would leave Chenhalls at once. To return home. Her mother and Hettie Hayes packed for her but she refused to take Hettie on the journey. On Oliver's arm she walked downstairs, out of the house and past Gabriel without a word.

'I'll . . . I'll give her a few days of solitude. I know what it feels like to need to be alone,' Gabriel said forlornly to Kerensa. 'Then I'll call to see her. You'll send for me at once if she needs me?'

'I promise, Gabriel. Just give her time. I know how upset you are. You have grown fond of Kelynen. Her father and I had such high hopes for your marriage. Hopefully, when she's had time to come to terms with the new situation she'll be her old self again.'

'I feel more for Kelynen than fondness.'

'I'm pleased to hear you say that. Kelynen has a fondness for you. She really does. You must cling to that.'

'What I shall cling to,' Gabriel told himself, after the Pengarron coach clattered away over the cobbles, 'is that she has a love for Chenhalls.'

He went back inside the house – his house. He had hated the place, but Kelynen's enthusiasm for it – and then the responsibilities he had lately undertaken for the estate and its people – had begun to captivate him too. In the music room he sat at the spinet but didn't feel like playing. How could Kelynen have turned against him like that? Their months together, the times of loving they had shared, the plans they had made, meant nothing to her now. Only the belief that she was to bring up his uncle's heir had kept her here. She had not even said goodbye to Aunt Portia. Chenhalls no longer meant anything to her. She would never come back.

An atmosphere of gloom, in which there seemed to be a sense of gloating, pressed all around him. He tried to ignore it but the brooding impression gained strength and felt like a living force all around him. He knew he would find it in every room – in the gardens, the courtyards, in the tower folly, and even the chapel.

He threw up his hands and yelled at the house itself. 'All right, you win! No Tremayne will ever find lasting happiness under your roof. I hope all your walls fall down, stone after stone!'

Twenty-Eight

'Take me with you?' Sol Rumford's fifteen-year-old daughter said, her quick, dark eyes on the trunks in the bedroom of Josiah Tremayne's lodgings, packed for departure.

'Don't be ridiculous!' Josiah said, adding a foul oath. He had been drinking all day, had used the girl's skinny little body out of habit rather than need and he wanted her to go.

Netta Rumford sat up in the bed. Mr Tremayne had complained of it being lumpy and bug-ridden, one reason she assumed he was so testy. To her, used to sleeping on sacks of straw, it was pure luxury, as was the room, which was the size of her father's entire cottage and had more than half a dozen pieces of furniture in it. There was a high, carved mantel over the fireplace, which had baskets of seasoned logs on either side. The shiny brass lanterns contained fat beeswax candles and there were candlesticks made of bronze. The smells in here were heavenly, of expensive perfume, scented tobacco and brandy – and lots of food. She was hoping for a feast when they got up and dressed. Mr Tremayne had worked up a sweat, but it was not stale. She liked to sniff him. 'I didn't mean as your mistress, I wouldn't expect that. I was hoping to go somewhere different, that's all.'

'Shut up, I'm trying to think.'

Netta's father talked a lot about hope. He was a devout Methodist, strict yet kindly and encouraging. Although he said it was unlikely, he often said he hoped she'd marry someone who'd take her out of his hard way of life. Nice of him, but Netta was a realist. She reckoned she had to make her own good fortune. The most obvious route was through a wealthy man. She was as perceptive as she was hopeful and she moved away from her lover's warm firm body, watching his expression vary from angry, to smirking, to panicky and cunning. One thing was sure: he wasn't thinking about her request.

Josiah was keen to get away but he was furious to have to skulk off, humiliated and impoverished, thanks to his half-brother. At least Gabriel had been aptly rewarded, tying himself to the burden that was Chenhalls all for nothing. Uncle Rafe had apparently not left a child behind after all. Fear suddenly caught at Josiah's gut. Uncle Rafe would have forgiven him his deceit eventually and there would have been a place for him to return to. He'd have to live on his wits from now on. He hoped he was clever enough to accomplish it.

In a couple of days he would take the post coach up to London. But now it appealed to him to go overseas. He fancied a hot country. Africa. Perhaps he'd see how he got on there. He'd had a beautiful black mistress once, in Florence, the closest experience he'd ever had to being in love. She'd told him all about her homeland and the Zulu tribe she'd belonged to. It had sounded fascinating. Perhaps he'd find someone to ease the chill from his bones out there. First he'd go to Chenhalls, but definitely not to say goodbye to anyone. Now that his sharp-natured sister-in-law was no longer there, and Olivia Lanyon had finished his aunt's portrait, at last he might be able to get his hands on the horrid old mare's priceless collection of jewellery.

Netta thought it was time to move in close to him again and make one more appeal. 'Please take me with you, Mr Tremayne. I'd be no trouble, I swear.'

He found her hot moist breath on his face, the way she

snuffled all over him, offensive. She touched him. He shoved her away violently. 'Whore! Get out. You won't get a shilling off me today.'

She leapt off the bed and pulled on her clothes, glaring in return at his vicious gaze. 'Keep your rotten money. Bastard! No one'll miss you. Everyone knows you're bleddy useless now Sir Rafe's gone.'

'Bitch!' He hated being reminded that he had no one to take care of his mistakes now. 'Get out before I kill you!' Josiah picked up the empty brandy glass on the bedside cabinet and hurled it at her. The glass hit her face, broke and cut her chin.

Howling in pain, Netta rushed out of the door. Once she was outside, tears of humiliation and fury got the better of her. There was nothing for it but to trudge home. She didn't want her father to see blood on her so she pulled a scrap of cloth out of her apron pocket and mopped around the cut. She had found the ripped cloth while wandering about near the old disused mine shaft and had secretly washed it, hoping that one day she might wear clothes of similar quality. She'd wash it again before she got home, her precious piece of fine pink silk.

The tide was out on Perranbarvah's beach, exposing parts that would be under water within the next few hours. It was an area Luke had never ventured to before. He crept up behind Livvy. Under the shade of a parasol, she was sitting on a stool before her easel, painting a group of grubby, ragged children scampering among the rock pools.

'Should you not ask them to keep still?'

'Oh, Luke! How good to see you. No. I prefer them to be natural. They are easy enough to place.'

He took a closer look at her work. 'Such charm, such perfection you've captured, Sister, dear. You surpass yourself in this. It's no wonder you are gaining much admiration now, and deservedly so. I hear you've been busy making illustrations to accompany the lessons at the school. Our parents are justly proud of you. Do carry on, I shall not disturb you.'

'Timothy is greatly impressed with what I do now. I think I have found my forte at last. But when I next present my work to the art world, sadly, I must distinguish myself at first as a man. Only then do I hope to be taken seriously. What brings you here, Luke? How did you enjoy your stay at Truro?'

'It was little more than interesting.' Luke flopped down on a stretch of rock, his eyes set on Livvy's quick clever strokes with the brush.

'Oh?' She mixed ochre and white, to highlight the effect of the sun gleaming on the sand. 'Was Sophie not delighted? It's quite the place to promenade and show off one's latest gowns. Did you attend the assembly rooms? I've heard there was a very fine mayoral ball there.'

'We went out every hour of the day and night. We went to the ball, and a splendid theatrical play, several musical events, and soirées by the dozen. We took tea, or dined, or danced in all the big houses, from Comprigney to Malpas to Killiow to Trelissick. Not one of the new stately homes we did not enter, even those built on the fortunes of those from the lower orders. My wife enjoyed every minute of our outings. She exclaimed over the quaint surrounding hills of the town and its numerous streams and leats. She found the necessary abundance of bridges a joy to walk over. All she wanted was to be noticed. She's happy with the new friends she's made and the many invitations she has received for future engagements. Indeed, she has invited many prominent people to Polgissey. She was very happy in Truro.'

It was him she was not altogether happy with. He had not been fooled by Sophie's responses to him at night in the port and coinage town's principal hotel. He had previously enjoyed love-making in the same bedchamber, facing

the wide Boscawen Street, with willing and generous partners. Faced with the secret flirting of one of his old amours,
he'd missed all the fun and the passion. Sophie had declared
Lady Ariadne Truscott an aging scarlet woman. Damnable
jealousy. Ariadne was only thirty-three and just as discreet
in public as she was ardent in private. She had not received
an invitation to Polgissey, but had whispered she would
write to him. Luke was beginning to hope that she would;
just to talk about old times would be good.

A picture formed in front his eyes, of a letter. Not one
from Ariadne but one written by himself, suggesting a quiet
meeting with her. That meant only one thing. He blinked
hard to dismiss the vision. Surely he could not possibly be
contemplating being unfaithful to Sophie – not this early
in their marriage. He loved her too much, or had thought
he did. But it wasn't easy to keep an unlimited supply of
love at its highest point when you were continually rejected
where it mattered most.

'I'm sorry you didn't enjoy it more, Luke,' Livvy said.
She washed her brush in the little jug of water. 'I hope you
don't mind me asking – is everything all right between you
and Sophie? She can be rather . . . Well, what I mean to
say is, she hasn't fitted in easily with the family.'

Luke was still thinking about the lack of an exciting,
loving bedroom life. Whatever the reason for Sophie's
excuses, he knew she would never allow him to talk to her
about it. She'd cut him off at the first word, insisting all
was well. And anyway, Sophie didn't love him and was
unlikely ever to do so. Wintriness reigned in a heart that
could never be warmed up. Luke sighed. He saw things
clearly. Sophie hated him anywhere near her and was
unlikely to make the effort to change. He felt as if his
insides had been struck with a tremendous blow. But he
didn't know despair, just a terrible disappointment. Yet
Sophie, with her beauty and grace, was a good wife, and
she'd probably make a better one out of gratitude if he

sought her bed only once a week. She was always more amiable when he made it plain he wasn't about to make an intimate approach. And there was one good thing about her frigidity: she would never seek a lover. Thoughts of nights away from home, of raucous fun with his former set, and wild and satisfying liaisons, made him smile.

'We are happy enough,' he said cheerfully. 'We mustn't expect too much from her. Dear Sophie has been through hard times. Now then, what I really came to talk about was Kelynen. What can we do to lift our poor sister out of her melancholy? I called at Chenhalls before coming here. Gabriel is beside himself. His manservant told me he does nothing but pine and he's worried he may shut himself up again in the tower. Gabriel is so miserable. He goes loosely about his business. He has not the heart for it. He hasn't even turned to his music, so he must feel even more wretched than he did over the death of the Austrian dancer. He mentioned to me that if Josiah wasn't a blackguard he'd sign Chenhalls over to him.'

Livvy was puzzled by what she saw as his shift in moods, but she was glad to see him light-hearted about his own concerns. 'He's said as much to Lady Portia. She's so anxious. If only it was Rafe's baby Kelynen was bearing. Poor girl. Poor Gabriel.'

'Kelynen has us, her family. Gabriel's got no one. He might sell up and return to Vienna. I wouldn't blame him if he did.'

Livvy was so worried she jumped up from the stool. 'But what would happen to Kelynen? Her marriage would be over and she'd be left with a baby she has no wish for. This is too awful, Luke. I agree, something must be done, but in Kelynen's case, talking is of no avail. She listens to no one, not even Papa. If Gabriel did sell up, would you consider buying Chenhalls, Luke?'

'Not I,' he said vehemently. 'I've no wish to acquire a cursed property.'

Twenty-Nine

Panting, gasping, struggling, yet determined, Beatrice lumbered into the study at Pengarron Manor. She snorted in dissatisfaction and regret at what she saw there. In former days she would have expected to find Kelynen seated behind the desk, head bent over reams of documents, quill scratching in rapid neat script, enthusiastic, concentrating, reluctant to be disturbed. Today she was curled up tight on a dark reddish-brown leather sofa with Rex, shoes off, feet tucked up, staring into space, unaware that she had company. Dark shadows spread a sorry story under her eyes, which were red-rimmed from constant crying. Her cheeks were pale and sunken, hair dull as straw, dress crumpled. She wore no jewellery save her wedding ring.

'Can I join 'ee, m'dear?'

Silence.

'Kelynen. Please. Me ol' legs won't hold me up much longer.'

As if something clicked inside her head, Kelynen blinked. 'Oh, Bea, come and sit down.' She eased Rex's head off her lap, and he watched, mournful and anxious, while she plodded wearily over to the old nursemaid. Kelynen gripped Beatrice's elbow and helped her shuffle to the nearest easy chair. Beatrice fell down into it with a wallop, threatening its stuffing, its back and legs. Her nose dripped, but Kelynen didn't bother to search for the old woman's hanky in her grubby stretched sleeves, as once she would have done. Beatrice lifted her grubby tartan

254

shawl and thoroughly rubbed her fat bright-red nose, leaving behind on the wool the appearance of a snail's trail.

Kelynen went back to the sofa, sat with her feet dangling, white and bare. She clutched a plump cushion to her chest, let her head drop down on it as if she found it too heavy to hold upright. With unconscious fingers she tugged on the untidy length of her hair.

'Did 'ee have summut to eat midday, my handsome? Kelynen, can 'ee pay mind to me. 'Tis like talking to a deaf ol' horse who don't want to take 'ee to market.'

'Pardon?' Kelynen drifted out of her trance.

'Do 'ee reckon Sur Gabrall will come today?'

'I suppose he might.'

'He comes reg'lar, every other day to see thee. Good of him.' Beatrice sniffed noisily as the dripping started its habitual journey downwards again. 'He's a pleasant young man. Cares so much for 'ee. That's a comfort, isn't it?'

'I suppose.'

'You're not so angry with him now then?'

'Am I angry with Gabriel?' Kelynen looked as if she didn't know or care.

'Seems to me you was proper mazed with him when you first come back to stay. Refused to see him for days.'

'That was unkind of me,' Kelynen said without emotion.

'It was a mite unkind. He understood though. He's a good man. I like him. A lot.'

Kelynen raised her head very slowly. 'I know what you're trying to do, Bea. But I want to stay like this. Feeling nothing. Otherwise I couldn't stand the pain.'

'But 'ee can't stay like this. Not forever. You'll go off your head! I've seen it afore. You don't want that, surely? Kelynen, my little bud, you're not a coward.'

'I don't want to be anything, not now, not ever.' Kelynen let her chin press down harder on the cushion.

Beatrice's worries for her turned into anxiety. Kelynen

hadn't even sighed in irritation. 'Think this is what Sir Rafe would've wanted for 'ee?'

'Don't bring up that line of argument.' Kelynen's voice rose at last but only to scoff. 'Others have tried it. Rafe is dead. I loved him. I adored him. I could only face life without him when I thought I was having his baby.'

'And now you're having Gabrall's.'

'Don't remind me!'

Beatrice wagged a fat knuckly finger at her. 'Well, someone's got to! If thee don't start looking after yourself it'll be born sickly and you're risking your life. That's not the Kelynen I've always known. She used to care for everyone.'

'Well, I'm not that person any more.'

'No. You're not, and you should be ashamed to admit it. You were a clever, pleasant, duty-conscious, pretty young maid. It's what made Sir Rafe fall in love with you. Enough to want to marry you.'

Lifting her head up sharply, Kelynen was now paying full attention.

'Sir Rafe doted on his nephews, so I'm told of it, even the one's that's a rogue. It might not be Sir Rafe's baby your carrying, but 'tis his nephew's and he wouldn't want no harm done to it. And that's what you're doing to it, delib'rately so. Sir Rafe'd never wish any harm on thee, would he? Eh? He'd turn round in his grave twice a day and thrice on Sundays if he knew what you've become over his death. Be more 'n' a mite disappointed in thee, I shouldn't wonder.'

Gradually, Kelynen's mouth sagged open as she took in Beatrice's chastisement. Gone was the old woman's ugly indulgent grin. She was choking and spluttering with the urgent delivery of her harsh words. 'And he wouldn't like for you to be treating young Gabrall so. You nursed him back to health and vigour backalong. Want to see him going into a decline again? You must stop being so selfish, cruel even, Kelynen. I for one don't b'lieve the poor man deserves it!'

Kelynen went limp and the cushion dropped from her hands. Rex whined, and she reached for him and cuddled in to his warm, broad head. 'It's all right, Rex.'

'Is it?' Beatrice asked. 'Will everything be all right, Kelynen? Or are you going to go on making everyone's life a rotten, uncalled-for misery?'

Kelynen kept quiet for some time and there was no telling what were her thoughts. Then, in bland tones, she said, 'Just as you have said, Beatrice, I am duty conscious. I'll send for some food and for my things to be packed. Before nightfall I shall return to Chenhalls.'

She heard Gabriel's music coming from outside. Afraid he was once more wasting away in the tower folly she ran through the house. He was there on the lawn with his violin, his back to her, his hair draping long and free. She couldn't bear the tune. There was something sinister and morbid about it and it chilled her to the bones.

Reaching him she put out a hand and touched his arm. 'Don't! Don't, Gabriel.'

He stopped with the bow halfway across the strings, the last note echoing eerily all the way down to the sunken garden. He looked sideways, not believing his eyes, as if seeing a ghost. 'Kelynen?'

'Yes. I'm back. Come inside. It's getting dark and there's a chill gathering.'

A short time later she went to him in the library. He had only a few candles lit, their glow casting gloomy shadows and menacing blackness in the depths of the room. 'Jacob told me you have taken up domain in here.' She put a tray of food down on the desk where his hands were folded dejectedly on top of some papers. He's also told me you've given up on meals again.'

'I eat,' he said simply.

She knew there was an element of wariness in those two carefully polite words and she felt wrung out, hardly able to cope with the guilt of what she'd done to him along with her own sorrows. But she would try to take care of him, and the house, and all those under Tremayne benefaction. She would work hard, give over her every thought to them, and exhaust herself every day in the hope she would sleep through every night and give herself no time to think and grieve and give way to panic. That way she might somehow get through the rest of her life. 'Apparently you pick and then leave most of what's on your plate.'

He glanced at the steaming-hot lamb stew, cold duck meat, vegetables, fruit, nuts and cheeses, and half a cottage loaf. There was also a pint tankard of porter. 'I thank you for this.'

She moved round the desk and looked down on the report beneath his hands, of the installation of tunnel props in the Wheal Lowen. 'The mine is fully operational again?'

'It is?' He fiddled with the quill, his eyes darting uncertainly.

'You have done well.'

'I hope so.'

'I'll cut the bread and stay and eat with you.'

'This is not the place for consuming food. There are too many valuable books and papers. Ring for the tray to be removed to the hall. I'll join you there. Later.'

'If we're careful we'll not make any harm.'

'It will encourage mice.'

She stood in front of him but he would not meet her eyes. 'I'm sorry, Gabriel. Sorry that I've hurt you so badly, I mean.'

'Fate has been cruel to both of us.' Carefully he put the quill down. No sigh. No dramatics.

It cut through every inch of Kelynen's heart. The fateful mistake she had made in assuming she was pregnant with Rafe's child had cost him as dear as her. Beatrice had said

258

there were many reasons why nature sometimes paid a late visit to a woman – a change of circumstances, a fright, an illness, excitement, or simply the unexplained. There was no point in making a catalogue of 'if onlys'. The thing she shouldn't have done was to accept so readily Gabriel's compassionate offer. She had been selfish, almost conniving. Not far at the back of her mind she had always wanted Chenhalls, and she hadn't wanted to leave Rafe, even if all that was left of him was in a tomb. Gabriel didn't deserve this. Guilt, humility and recompense would make her a good wife to him. Gabriel was so good and caring that likely he would forgive her. 'You would have been in Vienna by now.'

'Yes.'

'Content.'

'Perhaps. But I know now that I did not love Caterina.'

'How do you know?'

He stared at her, gravely. 'Because I now know what it is really like to be in love with someone.'

'You mean with me?' The horror was etched on her face. Before she could speak, he got up and raised his hands to silence her. 'Kelynen, I have removed my things from the master bedchamber. I am back in my old room. Excuse me. I have formed the habit of walking with Digory about this time every night.'

Her tears were now for Gabriel. 'Oh, God, what have I done?'

Thirty

L ivvy was on her way to Chenhalls. Lost in thoughts
about how she could possibly cheer Kelynen, or even
Gabriel, she was startled by movement behind a bank of
gorse and tall ferns. She thought it was a small animal but
then heard giggling. She reined in. A group of mucky, saucy
young faces popped up one at a time and disappeared in
the same way as if being pressed by some mechanism.

She laughed and called to the children to come out. They
did so, scrambling through the ferns and defiantly stamping
over brambles, ignoring the close proximity of the gorse's
barbarous spines, finally presenting themselves in an untidy
huddle beside of her pony. With the Wheal Lowen not far
ahead, she presumed they were miners' children. The eldest
boy among the eight of them wiped a hand on his thread-
bare shirt, all eyes on her expectantly, hoping for a farthing
or two, or a sweetmeat.

'Good morning,' Livvy said, her eyes roaming over their
faces. She could pick some good subjects to paint amongst
this lot. Some had coarse and tanned skin, some were gaunt
and pale, and some had the scars of illnesses. Their ages
ranged from about three years to nine, their sizes skinny to
stocky. The eldest boy, who must be their leader, for he
stood a few commanding inches in front of them, had raven-
black hair and had the look of the Tremaynes about him.
Seemingly either Rafe or Josiah had dallied with a mine
maiden. There were rumours of a lot of illegitimate
Tremaynes in Mount's Bay. With Rafe dead and Josiah

about to leave at any time, the possibility of any more in the future would come to an end. She thanked heaven she had not encountered the obnoxious Josiah again.

'Do your parents work at the Wheal Lowen?'

The eldest boy shrugged his shoulders, wary, insolent. 'You going to see Sir Gabriel?'

'I might be. Is he at the mine now?'

'He might be.'

Livvy raised her head to show that she was the superior here. The boy copied her. Here was a proud individual, quick-witted and intelligent, she thought, and he'd look perfect in his tatters perched on a high set of granite, with the mine buildings and then the sea in the distance. She produced a penny and held it up between finger and thumb. 'Is he?'

In a flash the boy had transferred the penny into his own rough paw. 'Ais, been there since day breaked.'

Livvy was about to ask if he was going to be a miner, but then she noticed, with a small shock of horror at what would have been an insensitive blunder, that his other hand was missing, the result of some grisly accident judging by the scars on his dangling stump. She saw that some of the other children also had disabilities; one had a humped back. She hoped they weren't considered misfits and unloved, but they seemed cheerful enough. Then she remembered Kelynen had mentioned she and Gabriel were hoping that the school, soon to be completed at Trewarras, would provide the necessary education for a number of disabled and sickly children to find some suitable work. 'You know all the comings and goings at the mine then?' she said, to keep the boy's interest.

'You hoping to meet someone partic'lar?' He raised an eyebrow, seeming older and wiser in a way he should not – he definitely had Tremayne blood in him.

'I'd like to meet your parents,' she replied evenly. 'I'd like to make a painting of you. Do you think they'd allow me to?'

The boy wrinkled his nicely proportioned nose. 'Get paid, will I?'

'I'd make the arrangements with your parents. I presume they live in the mine village?'

'They're both at the workings now. Mother's cobbing ore. Father's down shaft. Go 'n' ask Mother. She'll say 'tis all right, certain sure . . . Missus Lanyon.'

'You know my name, but that does not surprise me.' Livvy smiled at his attempt to look cunning. 'What are you called?'

'I know lots of things.' He tapped beside an eye. 'Got two gooduns of these, I have. I see a lot. My name's Jowan Bray.'

'Well, Jowan Bray,' Livvy felt in her purse for some small coins for the other children, 'I'll probably be seeing you again.'

She rode on, leaving the children to exclaim over their unexpected good fortune and the exciting prospect of posing for the lovely lady. She wouldn't go to the mine but would leave word at Chenhalls asking Gabriel to present her proposition to Jowan Bray's father. She couldn't bring herself to go to the Wheal Lowen. It was a dirty, dusty, noisy, frightening place. And she needed to see Kelynen. Perhaps it would cheer her to learn that things seemed more settled between Luke and Sophie, especially now Luke had some kind of new diverting business in Truro. How could she encourage Kelynen to seek contentment with Gabriel? Actually, Kelynen *was* making endeavours, out of guilt and compassion, Livvy supposed, to form a good marriage. It was Gabriel who seemed to want to keep a distance, understandable after the way he had been hurt.

Livvy rode on a few more yards then swung her pony round to head for the mine. She decided she must forget her distaste for the mine and seek an audience with her brother-in-law. Gabriel must be feeling that he had no one to talk to, and it was probably just what he needed to do.

Gabriel was told of her arrival and he hurried out to her at the fringes of the workings, where the noise was not so ear-splitting and the air was more breathable. 'What brings you here, Livvy? Is something wrong?'

Before answering, Livvy waited for him to give her the customary kisses on both cheeks. His lips were warm and firm and he was always good to be close to. Kelynen needed to find a way to break through his diffidence or another woman just might manage to do so. Few women in the bay had seen him, but he was gaining a soulful character that was enticing. Some declared they'd liked to console him. Many found his desire to go readily down the mine depths daring and exciting. There was much talk about his fair good looks. He had even been approached to write music for a lady. Knowing the person concerned, Livvy knew the request was in the hope it would be a personal dedication to her.

'I'm concerned about you, Gabriel, you and Kelynen. Please don't tell me not to interfere. I want to help.'

The little light he had in his eyes drained away. 'I'm not given to talking about my private life, Livvy.'

'You might feel better if you tried.' She was relieved that he was not dressed to go underground. 'Could we not go somewhere and talk? I was on my way to Chenhalls but it's an unplanned visit so Kelynen is not expecting me.'

'It wouldn't do any good.'

'You must forgive her, Gabriel.'

'I have,' he sighed, swinging his head hopelessly. 'I understand why she behaved as she did. She doesn't want my baby and she'll never stop loving my uncle. Chenhalls is running well, the mine isn't doing too badly, the living standards of the people are being raised daily. That's all that matters.'

'No, it isn't. Neither you nor Kelynen can go on living like this. You'll end up destroying yourselves. You both need love. You both need to find a way to comfort each other, like you did before, or everything inside you will shrivel and die. You're both working hard for the estate, but while everyone needs a purpose in life, it needs to be done for the right reasons, for personal fulfilment, or you'll only ever live half a life.

'Kelynen was cruel to you, but she didn't mean to be. It was a shock to her, learning the child wasn't Rafe's. I believe, and so do Timothy and all my family, that her feelings for Rafe were mere infatuation, that eventually she would have been dreadfully unhappy with him. Rafe was kind and fun but he was also selfish. He was going to take Kelynen away from everything and everyone she held dear and she would have lived a life unsuited to her. Fate, in a grim way, has been kind to her. Given the right circumstances, she'll see it too, I'm sure she will. She is trying to make amends, to make a future for you both. I beg you to respond, Gabriel, before she stops trying, or there will be two empty shells living at Chenhalls.' Livvy suddenly shuddered. 'I find that frightening.'

'So do I,' Gabriel said sadly. He didn't believe he could feel any emptier, but he didn't want that for Kelynen. She had showed she cared about him in many ways. Last night she had come to him in the music room and waited for him to finish playing the violin.

'That was definitely one of your best pieces,' she'd said enthusiastically. 'It has a haunting medieval theme. It was wonderful. Luke will feel highly favoured to have such splendid music to complement his Arthurian play.'

He'd brought the violin down from under his chin. 'I suppose it will do. The carpenters will start on the staging next week.' He always kept the talk between them non-personal and she already knew this. He had gone ahead and made all the arrangements, including hiring the troupe of travelling actors Luke had recommended without consulting her. He knew she must have minded, but she had not shown it.

'The whole estate is looking forward to the play and the dancing afterward,' she'd said, omitting the other initial intention for the day – a late celebration of their marriage, inappropriate now.

He'd shrugged and placed the violin on top of the spinet. 'I think I'll take a walk. Excuse me. Come along, Digory.'

He thought now how rude he had been. She'd smiled, and he'd known she had been trying to make him recipro-cate, but he had not wanted any of the rigid corners of his heart to be softened. He couldn't bear her being nice to him just because she felt she should be. But Livvy was right. Kelynen had been trying to make something of their marriage. On the day of her return from Pengarron Manor she had abandoned the master bedchamber and returned to her former room. She'd kept the door on her side of the dressing room unlocked, but he had never strayed into her territory and his aloofness had made it clear that he had not wanted her in his. But he did! He wanted to be with her in either bed. He wanted more than anything to make love to her again. He wanted her to love him back. But that would never happen if he went on being miserable.

One day she had come to him in the summer house. 'I've a surprise for you. I hope you approve. I've commissioned Livvy to paint your portrait.'

He'd shaken his head. 'It's a kind thought but I've no wish to have my likeness placed in this house.' He felt he didn't belong in this horrible place.

'Very well, I'll tell Livvy.' She had gone away quietly. But what if she never thought of kind ideas for him again? What if, instead of going away quietly, she never came to him at all? What if she stopped listening to his music? Or locked her connecting bedroom door?

Gabriel grew frightened and now, more than anything, he wanted his terrible emptiness to go, and he hated himself for stubbornly staying so detached from Kelynen. He real-ized that he had been punishing her for her reaction to Dr

Menheniott's shocking confirmation about her baby's dates. Suddenly he longed to go home – not to return to Chenhalls, as he'd previously thought of it – but home to his wife. To tell her he was sorry and that he wanted a new understanding, a chance to prove he was worthy of her and all her consideration.

'Livvy, stay here; I'll fetch my horse and ride with you. But I beg you to call on my aunt. I want to talk to Kelynen alone.'

Moments later, while she waited in hopeful anticipation that her talk with Gabriel would prove worthwhile, Livvy was greeted by Dr Menheniott, who was taking his leave after the monthly clinic. 'I'm pleased to see Sir Gabriel at last looking purposeful,' he said, pulling his timepiece out of his waistcoat pocket. Something caught in the long silver chain fluttered down to the ground.

'What's that?' Livvy asked, feeling she should recognize the scrap of pink cloth lying there.

'Oh, this?' The doctor picked it up and frowned at it. 'I found it on the floor after one of my patients had left and I tucked it away lest the wrong person claimed it. I forgot about it. Something pretty, I suppose, to brighten up an ordinary girl's life. I suppose I'd better take it back to the office.'

Livvy held out her hand. 'May I see it?' Shortly afterward, she told the doctor and Gabriel, 'We need to speak urgently to whoever it was that had this piece of silk.'

Thirty-One

Kelynen was in Lady Portia's bedchamber. She had arranged with Mrs Barton that as soon as her ladyship went out into the gardens with her entourage, the carpets would be scrubbed and disinfected to rid this corner of the house of the offensive dog smells. The maids had done an excellent job, and Kelynen was feeding the fire with logs to help dry the damp carpets.

She made sure all the windows were wide open, and saw Lady Portia sitting in the rose arbour, where she liked to linger near the multi-coloured, highly scented blooms, and remember Rafe posing there for his portrait. It was a pity Gabriel had refused to have his portrait painted. His handsome fair features would have added something special and wonderful to the Tremayne gallery. She was surprised to think of the words special and wonderful, but that was what Gabriel was. And so much more. How could she have forgotten that? How could she have treated him so callously? He had never done anything to hurt her, yet she had screamed at him that she didn't want him near her. She was confident he had forgiven her. Gabriel didn't bear grudges, but probably because he was afraid of another rejection he remained determined to keep his distance.

There was one evening she would never forget. She'd come upstairs to bed and met Jacob Glynn in the corridor. 'Has Sir Gabriel already retired?' She was trying to think of a reason to go into Gabriel's room, to show him she wanted his company. That she was willing to fulfil the most intimate of a wife's duty. She missed loving with him, missed the passion. There had been a lot of love in their unions. His love-making was different to Rafe's. There had been nothing demanding, nothing selfish. She hadn't realized until now that Rafe had been selfish with her, in relation to their intimacy and in other things, which had all been done mainly on his terms. Disturbed, and as if her heart had strangely slowed down, she saw how overwhelmed she had been by Rafe, how she had been willing to forsake so much – too much – that had been important to her.

'He's fixing to get roaring drunk,' Jacob had replied disrespectfully, carrying a jug of rum. 'Although in his case there won't be any roar to it. He's like a star fading away. 'Tisn't fair.'

She'd heard Jacob's anxiety. 'I'll go into him. Don't bring in the drink. I'll tell Sir Gabriel I've ordered you not to.'

'Yes, milady.' Jacob dragged his feet away, glancing back at her often, as if willing her to put things right. She would try to.

She found Gabriel leaning out of the window. It was a habit of his to stare out across the sea, watching the ships. She presumed he wished he was on one of them, travelling far away from here. He was gazing down at the ground below. It was a long, long drop. Instant death if he fell. Or jumped. A sudden end might appeal to him. Perhaps he couldn't bear to go on with a woman who'd behaved as if she loathed him, who'd said she didn't want his child in her belly.

He'd leaned out further, sighing. Horrified, believing he was about to jump, she'd rushed to him, grabbing his shirt with such force to haul him back inside that he banged his head on the hard stone.

'For goodness' sake, Gabriel what were you thinking of? Things aren't so bad you wish to end your life, are they? I'm sorry if I've made you depressed, I'm so sorry.'

'Kelynen, I wasn't about to jump.' He grimaced in pain. His head was bleeding on the crown. A dramatic bright red trickled down through his hair.

'Well, you shouldn't be hanging out of the window! I've never been more frightened. You shouldn't be so thought-less.' She hadn't meant to make it sound a harsh reproach. She'd been shaking, thinking what would she do if she lost him. She couldn't bear it. She didn't want her child growing up knowing it had lost its father because he felt he'd had nothing to live for. It wasn't fair to the child. And she had been unfair to Gabriel. He had suffered enough already with Caterina. She had come across Gabriel's unpacked travel-ling chest and inside it had found a small picture of Caterina. She had been shocked by the wilful expression in the dancer's beautiful face. She had looked hard, malicious and egotistical. It was no wonder Gabriel had been reduced to such an appalling state of self-neglect by such a woman. 'I don't want you to be hurt.'

Gabriel had stared at her. 'I've no intention of harming myself. I'm fully aware of my responsibilities and have no intention of shying away from them. I was merely hoping the cool night air would clear my head.'

'I see. I'm sorry.'

'I'm sorry you were frightened.'

They were both apologizing, yet it seemed like a new distance had opened up between them. She should smile, say something nice and perhaps the chasm would start to close. But her mind went blank as minds so often do when they're called on to produce something vital, and she could think of nothing, so Gabriel turned away.

Now, as she stood watching Aunt Portia down below, she knew just how bereft she really would have been if Gabriel had fallen out of his window, more bereft than on the day she had learned that Rafe had died.

She wasn't given time to think through all the implica-tions of this. There came a howl outside in the corridor

269

from one of the cats. Something heavy hit the bedroom door and the cat went squealing off. Someone had kicked the cat viciously against the door. Kelynen made to run out of the room and rail against the cruelty – probably, she thought, performed by a servant – but the door handle was being turned, very slowly. Something made her freeze.

The door was opened a crack. 'Hello? Hello? Aunt Portia? Jayna Hayes?'

It was Josiah's voice. His calls could only be a precaution – he must know his aunt and her companion weren't here or he wouldn't have hurt the cat. Kelynen slipped behind a curtain and held her breath.

Thirty-Two

Kelynen watched Josiah from behind her hiding place. He was carrying a large leather bag by a long shoulder strap. He gazed about suspiciously at first, obviously surprised at the fresh smell in the room, and then he went straight into Lady Portia's dressing room, closing the door behind him.

Frowning as she heard him opening drawers and clothes presses, she arrived at the conclusion that he was here to steal from his aunt. She knew that could only mean her jewellery, and he was looking for the key to the safe. She crept to the dressing-room door. There was no key in the lock but if she was quick she could pull a heavy chair across and jam it under the handle to trap the thief.

She had her hands on the back of a plump upholstered chair when Josiah came out of the dressing room. Thinking rapidly, she said, 'Oh! Josiah, you surprised me. I was just tidying up. I'm afraid your aunt's not here, she's outside in the rose garden.'

She could see he was nervous – no doubt his reason for slipping out of the other room was to check all was clear. He rearranged the shock and panic on his handsome face into an innocent expression, and before Kelynen could think about making an exit, he stalked across the room and stood in front of the door. She knew she had to keep her nerve. He had made her a prisoner. He must be desperate to come here and steal, and he was unlikely to leave without his spoils.

'Kelynen,' he said, using false charm, 'you have greatly improved the environment in here. I shall go down to my aunt presently.'

'Are you leaving on your travels today?' She walked round the chair, keeping her eyes on him as she straightened the cushions.

'Indeed I am.'

'Gabriel will be home soon. We must share a farewell meal. You will write to him? I know things have been difficult between you of late, but he's most anxious that you'll keep in touch.'

The sounds of the gardeners chatting outside filtered in through the windows. Startled, Josiah cried out, a hand flying to his heart. Kelynen was not about to take chances. At any moment the panic could take its grip on him again. She was in danger. She headed for the fireplace and the long brass poker.

On to her, Josiah reached the fireplace at the same time. He grabbed the arm that was reaching for the weapon and twisted it round.

'Argh!' she cried.

'Make another sound and I'll hurt you even more!'

Kelynen took a deep breath to steady her fright. 'What do you want?'

Grinning superciliously, he brought his face in close, darkened and leering. With his other hand he grasped her hair. 'You've already worked it out with this famous clever brain of yours.'

Wincing in pain, she tugged at his clawing hands, trying to free herself. 'Then take what you want and go!'

'I need the key! I can't find it.'

'It's not kept in the dressing room. I think I know where it is. Let me help you. I just want you to leave. I don't want Aunt Portia distressed.'

'She's not your aunt!' He shook her, making her cry in pain. 'You have no stake in this house, nor does my peculiar, witless half-brother. I've lived here all my life, until recently. I've worked hard for the estate.'

'You've never wanted Chenhalls. And you've robbed the estate. It owes you nothing. Gabriel owes you nothing.' Kelynen regretted her surge of anger. Josiah twisted her arm until she was sure the bones would break. He moved his other hand over her mouth to prevent her screams.

'You look very pretty with tears running down your face,' he breathed over her. 'It's no small wonder why my uncle and Gabriel enjoyed taking you. I'd delight myself in that same pleasure if I had time. But if you're truthful about expecting my brother home shortly, then needs must the devil drive. Where do you think the key is kept?'

'It's in here, in this room,' she cried frantically. Josiah let her go. She staggered and nearly fell to her knees. She rubbed at the agonizing pain in her arm, wrought bright red with the imprint of his fingers.

'Lead the way.' He placed his hands in a high, clawing, threatening position.

'O–over there. In a cubby hole in the bureau.' Kelynen hoped that when she got closer to the windows she could cry for help.

'What makes you think that?' he demanded suspiciously.

'It would be too obvious in the dressing room. I've seen Jayna Hayes put a little key away in a drawer of the bureau.'

Josiah pushed and prodded her all the way to the lumbering walnut bureau. He got a stranglehold round her neck and she knew it would be foolish to scream or cry out. His fear was making him dangerous beyond all reason.

'Which drawer?'

'The second one down.' She choked on his murderous grip.

He hurled her to the floor. 'Open it! Be quick!'

Gasping for air, shaking, Kelynen pulled on the stirrup handles of the wide concave drawer. Her arm throbbed and she groaned. Losing patience, Josiah shoved her to the floor and yanked out the drawer himself. 'Which side?'

'The left in the corner.' She tried to scrabble away, but he locked another arm round her neck and clamped her against his body while he searched among the miscellany of his aunt's keepsakes. He threw out empty perfume bottles, dried flowers, letters, diaries and books.

'I can't feel anything unusual.'

He tightened his grip and Kelynen started to choke. She tried in vain to loosen his arm. She thought desperately about Jayna Hayes' posture when she had put the key into safe keeping. 'It might be . . . incorporated in . . . the bottom of the drawer above.'

He leaned in closer to the furniture. Kelynen felt crushed and was sure she would faint. She was frightened for herself and her baby. She loved her baby then, and wanted it so much. She prayed Jayna Hayes would come – Lady Portia was always sending her up for things. More than anything, she wished Gabriel really were due home. If she was to die, she wanted to see him one last time.

Finally Josiah's search was rewarded. He gave a yelp of triumph as he located the cubbyhole and got his grasping fingers on a tiny ornate iron key, threaded through with red ribbon.

He dragged Kelynen into the dressing room and dumped her down on a high-backed chair. She teetered and clung to the seat for balance. Warning her not to scream, he ripped the robings off her bodice, then, while kneeling in front of her, he yanked her arms behind the back of the chair and tied up her hands. She forced back the terrified thought that he was about to murder her.

For a second he gazed into her eyes. Then he tugged through her disarrayed hair, making her head dip from side to side, until her hair rested on her shoulders. 'I do hate an untidy female. Don't worry. I'll soon be leaving you to the burdens of this horrid old house. Do you know, Kelynen, you are a handsome woman. I should have taken you for that walk round the gardens.' She tried to lean away from him, but he held her face, put his mouth over hers and kissed her deeply.

'Please, Josiah, just take the jewellery and leave.' While tears coursed down her cheeks, he tore the thick gathered lace off the hem of one of her sleeves and gagged her. Then he swung to his feet, opened the safe – which he had found during his earlier hunt behind a picture – rapidly transferred the jewels in their many velvet pouches from a large silver casket to the leather bag. That accomplished, he went back to Kelynen.

She veered away from him, her eyes glittering in fear, not trusting him to leave her unhurt or alive.

Josiah pulled the gag down around her neck. 'Goodbye, Sister-in-law. I hope you have a nice little baby. Don't look so frightened. You've been a pest to me, but I don't perform the ultimate sort of dirty deed, and there's no Mordecai Lambourne here to take you away and throw you down a mine shaft. And before I go, I think there's something you should know about Uncle Rafe.'

Thirty-Three

'You're lying!' Kelynen gasped in horror.

'No, I'm not. Uncle Rafe was good to me. He sorted out any little problem I had. Just as I said, he ordered the demise of the late, unlamented, bothersome Adelaide Trevingey. Now there's a nice little secret you can take to your grave. After all, you wouldn't want to sully your dead lover's reputation, would you? He would have soon tired of you, Kelynen. It's a trait we share. You're boring, and so is Gabriel. Have a pleasant, boring life together.'

'You're evil!'

'Not really.' He shrugged, smiling. 'I was just spoiled as a child. Now, don't cause a scene about the jewels or my indelicate treatment of you. If I'm apprehended, I'll hang. I might as well hang also for my involvement in Adelaide Trevingey's death, and I'll bring my uncle's name into the murder too.'

Before Kelynen could respond, he pulled up the gag and smilingly watched the tears she shed over Rafe's crime, the unknown deadly side of his character. Then he slapped her, hard enough to render her unconscious.

Gabriel hurried into the house with Livvy close on his heels. 'Where's your mistress?' he shouted at Jacob Glynn, who was wasting time with a parlour maid at the foot of the stairs. Gabriel had been about to ride to Marazion to confront his half-brother about the scrap of Adelaide Trevingey's dress that had been discovered by a bal maiden, a girl Josiah had badly beaten, near the old mine shaft. An encounter with young Jowan Bray had informed him and Livvy that Josiah had passed along the road on the way to Chenhalls.

Jacob suddenly shot to attention. 'I'm not sure, sir. Upstairs, I believe.'

'Is Mr Josiah in the house?'

'Aye, sir, he went up to her ladyship's bedchamber. I said her ladyship was outside, but he said he wanted to leave something for her.'

With Josiah's departure imminent, Gabriel thought it unlikely there was an innocent reason behind this supposedly generous gesture. He was worried about Josiah resorting to violence. Had he lied about Adelaide Trevingey seeking her fortune in the city? Had she in fact met some terrible fate at the Wheal Lowen? If he was up to no good in the house and Kelynen discovered it . . .

Gabriel pushed the startled valet out of his way. He'd got to the top of the first flight of stairs when he was faced with Josiah rushing down the corridor, a bulky bag slung over his shoulder. Gabriel threw the scrap of pink silk down on the floor.

'Would you care to explain this?'

'A piece of rag?' Josiah feigned incredulity. 'I've come to say goodbye to everyone. I haven't much time, I'm afraid. I'm shortly to meet the carrier taking my belongings out on the fork of the main thoroughfare.'

'I've spoken to Netta Rumford,' Gabriel said harshly, advancing on his half-brother, who backed away. 'Remember her? The girl you hurt so badly yesterday that she needed the doctor's attention. She told me where she came by that piece of pink silk. My sister-in-law, Mrs Lanyon, recognized it as the same cloth that was wrapped around the foundling her husband found on the church steps, the foundling that is your baby, Josiah. What happened to Adelaide Trevingey?'

'I've mentioned before that she went off somewhere,'

Josiah snarled, but his mouth twitched with nerves.

Livvy had raced up the stairs. 'Where's Kelynen? You must have been here long enough to have seen her.'

'I've no idea. I've been to my aunt's room. I saw her from the window with her companion in the garden. Perhaps your sister's outside somewhere too.'

'Her ladyship never left the house, sir,' Jacob Glynn shouted up the stairs. He had been questioning some of the other servants. 'Mrs Barton says she last saw her in Lady Portia's bedchamber.'

At that moment Rex dashed up the stairs from the kitchens and ran, whining, towards the old lady's room.

'What have you done to Kelynen?' Gabriel seized Josiah by the coat collars.

'Nothing!' Josiah blubbered. 'I swear I haven't seen her.'

Gabriel thrust him aside and ran after Rex, shouting over his shoulder, 'Jacob, don't let this man leave the house!'

Experiencing the worst fear of his life, he burst through the bedroom door. 'Kelynen! Where are you?'

Rex whined outside the dressing room and Gabriel dashed inside it. Kelynen was coming round. 'Darling! Oh, dear Lord, what has he done to you?'

Kelynen regained consciousness properly in her bed. She was in a nightgown, her arm was bandaged and there were the smells of Beatrice's soothing ointments.

'I'm here, beloved.'

She saw Gabriel then at the bedside and realized he was holding her good hand. 'I was so afraid,' she said. 'I thought I'd never see you again.'

'I was afraid for you, Kelynen. I couldn't have borne losing you.'

She smiled faintly and he leaned over and lightly kissed her lips. She kissed him back and whispered, 'Stay close. Stay close to me, always.'

He lifted her gently and sat on the bed, holding her. She

snuggled in against him, her face tilted so she could look up at him. 'Josiah told me—'

'I know, darling. I know all about what happened to Sophie's sister.'

'Where is he now? I hate to think of Josiah getting away with what he's done, but I don't want a scandal to defile the Tremayne name, for your sake and our baby's. I know now what Rafe was truly like. I also know that what I felt for him wasn't real love. I want him to be finally laid to rest. He and Mordecai Lambourne have paid for their terrible crime.'

'Josiah has been punished too. I've sent him on his way, under escort, out of the county, with nothing more than the clothes on his back. He's a rotten, snivelling coward. He must make his own way in the world from now on, but I don't believe he'll do it very well.'

Gabriel kissed Kelynen's brow, and again, tenderly, on her burning cheek where she had been struck. Then he kissed her lips. 'Kelynen, I'm sorry for being so distant with you. I want you to know that I love you, that I will do anything to make you happy.'

She took his hand and placed it over her middle. 'Did you feel that?'

'Yes! Was that the baby moving?'

'Yes, it was. Our baby. It's going to be a blessed little child because its parents are in love with each other. When I thought I was going to die, which meant our baby would have died too, I felt this overwhelming love for it and for its father – you, Gabriel. I'm so glad it's your baby. I do love you, Gabriel.'

Days later, while they stood arm in arm looking at the tower folly, he said, 'Do you know I've become rather fond of this old monstrosity, where we first met.'

'I thought perhaps you'd order it to be pulled down. We don't have to stay here at Chenhalls, Gabriel. Why don't we move to a new house, or go overseas if you'd like, make somewhere our own?'

'Yes, why don't we do that?' He saw her disappointment and kissed away her little frown. 'But we shall keep Chenhalls. If there was a curse here then our love has broken it, and we're already living happily alongside the ghosts.'

'There are no ghosts here.' She laughed. 'Just a happy future for us and the scores of children we're going to have.'

He looked at the tower, then looked at her and winked. 'Well then, while I've got you all to myself, why don't we go inside and warm up these old stones?'

'Yes, why don't we do that?'